PRAISE FOR THE
NOVELS ~~O~~

The Forever Drug

"A hard science fi... ... ... and believable hero . . . a substantially satisfying read."
—*Ft. Lauderdale Sun-Sentinel*

"A hard-boiled thriller with a SF setting . . . good entertainment." —*Booklist*

Spindoc

"Fast-paced . . . His future world seems very real. *Spindoc* is a fun read." —*Analog*

"A lively tale of intrigue, murder, and sabotage."
—*Booklist*

The Matador Series

"Perry excels at hard-boiled writing, flashing dialogue, and stripped-down action." —*The Oregonian*

"Effective and logical . . . recommended highly for all who enjoy intelligent, thoughtful outer-space adventure!"
—*Science Fiction Review*

"Noteworthy!" —*Fantasy and Science Fiction*

"Classic . . . Pick up one of Perry's novels. You won't be disappointed." —*VOYA*

THE DIGITAL EFFECT

STEVE PERRY

ACE BOOKS, NEW YORK

This book is an Ace original edition,
and has never been previously published.

THE DIGITAL EFFECT

An Ace Book / published by arrangement with
the author

PRINTING HISTORY
Ace edition / May 1997

The Putnam Berkley World Wide Web site address is
http://www.berkley.com

Make sure to check out *PB Plug*,
the science fiction/fantasy newsletter, at
http://www.pbplug.com

ISBN: 0-441-00439-3

ACE®
Ace Books are published by The Berkley Publishing Group,
200 Madison Avenue, New York, NY 10016.
ACE and the "A" design are trademarks
belonging to Charter Communications, Inc.

PRINTED IN THE UNITED STATES OF AMERICA

10 9 8 7 6 5 4 3 2 1

This book is for Dianne
And for my grandchildren,
Zachary and (sort of) Howard.

Acknowledgments

As usual, there were folks who had a hand directly or indirectly in stirring my potboiler to keep it from burning too badly. Thanks go to: Chris Warner, Michael Reaves, Vince Kohler, Jean Naggar, and Tom Dupree. With a big hello to Tim and Angela Combe, and a special thanks to Ginjer Buchanan for understanding that the birth of a grandchild outweighs the delivery date for a novel.

Therblig: The fundamental motions of the hands of a worker, made up of a series of divisions. These are: search, grasp, reach, move, hold, release, position, pre-position, inspect, assemble, disassemble, use, unavoidable delay, avoidable delay, plan, and test to overcome fatigue.

Frank Bunker Gilbreth and
Lillian Evelyn Moller Gilbreth

THE
DIGITAL
EFFECT

1

GIL WAS WORKING between heartbeats to tack the life preservers in place when the woman walked into his shop. Yes, the gyrostabilizers were supposed to compensate for biological motions like heart and lungs, but if you depended on them, you'd wind up with a model that looked as if it had been constructed by a blind dexy addict using a power shovel. Well, maybe not that bad, but certainly below his standards.

He knew she was there, but he didn't move to acknowledge her. The quad-Z scale model under the microviewer was delicate at best. It was the *Dona Paz*, a Philippine ferry that sunk after it collided with an oil tanker in the Tablas Strait on Earth in 1987, killing 3,400 people. He specialized in disaster ships and, until the Floating Casino City *Shanghai* went down in 2077 taking more than 12,000 unlucky gamblers with it, the *Dona Paz* had held the record for most lives lost at sea in peacetime. When finished, the model would be slightly longer than a centimeter, shorter than the trimmed nail on his little finger. Sneeze at the wrong time, and two hundred hours of work would collapse into a tiny—and worthless—lump of carbonex.

Lubb . . . press the bacterium-sized ring against the superstructure quickly, firmly, move the hand back in the waldo-field, and . . .

Dupp.

Got it—

"M. Sivart?"

"Cycle tools," he said. "Field sensors off."

The model table's voxax obediently froze the microscopic instruments under the holoprojic magnifier and killed the waldo-field. He removed his hands from the photoanimatronic light grids that translated his motions from gross to extremely fine, twisted his form-chair, and looked closer at the woman.

My.

She was moderately tall, probably around 173 cm, athletically built, maybe fifty-nine, sixty kilos, with long red hair in a thick braid. She had green eyes. A swimmer, dancer, gymnast maybe. Muscles looked hard enough to bounce ball bearings off them. The physique was easy to see because she wore a dark green spandex bodysuit and jazz slippers. She had a matching carry bag on a low-slung and wide buscadero-style belt, brown leather or a good imitation of it. Her face wasn't quite perfect, the nose a hair too long, the lips a little too full, but that added character. He didn't recognize her—he was sure he wouldn't have forgotten seeing such a woman. On a wheelworld the size of the *Robert E. Lee* with more than seventy thousand permanent residents, it was quite possible not to know everybody, even after five years.

Looking at her, Gil realized he needed to get out more.

"I'm Gil Sivart. What can I do for you?"

"My name is Patricia Blackwell. What you can do is find out who killed my SO and why."

He gave her a small smile. From time to time, he did favors for people. He didn't have any official standing, but helping some highly placed folk had earned him a few debts in return, and as long as he didn't get into the middle of official police business, they usually left him alone. He liked to solve complicated puzzles, the more complex the better. But right at the moment he had a backlog of model orders stretching eight months, an upcoming show of his work, and no time to indulge his hobby as an amateur investigator.

"M. Blackwell—"

"Trish."

"Okay. Trish. Well, you see—"

And before he could say another word, the shop's front window exploded.

Shards of the clear castplast plate clattered on the floor and counters, and a blast of chemical stink rolled over them.

He dove from the chair, caught her around the waist, allowed the tackle to take them both down onto the floor behind the front display counter. She struggled, surprised.

"What the hell is going on—?!"

"Be still," he said. "Somebody just blew out the window. They might still be out there."

He let her go, did a fast crawl toward the model table, grabbed his com from where it was hooked to his chair. Thumbed the Emergency button three times fast to trigger it.

The computer caught the call immediately.

"Nature of the emergency?" the vox asked.

"Gil Sivart, Sivart's Model Shop, Public Square, Main Level, Row Twelve." The computer would already have that from his com ID, in theory, but he wanted to be certain. "Somebody just blasted out my front window with an explosive device."

"Stay calm," the computer said. "A police trike will be dispatched." There was a pause. "ETA, two minutes or less."

Gil crawled back to where Trish Blackwell lay. He wondered if the computer was programmed to say "Stay calm" no matter what was said.

The station just blew the hull. We're all going to die! Stay calm.

Right.

"Cools are on the way. Be here in a minute or two. Here, take the com."

"What are you doing?"

"Going to take a quick look." He gathered himself, bounced up, glanced into the courtyard in front of the Row Twelve shops. He didn't see anybody. He dropped back into his squat.

"I think they're gone," he said.

"Are you sure somebody did that? Maybe it was some kind of freak accident."

"That's commercial-grade castplast plate," he said. "You could stand outside and throw bricks at it all day long without making a dent in it. It doesn't just blow up by itself."

For a moment, neither of them said anything. Gil heard the sound of a police trike's siren dopplering toward them. He looked at the woman lying next to him on the floor. Made a decision.

"After we finish telling it to the cool," he said. "Then we can talk about your problem."

The trike cool was a short, heavyset woman who moved with economical steps. She checked to make sure no hairy-eyed bombthrowers were still around with one hand on her dart pistol, examined the damage, took a few seconds of holographic digital video stills. She pulled a small digital sensor from her belt, an electronic molecule sniffer, waved it back and forth. She frowned at the readout.

"Detonex?" Gil said.

She turned the frown on him. "How would you know that, M. Sivart?"

"Characteristic odor."

Trish said, "Smells like bug spray to me."

"That's what Detonex smells like," Gil said. "Probably a fifty-milligram shaped charge. Newton-bleak. They use it for cutting heavy plastic pipe in exterior construction. About the size of a BB and usually rigged to go off on impact. You can set it and then hit it with a weight, or fire it with a jet of compressed gas into a narrow spot where you want the boom.''

The cool nodded. ''I guess it won't hurt to confirm that it was Detonex. You have any enemies, M. Sivart?''

Gil smiled. ''A few.''

''Anybody who'd want to do this?''

''Some who might like to see me sucking vac or shoved into a chopper and fed down the tubes to Recycling, but I can't imagine they'd be satisfied with blowing up my window.''

The woman looked at Trish. ''What about you, M. Blackwell? Enemies?''

''Not that I know of.''

The cool tapped her flatscreen, spoke a few words with it held in front of her mouth so Gil couldn't hear. Racked the screen on her belt. ''Well. I've logged it. Probably some kid got into his momma's construction kit, though that stuff is supposed to be accounted for. We've had some vandalism on the LL's and in the Square Park. Teeners with too much time on their hands. We'll have Stores run an inventory, but . . .''

Gil nodded. ''Appreciate your time, officer. Thanks for stopping by. I'll get Maintenance to fix this.''

''Insurance'll cover it,'' the cool said. ''Any more problems, call us.''

''Got it.''

The cool climbed onto her trike and pedaled away.

''Somebody throws a bomb at your shop and that's all the police do?'' There was a bitter tang to her voice. ''I guess it doesn't really surprise me. Not after what happened to David.''

''Why don't we go find some lunch and you tell me about it,'' he said.

''I'm an exotic dancer at the The Baron, it's a club on LL5.''

Gil nodded, sipped at the cup of tepid coffee in front of him. That explained the muscles. The sidewalk restaurant a few doors down from his shop was convenient, it overlooked the park and served decent sandwiches, but good coffee wasn't one of its virtues. As she talked, he scanned the walk and surrounding area, watching carefully. The bomber might be out there keeping an eye on them right now, and if anybody made any sudden moves, he was going to do a little dancing of his own.

"David—that's David Corderman—was my Significant Other. We hadn't formalized our living arrangement, but were about to when he was killed."

He glanced around, decided they weren't about to be blown up, looked straight at her. "What happened?"

"The police say he put his head under a stamping press and committed suicide. He was a roughneck in Heavy Engineering, he worked on E&M."

"You don't think it was suicide?"

"It couldn't be."

"Why not?"

"Like I said, we were about to formalize our contract. He didn't have any reason to kill himself. None. And he never would have."

"Could it have been an accident?"

"The police say not."

Gil swirled the coffee dregs around in the pressed-paper cup. "Sometimes when people die, their loved ones have a lot of trouble accepting it."

"I do have a lot of trouble with it, M. Sivart."

"Gil."

She didn't pause. "The reason *why* I have trouble is that somebody killed him. He wouldn't have done it."

She sounded so sure. But then, he'd looked into other deaths that friends and families had been certain were suspicious, deaths that turned out to be just what they appeared to be. He didn't say anything, but waited for her to amplify it.

She ranted: "David was young, strong, healthy. No history of mental instability. He thought I was pregnant when he died. We wanted children. Turned out I wasn't, but he believed we were going to have a baby. His parents killed themselves when he was a boy. The last thing he would have done to his own son or daughter would have been to give him or her the same background he had. He wouldn't have killed himself under any circumstances, he had a deep conviction about it. I lived with him for three years. I knew him.''

Gil nodded. ''I see.''

''Look, I make good money at my job, more than I need. Whatever it costs, please, I'll pay it. I have to know what happened.''

He looked at her. Young, beautiful, vulnerable. Got him every time. Stirred up his latent knight-in-armor tendencies, it did. Plus there was that window. Could be a coincidence, of course.

''All right. I'll look into it.''

Her smile was mostly relief, but there was some gratitude in it. She could thank whoever had taken out his front window, too. Maybe it was coincidence, but he didn't think so. If somebody had been trying to scare him off, they'd made a mistake. People who threw bombs probably had lots of things they wanted to hide. If any of those *things* pertained to the death of this woman's lover, Gil Sivart was going to find out just what they were.

2

GIL SHUT THE shop down as soon as the repairman finished installing the new window. He paid a little more attention to his surroundings than usual as he strolled along the shop fronts toward the local elevators. He didn't want to turn into some kind of paranoid, but somebody *had* just tossed a bomb in his direction, even if it was only a little one.

He skirted the edge of the park, admired the bonsai and the tiny stream that burbled over the plastic rocks, smiled at an old woman who threw bread crumbs to the koi in the lower of the two ponds in this park. The station's builders had been very clever with the use of space. The little park was not that big, but with some artful planting and path construction, as well as different levels, the creators had made it look a lot larger than it actually was. There was a nice tang of peppery pollen in the air. On Earth, in the northern hemisphere, it was summer. The plants remembered the seasons even if the weather on the station never really changed very much.

Most of the shops ringing the level were open. Save

for the smaller operations like his own, most stayed open on a twenty-four-hour basis. The *Robert E. Lee* ran on shifts, three in a day, and one man's bedtime was another man's morning. Gil usually kept his shop open during third shift. When he was working on a new model he sometimes stayed through half the next shift, though he didn't usually put that much actual time in on the table. Every couple of hours he had to take a break, as fine motor control got harder to maintain. His circadian rhythms, had he still been on Earth, would have made him an owl. He generally slept from about 0200 to 1000 or 1100, went to the shop at noon and knocked off at 2000 or 2100. He was a little early today, but he figured that could be excused. A bomb tended to make the rest of the shift anticlimactic . . .

There was a small group waiting for the local when he got to the platform. Gil looked at them a little more closely than usual. Was one of the dozen people there a bomb-thrower? If so, he couldn't tell. There were office workers, a couple of exotechs, an old man with a small girl, probably a grand- or great-grandchild. Not a shifty eye or guilty look in the bunch.

Gil smiled. You couldn't judge a playit by its package. Some of the most violent and psychologically disturbed people he had ever met looked like kindly and innocuous souls who'd go out of their way to avoid stepping on a roach. There weren't a lot of murders on-station, but Domás Misipree, the man who'd poisoned four coworkers and fed their chopped up bodies one small section at a time into the recyclers, had looked like an advertisement for the Grandfather of the Year.

Ugly was as ugly did, not what ugly looked like . . .

The elevator was one of the smaller ones, just room enough for thirty or forty people, and when he stepped on it was only about half full. Somebody had already lit his level, so he found a vacant spot and looked at the newswall as the safety doors closed.

News from Earth or the other wheelworlds ran in a multimedia crawl down the right side of the wall, on-station news flashed on the left. There was a superimposed holoproj of the *Robert E. Lee* floating against a black background in the upper left corner and one of a spinning Earth in the right corner, in case you couldn't figure it out.

Gil had always thought this particular wheelworld was ill-called such. It didn't look anything like a wheel; it looked more like a thick dowel encased in an old-fashioned toilet paper tube. And there to one side was the tiny dot of the powercast satellite in a tight orbit around the space habitat. Actually, one could argue that the REL orbited the powersat and probably be right. It was all relative up here. If not for the breakthrough invention of artificial gravity—though that wasn't really exactly what it was—such an extee habitat shape as REL wouldn't exist. To get weight, you'd have to centrifuge it, and big spin wasn't for everybody. A lot of people couldn't function on twirlworlds; they spent all their time in the fresher throwing up, despite the best antinausea meds.

You could read or watch the news holoproj but if you wanted sound on the smaller elevators, you had to activate your personal com channel and wear an ear button. Gil thought that was a good idea; after working a shift, a lot of people, him included, didn't want to be blasted by news or entcom or spam as they went home. A couple of the big spiral-floor cylindrical express elevators had full multimedia running, and depending on where you stood, you automatically got full visual and aural input from one section or another—unless everybody agreed to turn the damned wall off. And on the big lifts, there was always *some*body who just *had* to see and hear what was happening, on the station, downlevels on Earth, or maybe just the latest soap opera. It could make for a noisy ride.

Once, on an elevator mostly full of green coveralls—recycle workers—who all looked tired as they could be and still be standing, some uplevel twerp had insisted the wall be left on so he could watch the stats. One of the tired workers looked at the twerp. He wasn't very big, the green, and when he spoke, his voice was calm, quiet and not the least bit angry. He said, "Oh. You want to see the report about the guy who was killed on an elevator because he wouldn't shut the news wall off?"

The twerp looked around and realized he was not among friends.

The surround went quiet in a hurry.

Gil noticed on the visuals that his shattered window had made the local level 'cast. Must have been a slow news period.

His cube was on LL3, the bottom sublevel, just above the Public Square, so it was a short ride, just the one stop. As the living levels went, Three was better than a couple, worse than a couple. Upper-middle-class tenants, mostly, people who had to work for a living, though not as hard as some. He wasn't as wealthy as those on One, but then, he wasn't chipping micrometeor splash and living in a four-meter-by-four utility on LL5, either. He had a bedroom, a living area, a fresher and a kitchenette, and while it wasn't a stadium, it was big enough for a single man who tended to bring in guests one at a time—and rarely, then. His ship models had found an audience, and he charged enough for them so that selling one meant a nice upward shift in his credit balance. He could have moved up a level, but—what was the point? He'd have more room, but his bed wouldn't be any more comfortable and it would just mean one more level to commute to his shop on the Square.

"Living Level Three, sublevel one," the elevator said. The door slid wide.

Half a dozen people got off along with Gil and headed into the maze of halls. Visitors from Earth usually had trouble negotiating the living levels on wheelworlds without begging the computer for help via their coms or flat-screens—the halls had been likened to English hedge mazes by some—but after a few years, finding your way around was automatic. Gil wended his way along the corridors until he got to his cube's door, only a two-minute trip from the local elevator. He palmed the lock plate and the door slid open.

"Good evening, Gil," the cube's computer said in a deep and throaty female voice. "The time is eighteen-twenty-six and you have three messages."

The door slid shut behind him. "Play messages," he said.

"Hey, Gil, Winston. I'm postponing the twenty-three-hundred class, I've got a tax audit. See you tomorrow."

Winston was Gil's kaja-tangan teacher. The martial art, known also as "glass hands," was a combination of several soft or internal styles—pa qua, tai chi and chan gen—and Winston was the highest-ranking sifu in wheel-space. Gil was almost ready to take his black sash test. Or so he thought—that was up to Winston. He had been training in the kwoon for nearly four years. In the beginning, they'd worked a trade for lessons: a ZZZZ-scale model of the French steamer *La Bourgogne,* sunk when hit by the British sailer *Cromartyshire,* off Nova Scotia in 1898. After he'd joined the advanced class, Gil paid for his lessons by teaching the beginners class now and then.

"M. Sivart, please call F. Jessel at Procurement. Your order of carbonex has been delayed until next Tuesday."

Well. That wasn't a problem; he had enough to last for another week or two.

"Better mind your own goddamned business, Sivart, unless you want to wind up like your front window."

This last message was from somebody with a deep and warbly voice, probably disguised electronically.

"Computer, identify caller three."

"The call was made from a public com without ID entered, Gil."

"The location of the com for caller three?"

"Public Square, main bank."

So much for running that down. He shrugged. "Forward this message to the Police Department."

"Message forwarded, Gil."

He stripped, put on a pair of shorts, and did a few

warm-ups. He stretched a little to loosen his tight legs and back, did a few yoga asanas, then began the slow motion close-set whose name, *Hashara Litenask*, translated loosely to "bug in a little box." The entire form, which ran ninety-seven movements and took about half an hour to complete, could be performed in a space two meters by two meters. Like the wall attacks and the corridor defenses, close-sets were very useful on a wheel-world where space was often very tight. And, like tai chi, the steps had colorful and descriptive names: Insect Climbs Wall; Hide Under Rock from the Storm; Parry Spider's Kiss; Become the Leaf . . .

He had not been practicing the set long enough so that it was automatic. It still took concentration to do it without a misstep or loss of balance, and whatever else was on his mind had to go away or he would falter, maybe even fall. There were masters who could reportedly do calculus while executing the moves perfectly, but he had a long way to go to get to that level, much less no-mind meditation.

He shifted his weight, settled into a deep squat with his right leg extended—Avoid Chameleon's Tongue—and listened to his left knee *pop!* sharply. His knees always did that, even here where the artificial gravity was a hair less than TS. Loud enough to be heard across the room, the noise was like somebody snapping his fingers.

When he was finished, he dialed up a two-minute shower. Dried himself off with the warm air jets, padded naked into the kitchenette, and popped a frozen burrito into the microwave. He added water to a dried apple, watched it plump, and thought about the events of the day. Blown-out window, a new investigation for a client, the model was going along pretty good. He'd had considerably less interesting shifts . . .

After his supper, he sat in the web-back chair in his robe and lit the holoproj to the local news channel. They might be a bit cramped, the wheelworlds, the rules restrictive, but there were certain advantages. Today on the REL, there hadn't been any murders, not bad for a town of seventy thousand; neither had there been any riots, hurricanes, or red tides. Nary a volcano had let go, no famines swept the decks, no new toxic waste dumps had been uncovered.

And no giant resiplexes had collapsed, killing hundreds of workers, either.

Gil sighed, and shut the news off. He put the new mystery playit by Sharinga Kopurraba into his reader and thumbed it on. He sat the reader in his lap. "Page one," he said. "Words only."

The image shifted as the reader flashed the first page into a flat plane angled so he could read the words. The background music and illustrations remained off. He preferred to use his own imagination for effects.

"Since Inspector Targan had once eaten in Yunta's Cafe, he could easily understand why somebody might wish to kill the cook . . ."

Gil smiled. He loved Targan, the Sydney-based abo detective who harried the wicked across Australia. Targan used logic, the latest high-tech gizmos, and almost always, great intuitive, spiritual leaps into the Dreamtime to solve his crimes.

Targan perhaps enjoyed female company and good food a bit more than was healthy—especially since the women tended to be guilty of something by the time his investigations were over, and the food tended to give him gas—but other than that, he had few vices.

As investigators went, Targan was right up there with the greats like Holmes and Poirot.

But before the Inspector could determine who had murdered the cook, then later, the owner of the ptomaine cafe, Gil dozed off.

3

THE WORLD'S LARGEST resiplex took shape on the outskirts of Buenos Aires. An engineering marvel, the building known locally as *Negro Grande*—Big Black— was almost three-quarters finished and two months ahead of schedule in the extremely hot January of 2083. It was expected to be finished and ready for occupancy by winter, May or June at the latest. The workers had been lucky—the mild climate around the city had been somewhat warmer than normal, but the rains had been less, and little time had been lost to the weather.

In shape, Big Black was a *pirámide*, almost two kilometers on a side at the base, and rising more than half that high into the warm summer night. It had taken almost a year just to build the proper earthquake-resistant foundation to support such a massive structure. The pyramid's color came from exterior solar slabs, both active cells and passive panels, and even during a cloudy day, these were sufficient to supply the structure with enough electricity to run a small city, which in fact the building would be when occupied. At night, supplemental power would come through giant buried copper power cables run from far hydroelectric dams and the new nuclear power plant just started up, halfway to Patagonia.

Big Black drew on the experience of the wheelworlds, was self-contained, and at full capacity would house comfortably some fifty thousand people. It was the first of a planned score of monster SA resiplexes, though that name was something of a misnomer—people would not only live in the building, they would shop, eat, work, and play there.

Not poor people, at least not at first. No, these first self-contained cities-in-a-box would be limited to those willing and able to pay the stiff residency taxes and rents. People who wanted to get away from the squalor and crime of Buenos Aires but who did not want to leave Earth to live in a can in vacuum. And who could blame them?

An engineering marvel, the design. Big Black had few enemies. The building could flex, could give enough with special joints in the compartmentalized frame, shifting stress so that even a major terrestrial disaster would not bring it down. Hurricane-force winds would not move Big Black, nor hail break it, nor lightning mar the insulated walls. If a meteor hit the ground and shook it, Big Black would probably ride that out, too.

The structure was, as engineers and architects liked to say, bulletproof.

On that hot summer's January day, Gil Sivart stood on a hillock mounded of a small part of the dirt from the excavation of the foundation, a hillock already thick and verdant with neatly mowed grasses, and smiled at the *Negro Grande*. It wasn't really his project; he was simply one of hundreds of engineers signed on for a chance to be part of history. The biggest self-contained building on the planet.

He was standing right there, no more than two klicks away, when the resiplex fell down.

He saw the east wall buckle, blinked, and didn't understand. The sound took a while to travel the two kilometers, a few seconds, and it was a death groan, full of shrieks as metal and stone and plastic sheared and let go. He heard the communal scream of the workers from inside as the east wall fell in and sent forth a cloud of smoke and dust. This was followed in a kind of stretched time by the north and south walls shattering and folding, before the west wall lost its top third and caved in as if it were brittle wax. Oddly enough, the bottom section of the west wall held fast.

He ran down the hill toward the ruin, screaming, though he didn't remember that part too well. It was only later when he realized his vocal cords were damaged enough so he spoke in whispers for a week that he realized how loud he must have yelled.

Yelling did no good.

The resiplex was dead by the time he got to it—and it wasn't the only thing. Seven hundred and sixteen workers were killed outright and another hundred and sixty would die later. Plus two hundred more injured badly enough that many of them would wish they had died. Bodies were blended into a swamp of bone and flesh and steel and plastcrete. The survivors' yells were pitiful, and rescue efforts, while heroic, were overmatched. It was too big; nobody expected anything like this. There was a smell, like dust and spray foam insulation and—he imagined—blood.

It was a major disaster. The designers and crew of the *Titanic* must have felt the same kind of emotion. How could this have happened? It was impossible!

The project managers needed goats, and they quickly found dozens. They broke speed records passing the buck—*pasaron el fardo*, as the locals said. It was the fault of the suppliers, the inspectors, the workers, the Italians—anybody but those at the top. Eventually, the head of the Engineering Department took the biggest fall, but everyone knew it was the money men who deserved it. The millions in projected profit hadn't been enough, so somebody cut corners to make more.

The other projected resiplexes died at the same moment Big Black collapsed.

Later, in a bar in Buenos Aires where Gil worked to get and stay drunk, he found himself talking to a police captain. They knew who the real culprits were, the policeman said, but what could they do? The rich were more bulletproof than the design for Big Black. Had always been so. The policeman shrugged, said it was the way of things, and Gil bought him another drink . . .

Gil awoke in a sweat. The dream didn't come as much as it used to, but every now and then, it would take over his night. There were variations. Sometimes he was inside the pyramid when it came down and was one of the workers trapped in the rubble. Sometimes he was floating above it, watching in fascinated horror, his engineer's eye cataloging the collapse, noting which girders collapsed, which held, watching it all as if it were a holoprojic question on a final exam: *Tell me, M. Sivart, what could have been done to avert structural failure at this location, just here at this point?*

Specified material, Professor. Properly heat-treated extruded girders from a qualified and inspected foundry, there, sir, in that series of supporting cross-braces, right there, sir. Good steel, instead of cheap Thai crap from a factory where the metal was melted from old automobile frames and seasoned by the odd worker falling into the bucket. Sir.

Gil sighed. It wasn't his fault. He hadn't known. And he'd quit. No more big projects. That was when he'd gone into model making.

Nobody got hurt if a model the size of your pinkie's last joint didn't set properly—except in the pocketbook—and Gil was willing to give the money back to any unsatisfied customer who wanted it.

None of which made him feel any better when the nightmare galloped up and forced him upon her back for another ugly ride. He sighed. Might as well get up. Once the dream stole his sleep, it never returned it. Maybe he could go back to Australia and help Inspector Targan chase his demon again.

4

WHEN HE DECIDED he wasn't going to get back to sleep, Gil called and found that the officer in charge of the investigation into Corderman's death was a detective named Ramses El-Sayed. Gil recalled meeting the man a time or two at some social gathering or another. He had a memory of the man as black-haired and dark-eyed, about average height and weight, from Egypt or somewhere in the Middle East originally. Gil's hobby sometimes put him in contact with the REL's authorities. Some of them thought he did good work; some of them thought he was a pain in the butt and should mind his own business. Some of them didn't know anything about him. Offhand, he couldn't recall which group Detective El-Sayed might be in. Well. He'd find out soon enough.

Gil went to his refrigerator's freezer and removed a small can of whole roasted coffee beans. He put a tablespoon of the beans into a small hand mill and turned the crank until the beans were ground into a fine powder. He dumped the powder into a gold-mesh cone filter, then used a small paintbrush to remove the last of the dust from the mill. He set the filter over the mouth of a ceramic mug he'd brought with him from Earth. He put the water kettle on the inducer and turned it on. One of the few things he missed from living down below was his natural gas range, the visual cues of an open flame, but electricity and microwave cookers were much safer on a wheelworld.

He did a few stretching exercises while his water heated. He allowed himself a single cup of coffee each morning. Import prices were high; coffee wasn't one of the crops that grew well on the REL. Top-quality beans ran about sixty New Dollars a half-kilo, almost triple what it cost most places on Earth. People who vacationed on the planet sometimes brought back their entire weight allowance in such things as coffee or semilegal tobacco. Despite the cost of tobacco—a pack of cigarettes ran more than a hundred nude—the smoking room on the Public Square always had a waiting line to get in.

Though he could afford more, it was also a matter of discipline and appreciation that he held himself to the single cup of coffee per day. He didn't like to let himself get into sloppy habits. He ate relatively well, exercised, and once a week he fasted for twenty-four hours, nothing except water or a little fruit juice. And that single cup of freshly brewed coffee.

He finished his stretches, went and poured the water through the filter. Inhaled and enjoyed the aroma as the water dripped into the cup. When it was done, he took the mug to his chair, sat, and prepared for the first sip of the brew.

When he drank his coffee, that was all he did. If his com chimed or there was a caller at the door, he ignored it. He didn't read the newsfax, nor even listen to any of his favorite music. His one cup deserved, and got, his full attention. He'd once heard a story about a monastery on the top of some mountain in Japan or somewhere. After a long trek in the cold to get there, the monks would offer to sell you a cup of coffee. You had a choice: There was a two-dollar cup—or a two-*hundred*-dollar cup. When pressed to explain the difference, the monks were reported to say, "A hundred and ninety-eight dollars."

Gil smiled. Zen.

His mind cleared. He took a deep breath, let half of it out, then sipped at the brew.

Ah . . .

The main Police Station on the *Robert E. Lee* was just past the Magnolia end of the Main Park on the Public Square. The Square wasn't that shape at all, but round as were all the other levels on the wheelworld, but the name came from a time when towns had been laid out that way. Would have been just as easy to say "Public Circle," but for some reason, the designers had elected to keep the older term.

The coolschool was a floor-to-sub-ceiling two-story unit, three shop fronts wide. It included in it a small jail. Short-term criminals were either stored in the jail or cube-confined with a telltale bracelet to make sure they stayed home. Long-term prisoners were shipped down below.

The desk sergeant looked up and nodded at Gil. The man had been a trike cop before his promotion a year or so back, and he'd been involved in a case Gil had taken on. They got along okay. "M. Sivart," he said. "What can I do for you?"

"Sergeant. I need to see Detective El-Sayed if he's around."

"I believe he is. Hold on a second." The sergeant waved his hand over a com unit. "Ray? Got somebody here to see you."

Detective El-Sayed didn't rate an office; he had one of half a dozen three-walled cubes in a big communal space. When Gil arrived, he found the man hunched over a keyboard in front of an old 2D monitor screen. A personal portable fan plugged into an exhaust duct in the wall to his right droned and sucked into it most of the smoke from the pipe clenched in the detective's teeth. The pipe was shaped in a rounded L, with a slightly curved black stem and a bowl of smooth brown briar. A few vagrant wisps of the aromatic smoke drifted up where Gil could smell them. They had a kind of bourbony odor. He liked the scent.

"Detective El-Sayed?"

The cop kept tapping at the keyboard. "Yeah, just a second. Have a seat." He nodded at the only other chair in the cube.

Gil sat. He noticed a holograph of a dark woman and two children that looked a lot like her on one corner of the desk. The detective's service weapon, a black plastic Smith & Wesson compressed-gas pistol, lay snugged into what looked like a genuine sharkskin paddle holster next to the holograph. The weapon fired nonfatal shock darts; a high-voltage, low-amperage charge was imparted to the projectile as it left the barrel and was sufficient to knock a big man sprawling if it hit him anywhere hard enough to break the skin. Gil knew and had practiced with air guns, owned one. Winston taught projectile weapons as part of kaja-tangan; it was his contention that you could not claim to be a modern martial artist without some knowledge of guns. Especially since such things were a lot more accessible now than swords or rice flails.

Also on the desk was a misshapen, cold-castplast ashtray that looked as if it had been sculpted by a pair of eager but very young hands. The ashtray was a brilliant phosphorescent blue that wouldn't match any of the decor in the building—or in any other building Gil had ever seen. He smiled. Presents from one's children were beyond matters of taste. Next to the ashtray was a clear plastic pouch of pipe tobacco, a lighter, a tamper, and a packet of pipe cleaners.

El-Sayed tapped in a few final keystrokes, then leaned back. He took the pipe from his mouth and held it up. "This bother you?"

"Not at all."

The detective nodded, puffed on the pipe, blew the smoke toward the exhaust vent. "Even with all the carcinogens taken out, some people get bent if I light up around them."

"Some people don't have enough to worry about," Gil said.

"What can I do for you, M. Sivart? If it's about your window, I'm afraid we haven't made any progress there yet."

"It's not about the window, though I did upload a message I got last shift I think concerns that."

"I heard it," the detective said. "Somebody doesn't like you. Probably has to do with your . . . hobby."

Gil nodded. So El-Sayed knew who he was and what he did when he wasn't making models.

"We'll keep looking. So what *can* I do for you?"

"I need to know about David Corderman's death."

The detective puffed on his pipe again. Grinned tightly around the stem. "She's a good-looking woman, isn't she?"

"She is indeed, but that's not why I'm checking on it for her."

"If you don't mind my asking, why are you? Don't you think we know how to do our jobs here?"

The question was mildly delivered, but Gil caught the hint of ruffled feathers behind it. He said, "No disrespect intended, Detective. Every cool I've had occasion to work with has been competent and professional. I'm not accusing anybody of neglect."

"Your client seems to think we missed something."

"She lost her SO; she isn't likely to be objective."

"If you know that, why are you here? You make a pretty good living doing modelwork, don't you? Or is it something else you're trying to get from her, besides money?"

Gil smiled. El-Sayed knew more about him than he'd let on. And the implication was a standard cool technique, to apply a little pressure and see what happened. Nothing to take personally. What El-Sayed was saying was, in effect: *So, are you playing the sympathetic investigator so the lady maybe welcomes you into her bed*

*and shares her favors with you? Even if you don't think
there is anything worth investigating?*

"You believe in coincidence, Detective?"

"Sure. Unless it gets stretched too far."

"Okay, consider this: I haven't stuck my nose in anybody's business for months, didn't have any plans to do
so. I've been busy making models. So Trish Blackwell
comes into my shop, and while she's there, my front
window just happens to get blown in. Could be a coincidence. But then when I get home, there's a message
warning me to mind my own business—which I have
already been doing, so that's maybe a little odd.

"So it's maybe a coincidence, or maybe it's that the
bomb and call are connected to M. Blackwell's visit. And
I have to ask myself, if that is so, why would anybody
want to warn me off an open-and-shut suicide? What
would be the point?"

He looked directly at the detective, met his gaze. "Feel
like that might be a fair stretch to you?"

Gil watched him think about it for two puffs on the
pipe. "Maybe. Or maybe she's got a new boyfriend, a
jealous type, who doesn't want any competition."

"Maybe so. I'm not saying you screwed up," Gil said.
"If it walks, talks, and acts like a duck, that's usually
what it is. Probably Corderman's death was just what you
think. And there have been bigger coincidences. But I
have to check."

El-Sayed nodded. "Okay."

"So, what can you tell me about it?"

"I got the call when I was doing secondary. The guy
who would have caught it was out working a domestic
on LL1—stoned rich people beating on each other. I took
the express to the bottom sublevel of Engineering &
Manufacturing. Corderman was a roughneck, doing ro-
botwork—he ran a stamper or a metal fabber, did a little
precision sawing, like that. Coworkers found his body in
a stamping press. I got there before they moved the
corpse. He'd stuck his head under a forty-ton hydraulic
ram. From the shoulders up, he was a quarter-centimeter

thick and a meter wide. No sign of foul play, no chance
it could have been an accident. There was a scanning
security cam on the unit that showed before and after,
though it didn't show the actual event. We checked all
entrance and exit cams, the coworkers, did a background
looking for enemies and came up empty. He was in that
area alone, it was just before shift-change. This guy was
big, thick with muscle, and nobody's lap dog. Strong
enough to have picked himself up with one hand, according to people who knew him. If somebody had
grabbed him and shoved him into the machine and he
hadn't wanted to go, there should have been signs of a
struggle. There was no reason to believe anything other
than what we found—the guy wanted to die.''

''Autopsy?''

''Not a mark on him, except for the press. Drug screen
was clean.''

''So a man who was cold sober just undid a lot of
safeties and squashed himself,'' Gil said. ''It would have
been a lot easier just to step into a lock and blow himself
into vac.''

''Or take poison or an overdose of sleeping pills,'' El-
Sayed said. He shrugged, the pipe in one hand. ''A lot
of suicides don't take the easiest path. Only they know
why.''

''Could I have a copy of the report?''

''Sure. It's public record. Here's the number, you can
download it at your convenience.''

''Thanks.''

''Now what?''

''I'll talk to the medic. Maybe the people on Corderman's shift.''

''We didn't miss anything.''

''You've never made a mistake, Detective? Must be
nice.''

That got a grin from El-Sayed. ''When I was twenty-
two, I decided I wanted to be a cool instead of going to
work with my father in his shoe store. I sometimes wonder about that decision.''

"We've all passed that road," Gil said. He stood. Extended his hand. "Appreciate your help, Detective."

"Call me Ray," he said, offering his hand. "If you find something I missed, you'll let me know?"

"Of course."

If Ray El-Sayed was a bad cop, he'd want to know so he could cover his ass. If he was a good cop, he'd want to know so he wouldn't make the same mistake again. Either way, Gil would probably pass on what he figured out. Eventually.

It was a little early to expect any results, and Gil was just gathering basic information. Like collecting fissionable material, you had to scrape together enough of it to start a chain reaction. When what you had was a teaspoon, it took a while to pile up that many kilograms.

And that was assuming what you were digging up was uranium and not lead.

And a man couldn't run without fuel of his own. Gil didn't much like eating when he first arose, but after he'd been active a couple of hours, he didn't mind eating.

Breakfast, then he'd get back to solving this crime—if there really was a crime.

5

GIL WENT TO the Square, to Mona's Cafe. For his money, Mona's served the best breakfast on the station, and since that was all they served around the clock, you could usually get a seat if you picked a time in mid-shift to eat. It was a little crowded this early, but they found a single-seat table for him in the corner next to the bonsai display. He ordered soypro ham, defatted eggs over easy, and whole wheat toast with real imported butter. Before he talked to the medic, Gil thought he ought to see if he could interview the initial investigator on the scene of Corderman's death. As it often happened on the station, it wasn't a cool but somebody from Corporate Security who got the call. And as it happened in this case, Chaz Wells, the Chief of Corporate Security himself, had been the first man to lay hands on the investigation.

Gil knew Wells slightly; the man owned one of his sculptures, though he had bought it second-hand, and was on the list for a second piece. Gil put in a com to Wells's office.

"I'm sorry," Wells's secretary said, but M. Wells is quite busy this morning."

"I'll only need a few minutes of his time. It's important. Please."

The magic word got her to at least check. Probably she didn't hear it a lot while screening calls for Security. "Hold a moment, M. Sivart."

Gil smiled. His name wasn't likely to be on the put-it-through list of movers and shakers. Then again, Wells knew who he was, and if he wanted to get another of Gil's models, he was likely to at least think about talking to him.

The secretary was back in half a minute. "M. Sivart, if it would be convenient for you to see M. Wells in about half an hour, he can give you ten minutes."

"That would be fine. Thank you for you help."

"You're welcome."

His breakfast arrived, delivered by a fresh-faced girl of about sixteen. Likely a secondary ed student earning a little money between classes. Gil nodded his thanks and smiled at her. Just enough time to eat before he was to meet Wells. Perfect.

Chaz Wells was a bachelor, about thirty-five, a very fair-skinned blue-eyed blond. Gil thought Wells might be of Germanic or maybe Northlands extraction, a big man who obviously lifted weights to keep fit and had thick muscles to show for it. He wore a tailored silk business suit in a muted power blue over an open-necked straw silk shirt and handmade moccasins. He flashed a high-wattage smile as Gil entered his office, stood, and offered his hand. They shook hands, Wells's grip a little too firm, then he waved Gil at the chair in front of his desk. Both men sat.

Gil noticed what appeared to be a Thompson submachine gun inside a glass case mounted on the wall at eye level behind Wells's desk. It would have been hard to miss.

"Thank you for seeing me, M. Wells."

"Call me Chaz, please. It's good to see you, Gil. I

hope you've come to tell me you are about to start on my commission.''

''Not for another three months, I'm afraid,'' Gil said. He nodded at the wall decoration. ''Interesting weapon. An airgun ersatz?''

Wells gave Gil a pleased grin. ''Actually, no, it's a real one. Dewatted—that is, rendered inoperable—by Terran T&F, of course, so it couldn't be fired even if you could get the ammunition, but it's genuine.''

''A tommy gun,'' Gil said. ''Military issue? Late 1930's or WWII?''

Wells's smile faded. He had been all prepared to deliver a lecture, and Gil had just stolen his thunder. ''How do you know that?''

Gil said, ''That front stock instead of the pistol grip, the lack of the Cutt's compensator, a thirty-round magazine instead of the bigger drum.''

''You're very well informed.'' Wells sounded irritated.

Gil thought about it for a second, then decided he wouldn't tell Wells that he had once fired a weapon similar to the one displayed on the wall. After that experience, he had done a little research on such things. But, since he had already one-upped Wells more than he had intended, he decided not to rub it in.

He remembered the experience fondly. It had been in South America when he'd been working on Big Black, months before the collapse. Gil and a couple of the other engineers had been invited to the casa of a local rich man. Ortis Vega was owner of one of the larger metal jobbers locally, and he was also a gun collector. The collection was probably very much illegal, but among others, Vega had several esoteric and quite valuable weapons, including a Colt six-shooter, a German Luger, and a Thompson submachine gun, all of them in working condition.

After lunch, he invited Gil and the other engineers out to his personal firing range.

Illegal or not, wealth conferred certain privileges.

Gil was thrilled. He had never operated a gunpowder firearm, and he appreciated the mechanical efficiency.

Vega showed him how to charge the weapon, and Gil loaded the magazine for the Thompson. The cartridges were short and stubby things, brass shells encasing copper-clad lead bullets that were driven by gunpowder ignited by a little primer cap in the base. The entire cartridge was smaller than the last two joints of his little finger. The rounds were loaded into a circular metal drum that contained fifty of them, where they were wound by a key into place and held there by a powerful spring. To operate the gun, you locked the drum full of ammunition into place. A bolt inside the receiver—also spring-powered—slid forward when you pulled the trigger, stripped a cartridge from a slot in the magazine, shoved it into the chamber, and set it off by tapping the primer with a pin. The force of the recoil pushed the bolt backward, a small metal hook extracted the spent shell and threw it several meters away, the bolt spring compressed and shoved the bolt forward again, and the entire action was repeated.

As long as the trigger was held down, Señor Vega explained, the gun would continue to fire.

Even with headphones to block out the sound, the exploding propellent was loud. The butt stock of the Thompson was braced against Gil's shoulder, but the recoil raised the end of the barrel in little bouncy moves as the bullets zipped out.

"You should fire in short bursts," the owner instructed Gil. "Pull and release the trigger so only three or four rounds go off, then realign the sights on the target again."

Gil did as instructed. The targets were four-liter plastic bottles full of water, set forty or fifty meters away, backed by a large hill.

Each time a bullet hit one of the water bottles, the plastic shattered and spewed water like a small bomb. The burned gunpowder smell and tiny flecks of unburned powder sprayed his face.

It took only a few seconds to shoot all fifty of the cartridges. A dozen bottles of water exploded and erupted, creating miniature and short-lived rainbows in the warm afternoon sun.

Altogether a satisfying experience on some primal level. He felt like a federal agent in some old style flat-vid thriller. Take that, you bootlegger!

Later, Gil's shoulder had been sore, and when he looked at the place where he had braced the gun's stock, there were half a dozen little hemorrhages, bruises, where the recoil had hammered the wooden butt against his flesh. He hadn't noticed it at all when he'd been shooting . . .

"I heard about your window," Wells said, breaking into Gil's memory. "We'll be glad to help the station cools in any way we can."

"Thank you. Actually, I'm not here about that. I'm doing a favor for someone, and I was wondering if you would mind telling me about the death of one of your employees a couple of months back, M. David Corderman?"

Wells blinked and looked puzzled. "I'm afraid I don't place the name."

"Killed under a stamping press?"

"Oh, yeah, that guy. Not much to tell. Open-and-shut suicide. Pretty grisly."

"No signs of foul play?"

Wells raised his eyebrows. "No way. Guy was an ox, it would have taken a dozen men to hold him there. He did it to himself. Crazy as a rat in recycling."

Gil nodded. "That seems to be the official position. Well, thank you, Chaz. I won't take up any more of your time." He stood.

"No trouble, Gil. How come you're interested in a suicide?"

"Corderman's SO has some misgivings about it."

"She probably drove him to it, you know how some women can be. Uh, look, would it insult you to offer a bonus to get to my commission a little faster?"

"No, I wouldn't take it as an insult. I have to finish them as they come in, though, sorry."

"Well, no harm in trying."

"Thanks again."

Gil smiled at the receptionist when he left.

Time to go see the medic.

The Assistant Coroner was one Doctor Basilio Alicante. According to the official bio Gil read on his way to the small medical complex on the Square, Alicante was from Spain, and his primary practice was in pediatrics. Gil wondered how one went from taking care of live children to doing autopsies on bodies.

Gil planned to make an appointment to see the medic, but as it turned out, Dr. Alicante had a cancellation and could talk to him immediately.

Gil was ushered into a small office by a medical assistant.

Alicante was a short, slight, young man. Late twenties, Gil figured; black hair worn short, brown eyes, maybe 166 centimeters tall and probably under sixty kilos. He wore disposable surgical blues, a short-sleeved shirt and baggy pants over throwaway silicone shoe covers. There was a pleasant, musky scent overriding the normal sterile smell Gil associated with clinics.

"Thank you for seeing me on such short notice, Dr. Alicante."

"You're the artist who does the microsculptures, aren't you?"

"Yes."

"Nice work. Wish I could afford one. How can I help you, M. Sivart?"

"I understand you sometimes act as an assistant coroner?"

Alicante grinned and nodded. "Sure. When Doc Steward is too hung over or down below on vacation."

"Long way from treating kids with station-pressure ear, isn't it?"

He shrugged. "I got interested in forensic medicine when I was at Harvard Medical. A lover of mine went on a trip to New York and was murdered. They caught the killer because a sharp pathologist was able to run down and match DNA from skin found between two of Eduardo's teeth when he bit his attacker. For a time, I considered going into the field, but my parents had a family practice in Cordoba and they prevailed on me to join them there instead.''

"And it is a long way from Cordoba to a wheelworld, too," Gil said.

"My parents died in a jetliner crash in eighty-six. I had no reason to stay there. I sold the practice and moved up. You want to see my appendectomy scar?"

Gil smiled. "Sorry. Bad habit, asking personal questions."

"De nada."

"I'm investigating the death of David Corderman. You did the autopsy on him."

"Ah, yes. The worker killed by the machine. Ugly matter. How is it your business, if you don't mind my asking?"

"Seems only fair. His SO is having some trouble with the manner of his death. She asked me to reexamine the details."

"This I can understand. It would give me nightmares had he been my SO, God forbid." Alicante said. "I can give you a copy of the autopsy."

"Thank you, I've downloaded that already. Any observations that you might recall that did not make it into the official report?"

The young doctor shrugged again. "Not really. No signs of a struggle, no drugs in his system, no way it could have been an accident, given the mechanical and electronic safeguards. He had no history of depression— no medical history at all, except for a pulled muscle in his back six months ago and routine yearly physicals. Aside from what killed him, he was in excellent shape. I cannot say why he would do such a thing, but it certainly appears that he did."

Gil nodded. "Is there any way to tell if he was conscious when the press came down upon him?"

"What do you mean?"

"Suppose somebody whacked M. Corderman on the back of the head with a blunt object, knocked him out cold, then put him under the press. Is that possible?"

"Sure. There's no way to tell if he was awake when he was killed."

"And any evidence of trauma to his head from such a thing would have been hidden by the manner of his death."

"Not hidden, destroyed," Alicante said. "You have reason to believe such a thing happened?"

"No," Gil admitted. "It was just a thought."

"The police and Corporate checked all that," the doctor said. "M. Corderman was alone in that area, so I was told. You should talk to them."

"I already have. Thank you for your help, Dr. Alicante."

"My friends call me Base," he said. He smiled. "Pardon another personal question, but are you by any chance a man's man, or bi, M. Sivart?"

" 'Gil,' " he said. "My preference is hetero, I'm afraid."

"Ah, too bad. My current SO Anton keeps threatening to leave me and return to his bullfighter boyfriend in Gijón. Seeing me with a handsome artist would do wonders for his attitude." He smiled.

"Thank you for the compliment, Base."

As he walked toward the park on the Square, Gil pulled his com and put in a call to Trish Blackwell. Perhaps they could meet for lunch?

That was agreeable, but she was working. Could he come to the club and speak with her there?

Yes. He could.

6

DOUBTLESS THE INTREPID Investigator Targan would be much farther along than Gil was by now, but unfortunately Gil wasn't blessed with the abo's mystical intuition. Gil was fairly logical, and logic was a superb tool—Sherlock Holmes certainly proved that—but then Holmes had those wonderful powers of observation to go along with it. Gil wasn't in that class.

What Gil had seen so far would probably have Targan and Holmes laughing themselves silly at his blindness, but if there was any evidence of murder there, Gil couldn't spot it.

He took an express elevator to LL5. It was a fairly run-down area, as run-down as it got on a wheelworld. A lot of tiny efficiency cubes, eateries, a few clubs, most of them dives. The Baron was nicer than most; it catered to a mostly upscale crowd—you had to be to afford the prices. He knew where The Baron was, although he'd only been there a couple of times. There had been an unhappy dinner with an ex-girlfriend a couple of years ago, a bachelor party for one of the students in his martial

arts class a few months after that. He didn't much enjoy
the club scene. If he wanted to drink, he could do it much
cheaper and in a better atmosphere in his own cube. And
if he was out to find female company, he'd rather do that
at his kaja-tangan class or maybe a gym, rather than
stalking some half-drunk woman in a pub. At least in the
class or gym, he'd know he'd have something in common
with the woman to start off with.

There had been several exotic dancers at the party,
male and female, but he was pretty certain Trish Blackwell had not been among them. He would have remembered her.

The elevator opened on the right sublevel, and six or
eight people got off with Gil. The Baron was four turn-
ings away, left, left, right, left. The unpainted aluminum
girders had a patina of oxidation that made them mottled
and dusky gray; the plastic wall panels were scratched,
with long stretches of tagger graffiti, some of it quite well
done. A few of the overhead lights were out. The anti-
static carpet was worn almost through to the floor in
spots. The station was supposed to be maintained the
same on each level, according to the charter and official
policy, but the truth was that some parts were better
maintained than others. Artificial gravity provided an up
and down, even in space, and as in most places, the haves
lived on top and the less fortunate lived on the bottom.
Five was the lowest of the LL's, just above Recycling,
and while the official policy was that nobody could possibly smell the waste being treated there in the airtight
and closed sewage system, everybody knew better. Now
and then, a malodorous vapor would waft up through the
vents or the elevator shafts from below, and LL5ers
would get a good whiff of what people flushed away tens
of thousands of times each shift on the *Robert E. Lee*.

The unofficial and much frowned-upon name for LL5
was Fecal Town. And while it could be his imagination,
Gil thought he caught a hint of that smell as he walked
along the corridor.

A large man stood just inside the doorway into The

Baron. He wore tight gray thinskins, so there was no
doubt that his thick muscles were real, and he played with
a small electronic credit reader, flipping it into the air
half a meter or so and catching it. Gil pulled his credit
card from the card pocket on his pants. Once upon a time,
the little narrow pocket would have held a wind-up
watch; once upon a time, the man in the doorway would
have been called a bouncer, for what he was apt to do
with unruly patrons.

"Cover is two nude," the man said.

Gil nodded and held his card out. The doorman took
it, dragged it through the reader's slot, handed it back to
him.

"I'm supposed to see Trish Blackwell."

"Lucky you, she's about halfway through her set."

Inside, the club was smoky—especially for a public
no-smoking zone—and the main lighting was dim. The
shape of the large main room was roughly octagonal,
with a bar at one end of the octagon and an elevated
stage at the opposite end. Small circular tables and back-
less stools, all of them bolted securely to the floor, were
spaced around the interior. Along the walls to the left
and right of the stage were a dozen booths, each with
enough seating for six, and larger, rectangular tables for
serious diners. There were forty-five or fifty people at the
tables or booths, about a thirty-percent capacity, Gil figured, and several waitresses moved back and forth, serv-
ing food or drinks. The waitresses wore gray thinskin
sheaths much like that of the doorman, but with artfully
cut-out strips that revealed patches of bare skin over
breasts, thighs and buttocks.

The stage was awash in bright lights, including a tracking spot that followed a performer. Some dramatic and
classical-sounding music was playing, either a full
orchestra or a well-programmed synthband. It sounded
like something by McNeeley or perhaps Extrapolated
Bach.

Gil found an empty table and sat just as the woman
onstage began a short tumbling run. Her costume was a

dark, electric red that covered her completely save for her hair and eyes. Probably it was some kind of spray-on latex, but she looked almost as if she had been held by her hair and dipped in a giant vat of crimson paint. All of her skin was covered, feet, hands, face, and she had a matching, smooth triangular patch over her mons blended so well you couldn't see the edges. Gil found the overall effect more sensual than if she had been na-ked. She did a round-off, two back handsprings, and a high, arching backward dive that ended in a stretched-out body roll to a full side split. With her legs spread wide, she leaned forward and laid her torso flat on the stage, turned her face to the left, then the right, then put her head down, hands pillowed under her hair. She looked as though she had fallen asleep for a beat, then she sprang up, leaped high and twirled, her long hair flying, and landed on one foot. Settled slowly into a one-legged squat, her other leg extended straight in front of her until it was parallel to the floor, toes pointed. Held the pose for ten seconds without any sign of a quiver in her muscles. Smiled at the audience she wouldn't be able to see for the light in her eyes. Her teeth flashed white against the dark red of her second skin.

The music died, the tracking spot winked out, and the other stage lights faded slowly until the stage was dark.

Gil smiled, impressed. Very nice. Exotic, erotic, ath-letic, and unique. He would guess it was Trish from the hair and body and the doorman's comments, but he couldn't be sure.

When the stage lights came up, the stage was empty.

A waitress arrived at his table a few seconds later. "M. Sivart?"

He looked up at her. "Yes?"

"Trish is in her dressing room. Through that door over there and down the hall, last room on the right. She asked if you'd meet her there."

Hmm. Maybe she could see past the spotlight. She knew he was here. "Sure. Thank you."

Gil stood. A brass fanfare, something Spanish,

sounded, and the stage lights went on. A man stepped
out onto the stage, dressed in a matador's suit of lights,
carrying a red cape. That could be interesting.

Gil glanced back as he approached the door to the side
of the stage, saw the doorman and the bartender watching
him. The bartender held a small remote in one hand. The
door's lock cheeped electronically, and the door slid
aside to admit Gil. He nodded at the bartender and went
through. Nobody was going to sneak backstage to bother
the performers.

There were four dressing rooms along the hall to Gil's
right, all of the doors leading into them open. In the first
room a pair of nude women sat in front of make-up mirrors, applying lip color or eye shadow. Neither of them
spared him a glance. The second room was empty. The
third room had two men in it, well-knit acrobats, a large
and small one, and they were practicing a balancing act,
the smaller man doing a handstand on the kneeling, larger
man's outstretched arm. Amazing.

Trish stood in the middle of the fourth dressing room
peeling strips of red from her body. The stuff was, as he
suspected, some kind of rubber or silicone compound; it
came off in stretchy translucent sheets as Trish tugged at
it. She was mostly bare on the left side of her body, a
little pile of the red gathered around her left foot as he
stepped into the room.

"Give me a hand, would you? Peel it slow and it
comes off without leaving any patches." She turned
around, presented him with her back.

My.

Gil stepped close to her, pinched the red material on
her right shoulder and the base of her skull and pulled
down slowly. A quarter-meter-wide strip of the stuff
came off Trish's body, came loose as cleanly as peeling
a banana. He gathered it into his hands, squatted, continued to remove the red, from over her tight buttock, down
the back of her thigh and calf, to her ankle.

With Trish working on her front, she was bare, save
for her crotch piece, in a few seconds. She gathered up

the strips of red and tossed them into a large bowl in the corner of the room. As Gil watched, the red plastic turned liquid in the bowl.

"Dermoplex," she said. "Osmotic artificial skin, used for burns. I got it from a medical supply place. Add a little dye and there you go. You can reuse it, over and over, though no matter now much of it I save, I always manage to lose some and wind up having to add another half a bottle for each new batch."

She stood naked in front of him and if she was bothered by it, Gil couldn't tell.

She looked at him. "You want me to put on a robe or something?"

"Not on my account. A thing of beauty is a joy forever."

She smiled. "You get used to running around naked and the stuff doesn't breathe as well as they claim, so I'm always burning up after a set. Have a seat."

Gil sat on a plastic chair, but Trish stayed standing, moving around and waving her arms a little to cool off. It was distracting.

"You are very good," he said. "The dance."

"Thank you. I work at it. The trick is to make it look easy." She stopped moving and looked directly at him. "You've found out something?"

He considered himself a man of the world but it was disconcerting to be sitting in front of a beautiful, almost-naked woman trying to have a business conversation.

"You cooled off yet?"

She grinned. "You do want me to put on the robe." It was not a question.

"Please."

She put on a thin silk robe and belted it shut. That was a little better. Now she sat in the chair across from him. "So?"

"So, I've talked to the cools, Corporate Security, and the doctor who did the autopsy, and the official line is that your SO killed himself. There is no evidence to suggest otherwise."

She looked disappointed. "So that's it?"

"Not quite." He told her about the threatening call he'd received.

"You think that had something to do with this?"

He shrugged. "I can't be positive. If it does, then something isn't right. Why would anybody want to warn me off a closed case—if all we are talking about is a suicide?"

He saw her hopes come up. "You're right."

He didn't tell her that he thought anybody who did such a thing would be pretty stupid. The smarter thing was to stay quiet and let it die. But then, people didn't always do the smarter thing.

"I'll keep you informed as I go," he said. "It might be a while before I find out anything."

She leaned forward and the silk robe gaped, giving him another view of her breasts. This was more erotic than her nudity, this quick glimpse of bare flesh. She took his left hand in both of hers. "You don't know how much this means to me, Gil. Nobody would believe me, they all thought I was crazy with grief, the poor bereaved girlfriend who couldn't accept the truth. I really appreciate this. Take all the time you want. At least you're trying."

Gil felt his lust saddle up to war with his principles.

The battle, while silent and short, was intense:

Lust rode forth, lance raised. *Reach out and take her, fool! She wants comforting, you know she does. You're both adults, you could be rolling around and breaking furniture, look at her, she's got the body for it! Her man is dead, she needs somebody. Help her put her grief behind her. It will make her feel better—and make you feel better in the process. The Big Dark is out there, always waiting. Unite against it, share your warmth. Who'll be hurt?*

But Principles said, *She is lonely, in pain and vulnerable. It would be taking advantage, and you know it. Another time, another place, on a level playing field, yes, certainly, but now? Now would be cheating. Now she is wounded, crippled, unable to defend herself. It will be a hollow victory. There is no joy in feeding on another's misery. You can't fool yourself that it would be anything else. You know it.*

Gil sighed mentally. Yes, dammit, he knew.

He squeezed her hand, smiled, removed his hand from her grip. Stood and nodded at her. "I'll chase it as far as it goes, Trish."

"What happens now?"

"I keep looking. Once you start wading through these things, stuff sometimes rises from the bottom muck to where you can see it. Something will come up. We'll just have to wait until we spot it."

7

THERE WERE OTHER avenues Gil could explore, and he went back to his shop to consider them. Might as well get some work done on his latest model while he was thinking about it, he figured.

And he could feel a little bit virtuous about how he'd behaved with Trish Blackwell while he was at it. Although it had been a few months since he'd been with a woman, and there was a certain amount of regret in walking away from what could have been a very interesting experience.

And a sure thing, too, fool!

Well. There it was. Some days the choices weren't easy and the victories were Pyrrhic at best. But you still had to look at yourself in the mirror when you rubbed the depil into your beard.

Inside the shop, the window looked as good as new, the glazier had cleaned up all the shattered plastic, and the shop was quiet. In fact, the window was better than new. Gil had augmented his insurance and opted for a thicker grade of castplast. The same strength device that had shattered the original window would probably spiderweb this one, but it shouldn't blow it out of the frame. He tapped the door lock button to prevent unexpected visitors and activated his table.

Modelmaking was, for Gil, like drinking coffee. Once he shifted into work mode, he tended to tune out everything else. Early on in his career, he would sometimes play background music, but he stopped when he realized he wasn't consciously hearing it. He would come out of the microscopic realm and notice that the recording had stopped and he had not been aware of any part of it. Once, the heating system in the station had gone awry and the temperature had dropped twenty or thirty percent, enough for breath-fog, and he had been so deep into placing the anchor on a German pocket battleship he hadn't realized it was cold.

But today as he placed and attached the final life preservers on his current project, the doomed Philippine ferry *Dona Paz*, Gil was distracted. Three times he had to peel and reattach one of the rings because he snarled the safety line or got it off angle. The waldo-field and magnifier were working just fine and the gyrostabilizers, while finicky, were no more so than usual. No, the fault was his. He couldn't concentrate.

"Cycle tools, field sensors off," he said. He leaned back and looked at the holoprojic image of the vessel. It was almost done, a few hours more and it would be finished, but he was simply not going to get it right today. If he kept going, he'd just screw it up.

He glanced at the front window. The Square was busy, the passersby going about their business. In deference to tradition, the lights on the Square were dimmed once a day to approximate night, and from the look of things, it was getting close to "dark." He sighed. Some part of his brain was tensed against the idea that whoever shattered his window might try something else.

Despite the locked door, he was in Condition Yellow.

Back in the mid-to-late 1900's, a professional pistoleer who had more or less invented the short-lived sport of combat shooting, one J. Cooper, had come up with a color-coded series of mental statuses for armed martial artists. The colors had probably changed and there were several variants, but the basics consisted of several states of awareness: Condition White, Condition Yellow, Condition Orange and Condition Red. Winston taught these as part of his coursework in kaja-tangan. Gil knew the system. Of course, knowing it was not quite the same as practicing it.

Condition White was a state of more or less complete relaxation. If you were sound asleep, you were in Condition White. If you were watching a vid in your own cube and so into it you couldn't hear the door chime, you were in White. Or, if you were making a model and unaware of music or major temperature changes, that would also put you into White.

Save for sleeping in a securely locked and alarmed cube, White was to be avoided if at all possible.

Condition Yellow was a state of heightened awareness, wherein you were very much cognizant of your surroundings, of any other people and any other thing that might present a potential danger to you or to those for whom you felt responsible. A trained martial artist was supposed to live in Condition Yellow nearly all the time. If you were walking in the park on a spring day, it was considered wise to look for possible attackers, places where they might hide or where you could take cover if a theoretical attacker leapt from the bushes and started blasting at you with a projectile weapon. Condition Yellow, it was pointed out, was not paranoia. It wasn't that you walked around *expecting* to be attacked, merely that you were aware that such things were *possibilities* and thus it was wise to be prepared as best you could be, under the current circumstances.

If you strongly suspected imminent danger, you shifted from Yellow into Condition Orange. A man walking toward you in a dark corridor who suddenly pulled a long-bladed knife and began waving it about was certainly something about which you should be concerned. Condition Orange prepared you to take direct action.

Condition Red was that state achieved when danger actually manifested close enough so that you had to do something. A bulkhead blew out, a mugger leapt at you, an escaped tiger from a zoo chose you as its next meal. Condition Red was when your training was put to the test. You were no longer looking and preparing for trouble, it was upon you—and you had to deal with it or perish.

Gil spent a lot more time in White than he should, according to the proper martial philosophy. It was necessary in his line of work and, until recently, being attacked in his shop had never really been a worry. Yes, when he walked down lonely corridors in places like Fecal Town, he carried himself in a higher state of readiness. People got mugged in such places. But until the window blew up, he had never been particularly alert in the shop. A public place, right on the Square? What danger could happen there?

Well. Somebody could launch a microbomb at your window, he now knew that for a fact.

What was to be done about it? He could keep the door locked when he was lost in work and admit customers only once he was aware of them. He could set the shop and his cube alarms when he was not around, or when he was asleep. He could consciously seek to be in Condition Yellow when he was out and about. These were simple precautions and easy enough to do. He didn't like the need for them, but he had to face the reality.

When Gil read mystery playits, it often bothered him that some of the protagonists were so stupid about their own safety. Not somebody like Inspector Targan, of course, who seemingly had eyes in the back of his head and always knew when the killer was sneaking up behind him, but many other detectives were not so gifted. Some villain shot at them or hired thugs to beat them to a pulp or rigged a bomb to blow up their electric carts. After surviving such things, sometimes much the worse for wear, a prudent investigator would surely keep a watchful eye out from then on, right? But—no. Very often, the hero of the story would blithely sail along, oblivious to demonstrated danger, taking no precautions, and never once worry that the villain would try again. It was as if the detective's memory malfunctioned, as if he had some-how . . . *forgotten* that he nearly died. And, of course, the villain nearly always *did* try to remove the hero again, sometimes several times in the same story.

Stupid. Not a survival characteristic outside of a playit where the writer could control the plot.

True, blowing out a window was not the same as a direct attack upon one's person. Gil didn't truly believe he was likely to get attacked physically by whoever had blasted an inert piece of castplast. Property damage was a long way from homicide. Still, since then, he had been paying better attention.

He opened the drawer under the work table and looked at the small air pistol therein. It was a Taurus, made mostly of spun carbonfiber, with a simple red dot holo-gram sight. The gun was legally registered, used in his martial arts training, and normally fired blunt, hard plas-tic target pellets at a velocity of maybe a hundred meters per second. A small tank in the handle was charged from a compressor and held enough gas to propel a half-dozen rounds. Such pellets would certainly sting if they hit un-protected flesh, maybe even bruise or draw blood, but unless they struck somebody in the eye, they would do little damage. Next to the pistol, however, Gil had a packet of semilegal fleschettes, sharp little darts that pro-duced and carried to their target a high-voltage, low-amperage electrical charge. They were similar to police shock darts, though not as potent. One would give a large man pause; two or three would knock him down and into a jittery, spastic tremor.

Of course, the gun itself was a deterrent—somebody staring down a barrel pointing at him would not know what manner of missile it contained.

Gil took the gun from the drawer, exchanged the mag-azine with its target loads for the more potent darts. The weapon was charged, and all he had to do was point it, put the glowing red dot floating slightly above it on the target, and pull the trigger. The dot lit when the handle was squeezed. Out to about fifty meters, the dot was superimposed upon where the dart would go. There was a safety built into the grip that would not allow the pistol to discharge unless it was firmly gripped. That way if you dropped it, it wouldn't go off and shoot you by accident. Simple and somewhat effective. Better than nothing.

He put the pistol back into the drawer and closed it. He wasn't quite ready to start hauling it around full-time hidden on his person. Technically, he could only transport the pistol to and from his cube or the class, but since he was one of the instructors and had complete access to the school, he could always claim to be on the way there to practice, should he have to explain why he had a gun concealed inside a cleverly designed com pouch rigged for that purpose on his belt.

So, the gun was prepared if he needed it, and he *would* take it home with him. In the meanwhile, at the least, he would try to stay in Condition Yellow—at least until whoever blew out his window was identified.

His shop com cheeped. Gil said, "Answer com. Hello?"

"Gil? Chaz Wells here."

"Ah, Chaz. What can I do for you?"

"Well, I just remembered something that didn't make it into the reports on that guy who squashed himself. Probably won't do you any good, but I figured, what the heck, I could pass it along."

"I appreciate it, Chaz. What have you got?"

"Well, M. Corderman had a couple of run-ins with people. Nothing serious, but I thought you might like to know."

"Run-ins?"

"Yeah. There was a guy he worked with, name was Victor Willow, down in the same section, they apparently both got some kind of reprimand from a supervisor a few months ago. I saw the notation on the computer file but the supervisor retired and went down below, so I couldn't give you any details from that end. I talked to Willow and he said it was nothing, so I let it drop."

Gil tapped the name into his flatscreen. "And the other thing?"

"Retired military man made a serious pass at Corderman's SO in that clip joint where she works. Corderman didn't like it. Nothing official got filed, but one of our security people talked to some witnesses in the bar, said it got physical. Guy's name is Emile Gauthier."

"He's retired, you said? An older man?"

"From the military after twenty years, so not too old, forty something. But maybe you've run into him. He runs the airgun gallery in the Arcade."

Gil said, "Thanks, Chaz, I appreciate it. Maybe I can hustle my work along and get to your commission a week or two earlier."

"I was hoping you'd say that, Gil. Listen, you need anything else, give me a call. I have to be honest, I don't think there's anything here, but keep me up to speed if you do find out anything about this, okay?"

"I will. Thanks again."

When he broke the connection, Gil looked at the two names he'd tapped into the scratchpad file on his flatscreen. Very interesting.

It was like he had told Trish. Now he had some things floating up from the murk. He would see if he could get a better look at them before they settled back to the bottom.

He stood. Thought about it for a second, then opened the drawer and pulled the com pouch out and crowed it to his belt. Opened it and put his com into one compartment, then the little pistol into the other slot. Better to have it and not need it than to need it and not have it.

8

GIL CALLED HEAVY Engineering and got the work schedule. It was interesting how much of what went on in Corporate and on the station in general was public knowledge. Most people wouldn't think to ask, but there was a lot of information there to be had by simply doing that—asking. Such as work schedules. Gil found that Victor Willow, whose worker classification M-HE—Miscellaneous, Heavy Engineering—probably meant he was a general roustabout and relatively unskilled, should be getting off shift in thirty minutes. Just enough time to catch him and see if he would answer a few questions.

Since he didn't have any official status as an investigator, Gil had to depend on a certain amount of good will when he poked around. Some people didn't feel inclined to talk to him, and he had to figure out ways to circumvent that when it happened.

Willow was a large, beefy man with a florid complexion and a spacer's buzz haircut. He wore lube-stained coveralls and work boots and he looked tired as he passed through the security scanner with the crowd heading for the elevators. He carried a thermos and a small cooler. Gil recognized him from the ID photo in the computer. Probably about thirty, thirty-five.

"M. Willow?"

"Yes?"

"I'm Gil Sivart. Would you mind if I asked you a couple of questions? I'm not selling anything, not looking for donations, not trying to get your vote."

The bigger man raised his lip in a small smile. "If you don't mind walking with me to the lifts. I promised I'd take my two youngest kids to the Mealy Mall after I got off work."

They headed for the main elevators, along with dozens of others.

"So, what's up, M. Sivart?"

"You remember M. Corderman?"

Willow looked at Gil. "David? Yeah, I remember him. I worked next to the guy for two years. A real shame. I feel sorry for him."

"You were close?"

"Nope. I have to tell you, I didn't much like him. But he's going to Hell, I wouldn't wish that on anybody."

"You thought he was a bad man?"

"Nope, not particularly, no worse than most. But he killed himself. Suicides can't get into Heaven."

"You're a religious man?"

The lifts opened, and a flow of humanity filled them. Not enough room for all of the workers waiting to get on, but next time Gil and Willow would probably make it.

"Yes, sir, I am. Revised Catholic."

"I understand you and M. Corderman had some problems."

Willow blinked at him. "He used to rag me about my faith. Thought I was stupid for believing in dogma. I must confess that sometimes I was a little slow in turning the other cheek. But we never came to blows or anything. It wasn't serious. He just liked to pull my chain, see if he could get any angry word from me. Sometimes he did. If I were a better man, I would have just ignored it. What can I say? I'm a poor sinner trying to do better."

The lift arrived, opened. It was already half-full from the level above it, dock and port workers going down-levels. Not quite enough room for Gil and Willow to squeeze into it. "Next one for sure," Willow said. "Three is the charm."

"Father, Son and Holy Ghost?"

Willow looked at him with new interest. "You a believer, M. Sivart?"

"No. My grandparents were Roman Catholic. My parents let it lapse."

Willow grinned again. "Once a Catholic, always a Catholic, lapsed or not. Always room in God's House for another."

"Thanks. Look, I appreciate your help."

"You a friend of M. Blackwell's?"

"Why do you ask?"

"Nobody else would still be poking at this. Man did what he did, she can't let it go. Too bad. They were going to make it legal, stop living in sin. She's a pretty woman, would have probably made David a good wife, maybe settled him down. A family does that. I have four children and they are a trial sometimes, but I wouldn't trade them for a barrel full of platinum, you know?"

Gil nodded.

"I'm not stupid, you know. I was off work on free days when it happened, so I didn't see it, but I heard it was pretty rank. I didn't have anything to do with his death. I'm a Christian. We don't believe in killing."

Gil was tempted to point out that the bloodiest wars in history were religious ones, many of them between two Christian sects. And that one of the early Catholic popes was reputed to have said, when asked about what to do with a group of prisoners, "Kill them all—God will recognize his own." But he kept silent.

The next lift arrived. There was room for twenty or so, and Gil and Willow were right in front of it. "Anything else?"

"No. Thanks again for your help."

"No problem." He stepped onto the elevator, turned, smiled.

Gil watched the doors close and nodded to himself. M. Willow didn't seem like a killer, despite Gil's lack of faith about Christians not committing murder. Willow probably wasn't ever going to be a Vice President, but he had his faith, a family, and a job, and he seemed content. There were worse ways to spend your life.

The Arcade was usually filled with children and at least a few of their harried parents, since most of the games were designed for those who were at least young at heart. At the air gun gallery, however, there was a minimum age of fifteen, unless accompanied by a legal guardian. A few of the adults let their children play the games while they sometimes went to plink at various holographic reactive targets with the air rifles and pistols, but it wasn't a popular attraction. Shooting was a much more analog kind of recreation. A fast hand waving back and forth in a waldo-field or thumbs-on old-style control buttons weren't sufficient skills to pick up a mechanical weapon that had to be manually operated. To be adept with an airgun, one had to know how to establish and hold a precise sight-picture, be able to control the trigger, and even one's own breathing. There was little room for error when tracking and trying to hit small targets at ten or fifteen meters. A degree or two off at the muzzle of the weapon resulted in a wide miss down range.

Gil had been to the air gun gallery a few times, though not lately. He tended to practice his shooting alone in the school's small range. He recognized the man running the gallery, both from his station ID image in the mainframe and from earlier visits. There was only one customer at the range.

Emile Gauthier was probably in his mid-forties, a thin man with receding gray hair cropped close in a military-style cut. He had an old unrevised scar two centimeters long that went through his right eyebrow at a slight upward angle to his right. He wore a khaki shirt and pants that were not, but that looked like a uniform on him. He was watching a young woman of about twenty-five shoot one of the air rifles. The rifles were attached to the counter by thin spidersilk safety cables on computer-controlled wind-up spools. A shooter could lift the airgun and cover all of the the targets on the range, but the weapon could not be removed, nor turned around to point into the Arcade.

The young woman was a terrible shooter. She fired ten times as Gil watched and didn't hit anything she was aiming at. Gauthier came around behind her. "Here, let me give you a hand," he said. He put his arms around the young woman, cupped her hands on the weapon, pressed himself against her backside. He put his face next to hers. They fired again and one of the targets gave a little chime.

"See, it's easy," Gauthier said. "Now you try it." He removed his left hand from where he helped her support the stock under the air rifle's barrel and when he pulled his hand back he appeared to accidentally brush his fingertips over the woman's breast. She jumped a little. Gauthier put his other hand on the woman's back, just over her buttocks. "Steady . . ." He slid his hand lower.

"Mom, mom!"

A little boy of about four came running up. The woman put the air rifle down and bent to talk to the boy. Gil saw what looked like a cloud of pure rage pass over Gauthier's face before the young woman smiled up at the man. Gauthier smiled back at her.

Gil moved in. "M. Gauthier?"

"Who wants to know?"

"I'm Gil Sivart. I wonder if I could talk to you for a few moments?"

The woman and small boy moved off.

Gauthier waved at the empty firing line. "I don't know. I'm pretty busy."

Gil ran his credit card through the reader on the counter and picked up the nearest air gun, a semiautomatic rifle. Aim and press the trigger; it would fire two dozen times before it had to be reloaded.

There was a row of small disks against the back wall, fifteen meters away, each disk about the size of a New Dollar coin. Gil fired. The disk went *chink!* and fell over. He lined up on the next disk, fired, knocked that one down. In quick succession, he fired and hit ten of the disks, *chink! chink! chink!*

Gauthier raised an eyebrow at him. "Not bad. You've done this before. You a military man?"

"No. Martial arts."

Gauthier picked up the rifle next to Gil and snapped it up. He fired a dozen times, a lot faster than Gil had, and each time got a noise from a target. He was good, better than Gil. He put the gun down.

"What can I do for you, M. Sivart, you said?"

Gil put his air gun onto the counter and turned to face Gauthier.

"You know a woman named Trish Blackwell?"

"Can't say as I recognize that name."

"She's a dancer at The Baron."

"Oh, you mean Red. Sure. I don't know her as well as I'd like to, if you get my drift."

"And I understand you knew her SO. David Corderman."

"The son-of-a-bitch, yeah, I—" He stopped. "*Knew* him?"

"He's dead."

"What a goddamned shame. Something painful, I hope?"

Gil stared at him, said nothing.

"We met once. I was just talking to Red in the club, we were having a polite and private conversation, enjoying each other's company, and her muscleboy stormed over and sucker punched me for no goddamned reason at all. I was disposed to kick his ass and would have, but the security guy started waving a taser. Getting hit with a taser gives me a bad headache. How'd he die?"

"It appeared to be an accident."

"Too goddamned bad. I hadn't heard. Well, well. Maybe I'll drop by and offer Red my condolences. Why are you asking about this?"

"There are some unanswered questions about Corderman's death. I'm looking into it for a friend."

"Unanswered questions . . . ?" He laughed. "You think I killed him over that dust-up? Sheeit, I've hurt myself worse putting my socks on. I'm not going to risk brain-burn over pussy, friend, there's too much of it available for that. Sure, Red is a nice-looking piece, very flexible, and I'd enjoy seeing how many ways she could stretch and twist, but one is pretty much as good as another. You're wasting your time here."

Gil nodded. "One other question. You know those tiny shaped Detonex charges they use for shearing pipe or for rough-cutting installed plate?"

"Yeah. We used it for construction in the service when we couldn't requisition anything better."

"Could an airgun be rigged to fire one of those pellets without setting it off?"

Gauthier nodded. "Sure. Takes a sharp impact to cook Detonex. Airgun acceleration wouldn't do it, but if it hit a hard surface with enough velocity, it would explode. Might be iffy with these guns, they aren't very powerful, but, yeah, it could be done."

"Thanks for your time."

Gil turned and left the gallery. He smiled to himself as he walked away. None of the guilty people he'd ever talked to during his investigations had ever broken down in tearful remorse and admitted his or her crimes to Gil. Later, under threat of a scan or after the police had questioned them to exhaustion or tripped them up in their stories, then some of them had confessed, but never to Gil. Sometimes, in retrospect, he believed he could tell somebody had been lying. Some nervous gesture or edginess in their voice, a failure to make eye contact, convinced Gil they weren't being honest with him. But that was hindsight, and it seldom worked well enough before guilt was established to be depended on.

Was Gauthier lying? Could be. He wasn't a particularly likable man, but that in itself didn't mean much. Were that the only criterion, a net dropped on any gathering just about anywhere would haul in all kinds of guilty souls.

Gil seldom had the bright flashes of knowledge that the great detectives depended upon. He just gathered facts, opinions, observations, and sometimes, when he had enough of them, he could assemble a puzzle that made a fairly clear picture.

So far, he didn't have enough pieces.

Corderman was dead, that was a fact. Somebody had blown out his window, that was another. Somebody had called to warn him off. And his gut feeling was that if somebody didn't want him poking into this business, that was the most compelling reason to believe there was more here than simple suicide. He hadn't been able to rule out the possibility of homicide, either with the police or the medic who examined the body. For now, he would continue uncovering things. Experience told him that if he kept looking, and if it was there to be found, sooner or later something pale and evil would scramble into the light when he lifted its rock.

9

GIL HEADED FOR his cube. Ahead of him was a section of corridor where one of the strip lights had gone out. It wasn't that dark, but the shadows were thicker than normal. There didn't seem to be anybody else around.

As he walked through the darker section, because he had ratcheted his level of awareness up, what could have been a complete surprise was not. He heard or felt, then peripherally saw, the two men, each holding a half-meter section of pipe as they slid out of a utility closet behind him.

Both men wore what looked like stretch stockings over their heads, holes cut out for the eyes. One mask was red, the other green.

Time downshifted from normal speed into slow motion. The two men moved as if they were mired in a swamp. The problem was, the slow time affected Gil, too. Even so, they probably weren't expecting him to do what he did.

He turned, pivoted on his right foot and threw a short,

choppy counter sidekick with his left just as the first man
stepped in with the pipe raised to strike. His kick caught
Red Mask under the armpit and stopped his forward motion. Gil snapped his left foot back down, then back out,
hit the attacker under the armpit again, but a little lower
this time. Jerked his foot back and stepped in, left hand
cocked by his left ear, and launched a hammer fist against
the surprised man's temple.

Red started to stagger backward. Oh . . . so . . .
slowly . . .

Gil grabbed the falling man's outstretched pipe hand
with both of his hands, turned slightly to his left, and
leveraged the wrist. Red twisted into Green's path.
Green slammed into Red, cursed, and tried to untangle
himself—

But Gil was already pivoting on his left foot, still
holding Red's hand, bringing his right foot up and
around, from the knee, a spring kick that put the ball of
his foot hard into Green's side, not really damaging him
but off balancing him even more, so that he stumbled,
hit the corridor wall hard and fell—

Both men were on their way down, slowmo, and Gil
felt a rush of power. He had this under control. He was
full of confidence, secure in his skill.

So much so that the third man, one wearing a blue
mask, who must have been waiting *ahead* of him, was
able to get close enough to bring his pipe down and catch
Gil on the left side of his neck, low on the trap, almost
to the shoulder.

Damn!

Gil released his grip on Red, twisted away even as he
felt the shock of the pipe's impact all the way to the tips
of his fingers. Jumped over the fallen man and spun away
as Blue reset himself for another strike with the pipe—

Gil squatted, picked up the pipe that Red had dropped,
stood, and flipped it at Blue with a back-wrist toss, spinning it like a disk at the man's eyes.

Blue batted at the incoming pipe and ducked at the
same time. He missed, but the pipe was high, just glanced

off his head, then clattered against the wall. Not enough to stop him.

Red tried to roll up. Green was already halfway to his feet. Blue cocked his weapon for another blow—

Time to leave.

Gil hit Green with both hands in a hard push, slammed him out of the way, and ran down the corridor. He was ten meters away before anybody could recover enough to chase him. He was round the next turning and running at speed before a string of curses got going good behind him.

He was a hundred meters away, almost to a bank of elevators and a knot of waiting people, before he remembered:

He had a *gun* in his pouch.

By then it was too late. When he went back, his hand on the hidden gun, the three attackers were long gone.

Damn!

They were in El-Sayed's office.

"You were lucky," El-Sayed said.

Gil nodded. Yes. He had been lucky. He'd survived a potentially lethal attack from three men, and that was good. But while his technique hadn't been bad, his tactical work had been flat-out crappy. True, he hadn't had time to access his weapon during the initial attack—even if he'd remembered he had it—but he could have run five meters down the corridor, pulled his gun, turned and taken all three men down.

That he *forgot* he was carrying superior weaponry was absolutely inexcusable.

He did *not* look forward to telling Winston about that.

In fact, had he been using his brain, he would have taken off at the first sight of the two men behind him. Of course, he might have run smack into Blue and caught a pipe across the face for his trouble; probably that was the intent. Still, the first rule of self-defense was simple: Whenever possible, flight is better than fight.

"And you didn't get enough of a look at any of them for an ID?"

"No."

El-Sayed nodded. "Odd thing about that section of corridor. Seems that the security cam malfunctioned, as well as the lights."

Gil nodded in return. "What a coincidence."

"No way to be sure it was aimed at you," the cool said. "They could have just been waiting for a target of opportunity. Somebody to stomp for thrills or their credit tab. A good code rascal can break a tab open in half an hour; they could have cleaned out your account before anybody found you."

He reached for his pipe, looked at Gil, raised his eyebrows.

"Go ahead."

Ray fussed with the pipe, packing and lighting it.

"I suppose it is possible the attack was a coincidence."

A puff of fragrant smoke drifted for the exhaust fans, but Gil got a whiff of it. He said, "You sure that's denatured tobacco? It smells pretty good for the harmless stuff."

The cool smiled around the stem of the pipe. "You a smoker?"

"A long time ago, back on Earth. I had to give it up. The real stuff cost too much and the denatured leaf had all the taste of dried lettuce."

"I'm an officer of the law. Real tobacco would be illegal, now wouldn't it?"

"So is spitting on a public floor," Gil said.

The two men looked at each other. Gil knew he'd been the intended target of the three, no doubt in his mind, and he was fairly certain El-Sayed believed that, too.

"Still, if I were you, I'd stay out of dark corridors in the future. And maybe consider arming myself."

Gil gave him a short smile. "Thanks."

•   •   •

Winston held a make-up class for the advanced kaja-tangan students during second shift.

The kwoon was on LL4, below the Square. It was basically four cheap living cubes with the interior walls knocked out to make one large workout room, a small office, and a fresher. As in most martial arts schools, the frequent turnover in beginners paid for the space. A lot of people started out with good intentions, wanting to get into shape or to learn to defend themselves, but good intentions often went astray. Winston didn't hold anybody to contracts, just on a month-to-month basis, and word of mouth was enough to keep the newbie classes filled.

There were mirrors on one wall, punching and kicking bags hung about the perimeter of the kwoon, mats for tumbling and falls, and airgun targets at the end of a narrow corridor opposite the mirror wall. Traditional weapons—staves, swords, chains, and the like—were racked on the wall by the entrance. Pretty standard stuff.

Usually there were eight of them in the advanced class, but scheduling problems evidently kept a couple of them away. Marko and Idella the black sashes were there, as were Abdul, Rosa, and Little Billy, the other brown sashes. They were all dressed in the school uniform: black cotton sweat pants, black T-shirts, and kung-fu slippers, plus their rank sashes, four-meter lengths of silk wrapped around their waists and tied in square knots. Beginners all wore protective gear under their uniforms, cups and breast pads, but advanced students did not. By the time you got to brown sash rank, you were supposed to know how to protect your vital areas, and if you missed a block or parry, the theory was you deserved to get tagged.

Little Billy, who was sixteen and able to drop into a full Chinese split without warming up, grinned at Gil as Gil went through a series of stretches.

"So, I hear you get to ride the tiger tonight, hey?"

Gil looked around. Marko and Idella were doing a sticky-hand set, and Abdul was upside down in the yoga asana Plow, but he noticed that Rosa was also grinning at him. Ah. They knew about his little altercation.

"I suppose," Gil said.

"Good luck."

Winston arrived, dressed in the same uniform, except that his sash was white. In kaja-tangan, the ranks went full circle: white, purple, blue, green, brown, black, then white. So a beginner wore the same sash as the head instructor, the sifu. Not that a watcher would have much trouble noting the differences between a beginner and Sifu.

Winston, who was a tall and muscular man—1.9 meters and over 90 kilos, TS, easy—moved like hot grease. In his younger days, when he was still on the freestyle fighting circuit, they'd called him Black Leopard, for his speed and skill and his dark-coffee-colored skin.

The six of them lined up facing the mirror wall. Sifu walked to the middle of the room in front of them. Nodded, slowly.

The class offered him a formal bow, crossed and uncrossed hands in front of their chests, dropping to cover their groins as they bent at the waists.

"Warmup sequence," Sifu said.

He led them in a series of twists and turns, hand, arm, leg, and foot rotations, bends, starting slow but increasing tempo rapidly. After five minutes, Gil felt his blood circulating faster, knew his joints were warmer.

"Yoga," Sifu said.

They went through the Ten Postures, slower, but not as slowly as Gil usually did when practicing alone.

"Two-person sets, one through ten."

The six paired up. Marko moved to stand opposite Gil. Marko was the most senior student in the class, and the strongest, though Idella was faster.

Gil and Marko gave each other military bows. For formal exercises like the two-person sets, the attacker always had his back to Sifu, as Marko did now.

"Hup!" Sifu said.

Marko stepped in and shot a full-power punch at Gil's face.

Gil pivoted, counter-sidekicked Marko under the armpit hard enough to stop him. Both of them *kiai*-ed, deep and guttural yells. Gil stepped in behind Marko's leading foot, threw a left hammer fist at his temple, dropped onto his right knee, and circled a scoop fist to Marko's groin, pulling both hand strikes so that he barely touched him. Leaped up and slid back into a defensive stance.

"Reverse," Sifu called.

Gil and Marko traded places.

"Hup!"

Gil lunged, punched at Marko's face. Had he not moved, the punch would have broken the man's nose, at the very least. Marko repeated the defense Gil had offered, stopped his forward motion with the counter-sidekick, followed with the hammer and scoop fists, jumped up and away.

Sifu put them through the rest of the basic sets. Then they worked the heavy bag, the dodge bag, the blocking dummy. Sifu made them do the three short forms as a group, then each student performed the first of the long forms, Crane Hunts Frog, individually. Crane Hunts ran eighty-two moves, and was the shortest of the long forms.

For twenty minutes, they did freestyle sparring, light contact only, rotating until everyone had a chance to spar with everyone else.

An hour and a half went by. By the end of the time, Gil was soaked in his own sweat and tired. Sifu lined them up, bowed, then said, "Everybody but Gil sit."

Gil could feel the grins, though nobody was stupid enough to let one show. A misplaced grin would get a raised eyebrow from Sifu—and some form of butt-kicking to go with it.

"Gil had a practical experience earlier today," Sifu said.

Riding the tiger.

It was the aftermath of what happened when, on the rare occasion it became necessary, a student had to use his or her skills outside of the kwoon. When Sifu heard about it—and he always heard about it, because a student was required to share such encounters with him if he wanted to continue to train—Sifu had the student describe the event in detail for the class, so that they might learn from the incident. Students were encouraged to offer nothing less than total honesty about the incident. Anything less was . . . frowned upon.

Once, in the intermediate class, when Gil had been a blue sash, a green sash student had been involved in a bar fight. The student offered his account of the combat. When he was done, Sifu stepped in and hit the man in the solar plexus with a short punch that dropped him to the floor. The green sash had been unable to breathe for more than a minute.

After a recitation, Sifu would sometimes add a little physical test of his own to see if the student had indeed learned from his "practical experience."

Or, in the case of the green sash, administer a lesson for being less than candid. Sifu had obtained a recording of the bar fight, and the student's version did not agree with Sifu's interpretation of the event.

One learned not to lie to Sifu.

"Gil?"

Gil took a deep breath. He faced the others, who all sat crosslegged looking up at him. He told them about the three men in the hallway. He told them what he had done, what he had failed to do, and how he felt about it. He described the setting, the events leading up to the attack, including the blown-out window in his shop, the commed warning and the most damning thing, that he had been carrying a pistol he had completely forgotten about.

The five advanced students kept their faces carefully neutral. To offer a smile or a frown or any negative emotion to a man riding the tiger was considered impolite by Sifu.

A student most definitely did not want Sifu to think she was impolite. No.

However, when the speech was done, students were allowed to ask questions. These queries were often helpful to focus attention on ways the practical experience might have been improved. These queries were also brutal at times. Often impolite. Or downright unkind.

Came the questions:

"How could you *forget* you had a gun?"

"Why didn't you run at the first sign of an attack?"

"Given the threats, why did you walk into a dark corridor alone?"

"Why did you throw the pipe instead of keeping it?"

"How could you fail to notice a third attacker?"

"What color condition were you in?"

And after he had answered as best he could the how-could-you-be-so-stupid questions, Sifu smiled. Said, "Since Gil now has experience with multiple attackers, we'll allow him to demonstrate for us how best to defend against a group attack. Everybody up."

The students came to their feet.

"Everybody attacks Gil. Bare hands, medium contact—bruises, no broken bones."

Sifu looked at Gil. "You may defend using any method you choose."

Gil nodded. Five against one. The best defense would be to be elsewhere, but he'd never get to the exit before they caught him. Already Marko and Idella had drifted toward the weapon wall, to make sure he didn't get a staff or a sword—or away. Little Billy and Rosa moved toward the fresher, to block flight in that direction. Abdul edged forward in a creep stance, hands raised in tight fists.

Without hurrying too much, Gil turned and walked to the corner where the extra tumbling mats were stacked. He saw Sifu raise an eyebrow. Putting yourself in a corner was a good tactical move if you had two attackers coming at you—neither could get behind you, and you might effectively do a two-person defense. But five coming in at once meant you had to move. Were you going to fight the ten thousand one at a time, you had to move quickly and keep moving. Boxing yourself into a corner was not the way to survive.

At the very least, it was a way to get the crap beat out of you, even in the kwoon.

Before anybody could get more than a meter or so closer to him, Gil squatted, reached between the top and second mat, and pulled out his air pistol where he had stashed it before anybody else had arrived. He stood, held the gun with both hands pointed at the floor in front of himself.

There was a long moment.

"The match is over," Sifu said. He nodded at Gil. "So. You did learn something."

Gil allowed himself a small smile—after he saw Sifu's grin.

Sifu lined everybody up, and they all bowed. Class was over.

When Gil finished dressing and started for the exit, he saw Trish standing in front of the weapon wall.

"Hello," he said. "Been here long?"

"I was in M. Jones's office, watching on the holo-proj," she said. "I thought it only fair that since you saw me dance, I should see you. M. Jones is most kind."

Gil didn't say anything.

"I'm glad you are helping me, Gil. You move very well."

He smiled at her. "Come on, I'll buy you a drink or dinner, if you haven't eaten yet," he said. "And bring you up to date on things."

10

THERE WAS A little hole-in-the-wall cafe about three quarters of the way around the circumference from the kwoon, a place called Matilda's. Gil offered to take Trish there for a late supper and she agreed to go.

In the original design of the REL, the living levels were supposed to be residential cubes; in practice, each of the five LL's had a variety of mixed housing and commercial shops. A lot of folks didn't mind having a bar or minimart or a small restaurant near where they lived. There were times when catching a lift to the Square to buy a drink or grab a quick meal was more effort than it was worth. Being able to toddle a few dozen meters to a local store or somesuch appealed enough so that few such places had any trouble getting the zoning regs relaxed enough to open up shop—as long as they kept the noise down. Those that were too loud or caused too much of a disruption tended to get closed quickly.

Actually, the lower the LL, the more likely a noisy place would stay open. In Fecal Town, you could party loud enough to wake a man in a coma and nobody would say much about it.

Gil and Trish strolled around the main corridor toward the cafe. He was tired but pleased with himself. Sifu liked to see his students be enterprising. Then again, that trick with the pistol under the mats probably wouldn't ever work again. The next time Sifu set a student astride the tiger, he might just check for hidden weapons. It would be quite unpleasant to reach for a stashed piece and find it gone. If his gun hadn't been there, the class would have thumped Gil hard. It would have been a painful lesson, one he would be unlikely to forget. Which is what Sifu wanted.

A middle-aged man and a woman came from the opposite direction. The woman laughed. The man, who gestured broadly with his hands, presumably had said something she found funny. They looked happy.

Gil watched the pair carefully. He had his gun pouch's closure untabbed. He could have the pistol out and working in a second and a half, maybe a hair faster.

The laughing couple passed without launching an attack.

Ahead of Gil and Trish, a single man turned down a side corridor. Gil edged a little closer toward the center of the corridor.

"Matilda's?" Trish said.

Gil smiled at her, kept a portion of his peripheral vision tuned to the side corridor. They passed the turning. The man had his back to them, was proceeding down the corridor, ten meters away.

"A fairly new place, been there about four months. Half a dozen tables, good food, an excellent home-brewed dark beer. I don't think there is anybody named 'Matilda' connected to it, the owner-cook is from Australia or Tasmania or somewhere. He makes a great seafood stir-fry."

Since the Hydroponics & Livestock Level, just above Stores, had a fairly extensive aquaculture facility, seafood was common on the station. Like shelves in a refrigerator, the aquaculturists had multiple levels of giant, shallow trays filled with circulating salt or fresh water. In the fish trays, they raised shrimp, catfish, trout, and tilapia. There were oyster and mussel and abalone trays, a couple of racks dedicated to squid and octopi. In the siltier, murkier water sloshing in the bottommost of the artificial ponds, even crawfish. Sea creatures took a lot less room and attention than the animals raised for food, those mainly rabbits and poultry. There were no cattle or swine on the station.

"Sounds good," she said.

The tables at Matilda's were full when they arrived. The cafe was basically two side-by-side medium-sized cubes. The kitchen and fresher and office were in one, the tables and bar in the other. A tangy, peppery aroma filled the air. There were a couple of empty stools at the bar. Gil and Trish sat. He nodded at the bartender, a short and hefty man who moved over.

"Hey, Gil. Usual?"

"No, Roy, I think I'll just have tea tonight. Trish?"

"I'll try the homebrew beer," she said.

Gil liked the beer, but wasn't planning on slowing his reaction time until he did something about whoever was trying to have him beaten up.

He didn't think whoever that person was wanted him dead—at least not yet. Otherwise the three thugs in the corridor could have used guns instead of pipes. Still, downtime in the hospital didn't much appeal.

The bartender was back shortly. He put a tall glass of iced tea in front of Gil; in front of Trish, he set a frosted pilsner glass. The liquid therein was darker than the tea, with a two-centimeter head of thick foam.

She sipped the brew. "You're right, it is good," she said. "You come here a lot." It was not a question.

"Couple times a week. Usually after a workout I don't feel much like cooking." He sipped at the tea.

"I can see why. Does your teacher do that every time? Have the whole class jump on somebody?"

"No. That's a reward for failure."

"Failure?"

"Winston's philosophy is that if you actually have to

use your training in what he calls 'a practical experience,'
you've failed as a martial artist.''

"I don't understand.''

"A true expert should usually be able to defuse most
fight situations. You bump into somebody, you apolo-
gize. If you can't talk them out of it, you leave. You
walk away from somebody pumping himself up to take
a swing at you. Run away if you have to.''

"That seems . . .'' She searched for a word.

"Cowardly?'' He grinned.

"Well . . .''

"That's the reaction a lot of people have. And they'd
be right, if you were actually afraid. But most people
fight because they are insecure. They feel as if they have
something to prove, they worry about losing face or being badly thought of. So they hit because they're afraid
not to.''

"Hey, Gil?'' the bartender said. "Corner table is
free.''

"Thanks, Roy.'' To Trish, he said, "Shall we?''

They took their drinks. She followed him to the corner.
He cataloged other diners at the tables as he passed them.
A couple of regulars he had seen here before; two young
men who were obviously a couple and lost in each other;
an old man and woman arguing about what to order.

They reached the table. It was to the left of the entrance to the kitchen. Gil sat with his back to the wall.
Tibbs came out of the kitchen, dressed in food-splashed
and oil-stained white paper coveralls with a matching
apron. Tibbs was a tall and thin man, black hair almost
all gone gray, face pockmarked from some old skin in-
fection. Probably forty, forty-five. "Gidday, Gil.'' He
looked at Trish, smiled, revealed perfect teeth.

"Tibbs, this is Trish. Trish, Tibbs. The cook and
owner here.''

"And sometimes waiter when the bastard who's *supposed* to be doing that job gets a bloody hangnail and
has to stay home to deal with the terrible pain of it. I
ought to fire the little beater.''

Gil grinned. The usual waiter for this shift was Tibbs's son, the older of two. Every time Gil had seen them together, Tibbs beamed, much the proud father, when he looked at either boy.

"Anyway, I'm right pleased to make your acquaintance," he said. "What'll it be, then?"

Trish looked at Gil.

"Your choice is chicken, shrimp, or rabbit stir-fry with vegetables," Gil said. "Plain vegetables if you don't eat flesh. Noodles or rice. You can't go wrong with any of it."

Tibbs grinned.

"What do you have the most of?" Gil asked.

"Well, we had a run on the rabbit, so mostly shrimp or chicken left."

Gil looked at Trish.

"Shrimp sounds good to me," she said.

"Two shrimps," Gil said. "Noodles."

"Right. You I know about, but how hot do you want it, Trish? We can spice it anywhere from tasteless to third degree burns."

"However Gil takes his," she said.

"He likes it warm."

"My mother used to eat pickled jalapeños straight from the jar," she said. "I can do warm." She gave him a big smile.

Tibbs laughed. "I'll bet you can. Back in a minute."

When Tibbs was away into the fragrant kitchen, she said, "So, go on with your explanation of failure in the martial arts. It's very interesting."

"The art I practice is called kaja-tangan. It means 'glass hands.' "

"That sounds fragile."

"Actually, glass can be made strong enough to use for hammers. The name refers more to the clarity of glass. If your hands are transparent, you can hit somebody before they see it coming."

"Ah."

"It's a bit of a stretch. It also refers to clarity in general. Anyway, once you get to a certain level of ability, you tend to lose your need to prove anything. I'm not nearly an expert; however, on a good night, I can block and dance well enough to keep Marko—he's the black sash you saw in class earlier, the one with the muscles—from pounding me into mush. Marko is very good. I can't do a lot of damage to him, but since the most basic goal of self-defense is to keep yourself from getting stomped, if I can keep Marko from hurting me, I figure I can manage that in a one-on-one with almost anybody less adept than he is. Which includes almost everybody I'm likely to run into anywhere.''

"I see. So, knowing that you can probably wipe up the floor with any loudmouth who has a couple too many drinks and takes off on you in the local pub keeps you from having to do it.''

"That's the theory.''

"That wouldn't really apply in the attack on you.''

"No. Talking wouldn't have worked, and running wasn't really much of an option the way they set it up. What I should have done is used the gun I forgot I even had, but I got rattled. None of the three who attacked me were as good as Marko or Idella or any of the other students in my class, even though they had clubs. But despite all the years of training, a real situation is never quite the same as one in practice. The brain knows the difference, and it kicks into overdrive when the danger is 'real.' ''

The swinging door to the kitchen opened, and Tibbs emerged carrying two plates heaped with steaming stir-fry and noodles. He put the plates down on the small table. The smell was wonderful.

Tibbs moved to a stand nearby and fetched back a pitcher of water and two glasses. "Enjoy," he said. He darted back into the kitchen.

Gil used a pair of the chopsticks on the table to take a big mouthful of noodles and shrimp. The heat flared in his mouth, cleared his sinuses quickly. Whooo.

Trish ate a bite of her dish, nodded, finished chewing, and swallowed. "Terrific."

If the spicy heat bothered her, he couldn't tell it. For some reason, this pleased him.

As they ate, he told her about his progress on his investigation.

"Doesn't seem like an awful lot," she said.

"Ah, but it is. Before, we weren't sure—at least I wasn't sure—about the manner of your SO's death. All this has convinced me it certainly wasn't suicide. Made the police stop and think, too. Somebody is worried enough about me poking around to do something to try to make me stop. And it's to our advantage, they aren't very smart."

"They were smart enough to make David's death look like suicide," she said.

"But not to let it lie. If they hadn't blown out my window and tried to scare me off, I would have hit a dead end pretty quick. Now, even if I can't see it, I know there's something to find. You can find a coin buried in a mountain of sand if you know it is there and you are willing to look long and hard enough."

"And are you that willing?"

Gil took another bite of his supper, relished the taste. "Oh, yeah. They have my attention now. I'm going to keep at it as long as it takes."

He looked at her. "But there are some things we need to worry about."

"Such as?"

Tibbs came out of the kitchen carrying more heaped plates to other diners. When he returned, he paused by their table. "Everything okay?"

"Superb," Trish said. "This is the best stir-fry I've ever eaten."

Tibbs grinned. Inclined his head slightly. "Thank you, ma'am. I'm honored you think so." He looked at Gil. "She's a keeper, mate." Then he was gone back into the kitchen.

Gil and Trish smiled at each other, Gil feeling a little

awkward but pleased by Tibbs's comment. He said, "I don't think you are in any real danger, but maybe you ought to consider a couple of basic precautions."

"Such as?"

"You could take a vacation to Earth."

She shook her head. "No."

"Take off work for a while? Stay in your cube and catch up on your reading?"

"I don't think so."

He nodded. He hadn't really expected her to go for either of those. "All right. How about you don't go down any corridors alone. Have somebody from your club escort you to and from the main lifts. Don't open your door to anybody you don't know well enough to trust with your life."

She said, "I can do those."

"You have any kind of defensive weaponry?"

"I've got a canister of puke spray. I've had a few people want to get closer to me after they've seen me dance. A couple of times somebody has followed me when I've left the club. I had to use it once. A long time ago."

Puke spray was pretty much what the name said: It was an emetic fluid, a blast of which in the face would almost always cause immediate, uncontrollable projectile vomiting.

It was hard to attack somebody when you were throwing up everything you had eaten since you were born.

"Keep it handy," he said.

"I will."

It wasn't ideal, but she was a grown woman and at least he had offered her the warning and advice. He didn't really think anybody would go after her—it was too far along for that to stop him. Plus if anything happened to Trish, the police would certainly take a renewed interest in her SO's death. Probably the killers weren't that stupid.

They went back to the serious business of finishing their meal. It was, as always, delicious.

Sooner or later, people were going to discover Tibbs's ability with a wok and hot oil, and getting in here to dine was going to be a problem. Probably Tibbs would have to expand the place.

Gil had a bit of money saved. Maybe Tibbs would consider selling him a part interest in the place. It would be worth it just to have a table reserved. Or maybe Tibbs would like a model. Gil had done pretty well with his bartering in that way.

It was something to think about.

Not that he didn't have plenty of other things to think about . . .

11

ALONE IN HIS cube, Gil sat in his web-back chair. He closed his eyes. He breathed slowly and evenly, let his mind drift toward a place of quiet. He meditated for a few moments on his breathing, counted the out-breaths. Focused until he was calm—as calm as he was going to get.

When he was ready, he conjured from his memory the attack upon him in the corridor.

—two men, each holding a half-meter section of pipe as they slid out of a utility closet behind him—

Best to concentrate on one of them. Which one could he see the best?

—Red started to stagger backward. Oh...so... slowly...

—put the ball of his foot hard into Green's side, not really damaging him but off balancing him even more, so that he stumbled, hit the corridor wall hard and fell—

—third man, one wearing a blue mask, who must have been waiting ahead of him, was able to get close enough to bring his pipe down and catch Gil on the left side of

his neck, low on the trap, almost to the shoulder—

Red, Green, Blue. Which one?

Blue, he decided. He could see Blue the best, because of the distance. Because for a brief period, he had all his attention focused on Blue alone—even though he shouldn't have.

He let his memory rule, and what he saw was the man's left hand. The hand was pale, and there was dark hair on the back of it and between the knuckles of the fingers. Fairly smooth skin, none of that crepe texture an older man would have. The fingernails were ragged. Bitten close to the quick. Odd that he noticed that.

Eyes still closed, he said, ''Computer, record voice input.''

The voxax system acknowledged his command. ''Recording,'' she said in her throaty voice.

''Male, aged twenty-five to thirty-five. Black hair.''

—Gil squatted, picked up the pipe that Red had dropped, stood, and flipped it at Blue with a back-wrist toss, spinning it like a disk at the man's eyes—

''Brown eyes. Height, approximately one meter eight. Weight, seventy-eight to seventy-nine kilos.''

—Blue batted at the incoming pipe and ducked at the same time—

Blue's coverall left a patch of bare wrist and arm as he raised his weapon. Anything there? Scars? Veins? Tattoos?

No.

—the pipe was high, just glanced off his head—

Hmm. The man might have a bruise or small cut on the right side of the forehead, just below the hairline, but that wouldn't help, unless he went to a doctor for treatment. And even if he did, Gil couldn't get that information. Well, it wouldn't hurt to check with Ray El-Sayed, maybe the cool could get it, though he doubted that, too.

—Blue cocked his weapon for another blow—

Wait, was that a flash of color under the upraised arm? What was that? Orange? A tear in the coverall that revealed something under it? Or some smear on the fabric? He couldn't tell.

He went over the attack again, then a third time. No more useful stuff, nothing he could add to the description.

He blew out a breath, opened his eyes. Memory depended on observation, and when he had time to do it properly, he was a pretty good observer. No Holmes, but neither was he blind. In the middle of a fight, however, the primitive hardwired-in-the-caves-fight-or-flight reactions drenched you, slurried thick with adrenaline, and sensory input got strange. Sounds went away, vision tunneled, and your mind focused on the oddest details.

He remembered that from the destruction of the resiplex.

And once, a cable car he'd been riding in high over downtown Buenos Aires snapped a support line and dropped like a big rock. For a heartbeat, Gil had known he was going to die. What he noticed, save for the sudden clutch in his belly, was a cameo pin on the blouse of a woman seated across from him.

The car fell a mere five meters before the emergency line went taut enough to stop it. There hadn't been any real danger, though his body hadn't known that.

When the cable caught and bowed, then rebounded, and they knew they weren't going to die, there had been a lot of nervous laughter and conversation among the passengers and operators of the car. He couldn't remember the specifics of what was said, couldn't picture the woman's face upon whose blouse it rode, but he recalled that cameo pin in photographic detail—a gold-rimmed oval the size of a small coin, the black background, the carved white profile, he could see still clearly years after the incident, as if it had somehow been branded into his memory. Like a final snapshot by a brain that thought it was going away and wanted to take something—anything—with it when it went.

Blue didn't present much of a picture he could use, but if he ever got close enough, he was pretty sure he'd be able to recognize the man by his hands, the chewed fingernails. Of course, getting close enough would be the trick.

"Computer, access public identification records of the *Robert E. Lee*'s population as of this date and look for matches who might fit the physical description just recorded."

There was a short pause. "Done," the computer said.

"How many possible matches?"

"Eight hundred and seventy-nine listed IDs fall within the parameters."

Jesus, almost nine hundred men. Was there any way to narrow that down?

"Computer, eliminate any possibles logged off station for the past twenty-four hours. How many does that leave?"

"Eight hundred and seventy."

Well. That was a big help.

"Computer, eliminate any men with recorded physical handicaps that would significantly impair normal leg or arm movement. How many left?"

"Eight hundred and fifty-seven."

This road was going to be a long, ugly trip, Gil realized. Even if he could cut the number of possibles in half, it would take months for him to track down and speak to all the remaining black-haired, brown-eyed men on the station. And there was the possibility that the man he wanted was younger or older than his search, or even a transient who could by now be back on Earth, drinking wine in a bistro in Lyons or lying with a street whore in the bad part of Seoul.

Well. You had to go with what you had. It was better than nothing.

The com chirped. "Yes?"

"Gil, Nicholas Higgins. How are you?"

Gil blinked, drawn away from his investigatory trance by the caller. Nicholas was the owner of the most exclusive art gallery on the station. The Higgins Gallery was on LL1 and you had to make an appointment just to get in the door. Most station artists would cheerfully set fire to their grandfathers to get a showing at the Higgins, and here Gil had forgotten all about the upcoming show.

His show.

"Fine, Nicholas. And you?"

"I'm great, really looking forward to your exhibition. Everything going okay? You need anything?"

"Things are going fine. I'm putting the finishing touches on the new piece, hope to have it ready in time."

"Don't wear yourself out," Nicholas said. "Aside from the five pieces you sent over, I've got more than a dozen owners committed to lending us their models, that includes Thurgood Ainge's three and Holly Mbutu, who's got four, so we're looking at twenty-five exhibits altogether."

Twenty-five models. That was more than half his professional output—he'd only completed forty-four pieces worth selling, and several of those were relatively crude early models he'd never let out of the shop now.

"You ready to talk price on the five new ones?"

Gil shook his head, realized that Higgins couldn't see him, and said, "Whatever is fair." Currently, Gil asked seven to eight thousand for his pieces and he limited his waiting list to six commissions. He liked to allow five or six weeks for each piece, though he could generally complete them faster than that. It averaged out to a hundred and fifty or two hundred hours per model, some less, some a little longer. Seven or eight thousand for a month to six weeks work, well, that certainly was decent money. It was about two and a half times what the average wage was overall on the station.

Higgins laughed. "Fair? We're talking about *art*! There's nothing *fair* about it! You have a talent, a skill, and you should be rewarded for it. Any sucko can push a sweeper. The medical schools turn out thousands of doctors every year. There are hundreds of super-class pro sports players, dozens of interplanetary vid stars, and the shorter the line, the more they get paid. How many guys are there like you, making these tiny models as well as you do?"

"Four," Gil said. He was pretty objective about how his work stacked up. There were only three other modelmakers whose work was in the same quality arena as his: LeDoux, in France, Warner in NA, Zuri on the wheelworld *New Capetown*. LeDoux did buildings and historical cityscapes. Warner specialized in battlefield recreations, Zuri did landscapes.

"Uh-huh. And how much do they get paid for their work?"

"Depends on the commission," Gil said.

"LeDoux gets twice what you ask, minimum. Warner more than that. Zuri doesn't do anything for less than twenty thousand nude. Wöhler, we're talking eighty, a hundred thousand before he switches on a magnifier. Half a million for his major pieces."

"So?"

"So, you're as good as they are."

"Nobody is as good as Wöhler."

Johann Wöhler, the German, was in a class by himself, and so far above the rest of them that he was the sun to their moons. He did human figures, ships, buildings, wheelworlds, whatever he felt like, and his worst was better than anybody else's best. Wöhler was a perfectionist. He didn't think anything of scrapping five hundred hours work if he got an eyelash crooked on a background character nobody would ever look at.

Wöhler could have sat at the same table drinking with Michelangelo or Rodin or Picasso.

"Fine, we won't ask for as much as he gets."

Gil grinned. Higgins took thirty percent of anything that sold in his gallery, and that was reasonable; some galleries charged fifty percent.

"Whatever you think, Nicholas. I'm just the craftsman, you're the expert."

"We need to work on that attitude, Gil. The guy who repairs your plumbing is a craftsman. *You* are a goddamned *artist*."

Gil laughed.

"Come on by the gallery in the next day or two, take a look at how I want to do the displays."

"I will."

They broke the connection. He liked going to art openings; it gave him a chance to walk around sipping champagne and watching people, ever fascinating. But at this opening, he would be in the center of everyone else's attention, and so it wouldn't be nearly as much fun.

Well. A successful showing in the Higgins could lead to a show down below. Word was that the ear of the Metropolitan in New York and Nicholas Higgins's lips were never that far apart. Wouldn't that be something, to get a show in a major Earth museum? That could give a few of his old buddies heart attacks.

Abruptly, the thought struck him that Trish might enjoy attending the show. He should certainly have Higgins send her an invitation.

Better still, why didn't he invite her himself? It was a week away. Probably he would have something new to tell her about the investigation by then, right?

Come on. Who do you think you're fooling here, pal?

Well, hell, what was wrong with having an attractive woman to whom you could show off your work? No sin there, was there?

Not yet, anyway.

He grinned at himself.

He went to take a shower, attended to his teeth and beard, then headed for bed.

It had been a long day, but even so, sleep came hard. When he finally dozed off, he did so thinking about the man whose head had been crushed by a powerful press. He did not dream, or if he did, he didn't remember it.

12

WHAT GIL HADN'T seen was the actual place where Corderman had died. He might have had some trouble arranging that, but Chaz Wells was happy to help out. In fact, he was willing to take Gil on a tour of the site himself.

They arranged to meet between the end of second shift and the beginning of third, so they could look for a few minutes without getting too much in anybody's way.

The Engineering & Manufacturing Level was just below P&D—the Port and Dock, these latter being at the top of the *Robert E. Lee*. In zero gravity, such designations wouldn't matter, top, bottom, up, down, but in a station with gravity generators, up and down were as useful as they were on Earth. On the REL, the gravity generators were installed below Recycling, mounted on the aft hull, between the radiators that, when it sometimes became necessary, bled excess heat into space. People on Earth were sometimes amazed that a space habitat could develop so much excess heat, given that it was surrounded by all that vast, cold vacuum. And most of the time, most of the heat was recycled and put to good use; but every now and then, there was more than the station needed, and it had to go somewhere. The thermodynamic engineers tore at their hair when that happened—by their natures, they hated to waste a single calorie.

Like most, the E&M Level was multistory, with the heavier machineries on the lower sublevels. There were eight sublevels; the place where Corderman had died was S-1, the lowest. Down in the bowels of the beast.

Despite the harmonic cancelers, vibration dampers, and audiostik insulation, S-1 was noisy. Gil and Chaz Wells were issued hardshell caps, safety glasses, and electronic ear plugs before they went through the entrance gate. The hardshell would save your skull from a loose rivet or mishandled rotowrench. The polarized glasses were supposed to protect your eyes against blasts of grit and sudden flashes of light, and the plugs would let you hear normally, but would block any sound beyond the decibel level that would damage your auditory nerves. Workers' comp was a major expense wherever a human hand put a hammer to a nail or a driver to a screw, and the Corporation took precautions to avoid paying any more of the injured and unproductive than it had to.

A forewoman led Gil and Wells through a series of wide corridors lined with stressflex-carbon shelving piled high with various bins and plastic boxes full of metal or glass fiber components for fairly big machinery. Now and then the rows of shelving gave way to open areas with heavy equipment running.

Gil looked around, tried to get a feel for what it would be like to work here. As a former engineer, he'd been on a few work sites. There were dumbot assembly lines, welding, bolting, gluing things together. A few men and women monitoring computerized cutters or stampers or melders. A big fabber tended by both robots and people, bright blue lasers flashing and following material buildup as the fabber constructed items from whichever material tray was needed. There was a smell of burned metal, overlaid with a yeasty odor not too unlike a pie shell baking.

"This way," the woman leading them said.

The trio zigged and zagged a few more turns. They came to a large square occupied by several big machines, a couple of anchored dumbots and more complex robots on rails, an overhead crane, some large bins full of scrap metal—aluminum, brass, copper, steel.

There weren't any people in the section.

"This is it," the forewoman said.

Gil looked around. Nobody could see you from anywhere else; the floor-to-subceiling shelving surrounded the area. He looked for the security cams, spotted one. It was a sweeper, slowly panning back and forth, covering the work area. Looked as if it would take a minute or so to do a full cycle. They would have kept the recording of that day. He reminded himself to ask about that later.

"This is where we do sheet and plate fab," the woman said. "That's the big shear, there is the laser plate-saw, over there, the masher."

The masher, Gil assumed, was the name for the 40-ton press that had killed David Corderman.

Wells confirmed this. The three of them moved toward the machine. There was a triple rail of metal tubing from floor to chest height all the way around the machine, and a swing-up counterbalanced electric gate to allow access. The gate was up.

It was a simple-looking device. Mounted on a very solid-appearing pedestal to a huge footplate on the floor was a durasteel bed, probably tempered to an extreme hardness. The bed was flat, shiny, and square, two meters by two.

Four meters above the bed was the ram, a matching durasteel plate mounted on a hydraulic arm as big around as Gil. Around the outside of the square was a splash guard, also durasteel, a raised frame a third of a meter high and as thick as Gil's forearm.

"Show him how it works," Wells said.

The forewoman nodded. She went to a large plastic

bin and retrieved a fist-sized lump of a dull gray metal. "Tin," she said, waving the lump.

She went through the gate, put the chunk of metal on the press bed. Stepped back outside the surrounding fence. Went to a control panel, tapped in some settings that appeared on the flatscreen computer. Then she lifted a spring-loaded button cover and thumbed the red button underneath.

Nothing happened.

Wells gestured at the open gate. "First interlock," he said to Gil. "Unless the gate is down, the press won't operate." He nodded at the forewoman. She touched another control, and the gate pivoted down into place and locked audibly, a sharp *chink!* Gil easily heard through the plugs. A red light he hadn't noticed began flashing and a repetitive *beep-beep-beep!* alarm began. Not quite enough to kick in the sound suppressors, but certainly enough volume that you couldn't possibly miss it.

The forewoman thumbed the button again. The hydraulic ram still didn't move.

"Second interlock," Wells said. "Spray shields are down."

The woman tapped another control on her panel. From the floor, a series of linked, clear panels came up. Denscris or Lexan, Gil figured. There were scratches on the inner surfaces, a couple of dings. The panels came up just inside the fence, rose to a height of three meters, completely encircling the press. The gaps between the panels were maybe a centimeter wide. "Maybe one time in ten thousand something squeezes from under the splash guard, little bits that probably don't do any real damage, but when it does, the shields keep it from spewing the operator or anybody else who happens to be in the area."

This time when the forewoman hit the covered button, which certainly couldn't be pushed accidentally, the press came on line. There was a hiss, a rumble, a groan as the hydraulic ram began coming down. It settled very slowly.

"You could take a nap waiting for it to get all the way

down,'' Wells said. "Plenty of time to move out of the way. And watch this.''

Wells picked up a piece of scrap, some brass bar stock about a dozen centimeters long, as big around as a pencil. He went to the splash shield, shoved the thin bar through the slight gap between two of the clear panels, hard enough so the bar flew and landed on the bed under the settling ram.

The machine stopped. The warning beep changed tone.

"Third interlock. If something moves under the ram, the sensors stop it." To the woman he said, "Go ahead and reset it."

She tapped the control panel. The alarm went back to its earlier sound, started down again. It took ten seconds for it to reach the gray lump. The splash shield on the ram hid the lump of tin and the bar before the upper plate reached it. The ram settled. Reached the computer-set thickness and stopped. Hydraulics hissed as compressed air vented. The ram rose.

On the bed was a thin sheet of shiny silver—the former lump of tin—with a darker blot of yellow film—the brass bar—overlaying it.

"Tin is pretty soft," the woman said.

"So you see how it couldn't be an accident," Wells said.

"Yes," Gil said. "I see."

It wasn't an accident. It had to be murder.

Wells showed Gil where Corderman's personal locker was. "Still got some of his work gear in it," Wells said. "Coveralls, extra shoes, like that."

Gil was surprised the locker hadn't been reassigned and said so.

"Apparently the section is running more efficiently than the designers figured on," Wells said. "Got more locker space than people to use it."

Gil opened the unlocked plastic cabinet and looked inside. Wells said, "Feel free to poke around." He

waved at the locker, then turned to talk to the forewoman.
"We've already gone through it."

Gil cataloged the contents of the locker. There was a
spare coverall, some work boots, an emergency oxy mask
and bottle. Some accumulated trash at the bottom. Food
wrappers, worksheets, a little stylized Big Blue company
logo sticker that looked as if it had been peeled off the
front of a personal computer and tossed carelessly into
the locker. Gil bent, picked up the logo, looked at it for
a second, then dropped it.

Not much to show for a man's life.

He stood. Wells said, "You got everything you
need?"

"I believe so. Thanks for showing me around." He
smiled at the forewoman. "I appreciate your help, fem."

The forewoman waved him off. "No problem."

As he and Wells left, the security chief said, "I hear
you've got some new pieces in your upcoming show. If
I made an offer on one, would I still be able to get the
commission piece?"

"Sure."

Apparently the Corporation paid its head of security
pretty well.

"What do the new ones run?"

"Check with M. Higgins, he's working up the cata-
log."

"Ouch, that sounds like your prices are going up."

Gil smiled, but didn't elaborate further. Probably his
prices *were* going up, and it would likely sound disingenuous to say he didn't know what they were apt to be.

"Well, I got my invitation, so I'll be there. I'm looking
forward to it."

Gil nodded at Wells. It would have been appropriate
for him to say he was looking forward to the show, too,
but he found that in truth, he wasn't, at least not all that
much. Not that he'd have a bad time or that it wouldn't
be interesting. He'd make some money if any of the five
models sold. There would be a lot of ego-boosting to be
had, people going on about how much they admired his

work, and he wasn't immune to such flattery. Though he always felt a kind of puzzlement about people who told him such things. Why were they saying it? Did they really like the work? Or did they have some other motive? And if so, what? Gil didn't get a lot of opportunity to talk to other artists, but when he did, he found a common thread that seemed to run among them all. Artists who worked for the love of it, who would have done it if they never made a centimo from it, didn't consider what they did real work. It wasn't like a carpenter or a medic or a programmer who did something *useful* . . .

He grinned to himself. Man did not live by bread alone, he knew that. Knew that art and entertainment were necessary to most lives, that all work and no play certainly did limit one's horizons. Even so, it was still amazing to him that he could get paid—well paid—for something he so much enjoyed doing. It didn't seem real, somehow.

"Gotta run, duty calls."

"Thanks again, Chaz."

"Any time, Gil."

Gil went by his shop and managed an hour on his model, actually getting some work done. A few more touches, another couple of hours, and he'd be finished. That would give him six new pieces, even though the current project was a commission and thus not for sale. He didn't have time do a lot of uncommissioned work. One of the five unsold models had started out as a request, but before Gil finished it, the buyer had died in a traffic accident. A shuttle had come in too fast, slammed into a loading dock, killing a dozen passengers, his patron among them. The heirs didn't care for art. That model was of the *Lusitania*, a British Cunard Line steamer torpedoed by a German U-boat off the coast of Ireland in 1915, taking almost twelve hundred passengers and crew with it to Davy Jones's locker.

Most commissions were of well-known vessels, though

they were getting less so, since Gil wouldn't duplicate a model he had built before.

It wasn't as if he was about to run out of material. Since man had taken to the seas in watercraft, tens of thousands of ships had gone down to feed the fish and litter the ocean bottoms. More in the last couple of centuries alone than Gil could possibly ever finish even if he could build them twice as fast as his current output.

The four ships he'd built just because he wanted to had taken almost three years of spare time to construct, oddball projects of lesser known sinkings. They were the *Princess Alice,* a British steamer that went down in 1878 after a collision with another ship in the Thames River, costing 700 lives; the *General Slocum,* an excursion steamer that caught fire and burned in the East River near New York City in 1904, killing more than a thousand; the *Kichemaru,* a Nipponese vessel that sank off the Japanese coast in 1912, just five months after the *Titanic*'s ill-fated voyage, claiming a thousand lives to mark its passing; and the *Kiangya,* a Chinese refugee ship destroyed in a massive explosion off Shanghai, with more than eleven hundred souls, in the bitter winter of 1948.

Doubtless a psychologist would have no trouble making something of Gil's choice of model subjects and the destruction of the giant resiplex upon which he had once worked. Gil was not unaware of the parallel. Certainly he felt drawn to such events, and certainly he was not the only one. People kept souvenirs of such disasters, conversation pieces sometimes mounted under a glass dome in one's house or cube. That? Oh, that's a piece of metal from the frame of the lighter-than-air zeppelin *Hindenburg;* or a lump of coal brought up from the *Titanic*; or fragments of the engine from the orbital passenger lifting body *Bejeli Vjetar.*

What was so fascinating about such relics? It was hard to say. But Gil's theory was that many—if not most—humans still believed in luck. They might claim to be rational, might deny a belief in spirits or demons or winning the lottery, but he thought that collectors of disaster memorabilia believed—perhaps on an unconscious level— that there was a sort of . . . magic connected to an object that had been witness to a disaster, and that perhaps that magic might extend to the owner, to somehow protect him from similar happenings.

It was as good a theory as any he'd heard.

He leaned back in his chair, thought about his other work, the hunt for justice when none seemed to be available. The investigation into Corderman's death was still young. He had a few pieces of it, not enough to put it together into anything recognizable, but it wasn't at a dead end yet. Corderman had a life outside his job, and Gil hadn't begun to delve deeply into that yet. What he did when he was away from work might give Gil the missing pieces. He had some of that information he could check on; he would collect more.

It was hard to be patient sometimes, but working on tiny models where a too-fast move could ruin a month's work had taught him that slow and steady might not always win the race, but it usually would let you finish it.

He reached for his com to call Trish. This might not be the most pleasant chore, but it was something that had to be done, sooner or later. He would proceed as gently as he could.

13

TRISH WAS WILLING to have Gil come by and go through Corderman's effects. Since her work usually began on third shift, at 1600, there was plenty of time.

He called Ray El-Sayed's office, got the computer. The detective was off-shift. Gil left a message, asked if he could access the security cam recordings for the S-1 press area on the day that Corderman died. As he finished leaving his request and discommed, the unit chimed with an incoming call.

It was El-Sayed.

"Sivart? I think we need to have a conversation."

"Sure. About what?"

"Face to face. I'm at the catfish pond on H&L, you know where that is?"

"Yes."

"Why don't you drop by, if you aren't too busy?"

Gil shut the com off. Hmm. Interesting. Something the policeman didn't want to talk about on the com? Was that because he didn't want some bored kid with a scanner to overhear it? Or something else? The somewhat terse, "Drop by, if you aren't too busy," might be a more polite way of saying get your butt over here.

Well. He'd find out soon enough.

The Hydroponics & Livestock Level was split, not into a pair of neat half-cylinders, but rather more like the Oriental yin-yang symbol—viewed in cross-section from above, the level looked like two tadpoles chasing each other's tails. It had to do with distribution of weight— water was heavy and there was a lot of it on the level, on both sides.

Near the tail of the aquaculture section of Livestock was the public fish pond. You could rent gear, everything from a basic cane pole with a weighted and hooked line with a red and white plastic float, to state-of-the-art graphite rods and reels for fly casting. The limit was three catches per fisher, no matter what equipment you used, and the cost of the equipment and the license fees were slightly more than you would pay for the fish if you bought them in the market.

They didn't charge you just to stand and watch.

Gil saw Ray El-Sayed standing near the edge of the pond, behind the waist-tall safety fence. The surrounding deck was slightly elevated away from the water, like a shallow-rimmed crater. There was a wide apron of living grass carpet around the pond, a thick and deep green mat. Next to the detective was a small boy of about seven or eight. The boy, who was a younger copy of the cool, had to be his son. He held a three-meter cane pole out over the fence, and his attention was riveted on the little float in the water beneath the pole.

The float dipped halfway under, came back to the surface, made little ripples as it bobbed up and down, never quite going under.

Gil walked over but kept quiet. Saw El-Sayed acknowledge him but keep his attention focused on the float.

"Now, Poppa?"

"Not yet, son. Wait a little longer."

The float bobbed. Sank completely under the surface. "Now!"

The boy jerked upward on the pole, leaned back.

The hook cleared the water, brought with it a silvery white fish eighteen or twenty centimeters long.

"I got him, Poppa! I got him!" The little boy smiled, showing a gap in his top front teeth.

The flexing catfish cleared the safety fence, and the boy dropped him onto the grass. The fish snapped, bounced, popped, doing a little dance on the mat. It was grayish, had a white belly and whiskers, and a thumb-sized black splotch on one side.

"Okay, okay!" El-Sayed said. "Now, pull the hook, and watch out for the spines!" His grin was as broad as his son's.

Gil found himself smiling as he watched.

The fish flopped around a little more until the boy managed to pin it to the grass. He unhooked the fish, picked it up in two hands, held it up for his father to see. "Look, Poppa, look!"

El-Sayed patted his son on the back, then pulled a small camera from his belt. "I see him. Okay, hold him up so I can get a holo to send to Nanna."

The boy smiled into the camera's lens. His father clicked off three images.

"Better throw him back before he gets too upset."

The boy turned and heaved two-handed. The small catfish sailed over the fence, hit the water with a splash, disappeared.

"Well, it looks like we're out of bait. Run go get another packet of bread. Tell them to put it on our tab."

The boy darted off toward the bait shack.

The men watched him run, legs pumping.

"Good-looking boy," Gil said. "You don't keep the fish?"

"Nope. We're vegetarians. The idea is to catch it, not eat it. The hooks are barbless so it's a little harder to get them out of the water. Probably scares the devil out of the fish, but they get a bread ball for their trouble, then go back in the pond. It doesn't seem to hurt 'em much—I think we've caught that particular one a couple of times before."

"He your only child?"

"No, he has an older sister. Celene, she's thirteen, going on thirty." El-Sayed glanced upward, as if to the heavens. "A beautiful child and I love her beyond words, but she is a trial."

"Don't you remember how it was to be thirteen?"

"Apparently not," he said. "To hear Celene speak of it, when I was her age, dinosaurs still roamed the Earth and I couldn't possibly begin to understand with my fossilized brain how it is to be her age *now*."

Gil grinned. There was a small pause. Then the cool said, "So, tell me why you did a search of the station records for a black-haired young man."

"Ah." He hadn't made any effort to hide the search, so it would have been a matter of public record. Interesting that El-Sayed had a squeal program set to notice such things, though.

"I remembered something about one of my attackers," he said.

"I thought as much. And you thought you might try to locate him on your own rather than let me do my job."

"Sorry. I didn't think it was enough to bother mentioning."

Abdul came running up, a plastic bag full of mushy-looking white doughlike stuff clutched in one hand. "Here it is, Poppa."

El-Sayed pulled a device from his pocket. It looked like a melon-baller, only much smaller. "Okay, you make the bait-ball like I showed you."

The boy nodded, took the device. Looked up at Gil.

"This is M. Sivart," El-Sayed said. "He's helping me on a case."

"Pleasedtomeetchoo," the boy said, all one word. "I'm Abdul Nasser El-Sayed."

"I am pleased to meet you, too, Abdul Nasser El-Sayed."

The boy turned to his bread-balling, and Gil could have become invisible for all the further attention he merited.

"You were going to call and give me this information, but you hadn't gotten around to it yet, right?" El-Sayed said. "To do otherwise would have been withholding evidence in a criminal matter."

"If I had gotten the possibles narrowed down to a reasonable number, yes."

"Do you not think it proper that the police determine what is reasonable in such business? We have resources you do not, after all."

Gil looked El-Sayed straight in the eyes. "And would the police be willing to spend these resources narrowing down a list of eight hundred-plus possible suspects in an assault case? Given that I could not recognize the man's face?"

"Assault with a deadly weapon is a serious infraction."

"I agree. But I wasn't hurt—and you didn't answer my question."

El-Sayed flashed his teeth in a grin. "Between you and me, as important as such a crime is, we don't have that many resources to spare."

"I thought not."

"But still, I would like to know such things."

"I'll keep that in mind."

"I see that you called about the recording of M. Corderman's last moments. You may access it when you wish. I will have the code transmitted to your inbox."

Gil nodded. If he wanted to be difficult, El-Sayed could have denied him access to the recording, at least for a few days, or until Gil could have used another contact to circumvent him. And given that Gil hadn't told him about the black-haired attacker, El-Sayed would have probably been justified in feeling he could keep the recording from Gil. Tit for tat. By granting Gil's request so promptly, the cool had one-upped him. He was being gracious when he did not have to be.

"Thank you," Gil said. "If I uncover anything that might be of interest to you, I'll pass it along."

El-Sayed nodded, a short and lazy military bow. He seemed to hesitate a moment, as if weighing something. Decided, apparently, to say it.

"Word has filtered down from uplevel management that this death you are investigating was a suicide and that no officer is to waste any more official time on it. The case is closed, it is history, we have better things to do with our time."

"Really," Gil said.

"The rumor is that this unofficial recommendation comes from within the office of the Commission of Fire and Police Affairs. Maybe even the Commissioner himself."

"How interesting."

"Yes, isn't it."

Gil thought about that for a second. Why would anybody at the upper level of station management want to make that statement? It was Gil's experience that whenever political appointees who normally need do nothing but collect their pay each month began laying hands on the day-to-day operations of anything, something was wrong. And that El-Sayed would tell him this meant the cool knew something was rotten somewhere in the barrel. Very interesting indeed.

"It's ready," Abdul said. He held up the hook, baited now with a misshapen blob of white.

"Very good," El-Sayed said. "Okay, let's see if you can't catch Big Whiskers himself this time!"

The boy nodded, took the pole, and flipped the hook and sinker over the fence neatly.

"Have fun," Gil said to the boy. "See you later, Ray."

"I expect so, Gil. One way or another."

As it turned out, Trish's cube was on LL3, same as Gil's, though nearly one-eighty from him and up one sublevel. He walked through the small grassy park on the main floor, watched several children playing airball, then cut through the rose gardens, over the arched bridge that spanned the ankle-deep and narrow stream that gurgled in meandering loops on the main floor of the level.

He kept his attention sharp, but didn't see anybody watching him.

He bypassed the moving sidewalk and took the manual up the wheeled access ramp to the next sublevel. Found Trish's cube and touched the door chime.

"Come on in, Gil."

The door slid open, and Gil stepped into the cubicle. It was much like his own, but newer. Still had that fresh plast smell. The furniture was issue, except for a heavy plastic rocking chair made to look like wood. There were a dozen fiberboard boxes stacked against the wall. After a moment, Trish came out of the bedroom, carrying another box, a large one.

"Excuse the mess," she said. "I've only been here for a week. I used to live on Four, but the place had too many memories . . ." She looked around, put the box on the low coffee table. "I hate to move. Takes forever to get unpacked."

"You know the rule, don't you? If it's still in a box after six months, toss it, you don't need it."

"Sounds like a good idea."

She looked at the box on the table. "This—this is pretty much all I have left of David's personal stuff, here. I gave the clothes away, we didn't have the same tastes in playits or discs, his tools are in a locker. He built that rocker for me, I'm keeping that."

Gil looked at the chair.

"Um. Anyway, you can go through it. Most of the stuff is probably going to go away, too. There are a few things I'll probably hang on to."

Gil had done this a couple of times before, gone through the effects of somebody who had died. It was not a very pleasant experience for any family they had, but it was helpful to him. "Thanks. If you don't want to hang around . . ."

"No, I'm okay. I'm cried out."

"Thanks. You can explain things as we go. Also, I'd like for you to map out in your head a typical week for you and David. When you worked, where you might go when you weren't working, how you spent your time, friends, people you didn't get along with, like that."

"You think that's important? He was killed at work."

"In journalism, there are six questions a good reporter answers in every story: who, where, what, when, why, and how. People investigating crimes have to ask themselves the same questions. We already know the what, where, when, and how—or at least most of the how. What we need to know is who did it and why."

She nodded. "Okay."

"There's a classic triad in criminal activity, certainly in homicide cases—motive, means, and opportunity. Because he was killed at work doesn't mean it was necessarily connected to his job. Somebody had a reason to want your SO dead. If we can find out why, that will lead us to the who. Or the other way around. The answers might be found in something that happened elsewhere. When somebody is killed, most of the time it is by somebody they know, family or a friend. Usually it is an act of passion. Somebody gets angry, a yelling match escalates into violence, it gets out of hand. That didn't happen here. This was premeditated murder, and the killer is somebody with connections."

"Why do you say that?"

He looked at her. "I have accessed the recording taken by the security cam where David was working on the date he died. I can show it to you."

"No!" She swallowed.

"All right, I can tell you what I saw—"

She shook her head. Seemed a little calmer. "It's all right. You can show it to me. I'm okay."

He looked at her for a long moment. "Okay. Tell your computer to bring up this file." He gave her the number.

She did so. The holoproj lit. There was a still image of the large stamping press in Heavy Engineering, sub

S-1 of the E&M Level. The location was date-and-time-stamped in the lower right corner of the image.

Gil gestured at the couch behind them. They sat.

"If you'll let me run it . . . ?"

"Computer, accept voxax input from Gil Sivart."

The computer acknowledged the command.

"Computer, this is Gil Sivart. Run the accessed recording, normal speed."

The holographic image was clear and sharp, as good as a commercial entcom or edcom visual, though there was no sound. The scaled-down, three-dimensional image showed the press, panned to the left slowly. Numbers flashed in the lower right-hand corner of the holoproj, counting tenths of a second.

The camera came to David Corderman. He wore a green coverall with the sleeves cut off, a hard cap and safety glasses. They couldn't see if he had earplugs in. He stood next to the big machine the forewoman had identified to Gil as the shear.

Trish sucked in an audible breath. Not quite a sob.

As the camera continued to pan, they saw the man step on a long bar under the shear. A giant blade came down and sliced off a narrow section of an aluminum sheet under the shear. The cut strip fell into a bin in front of the blade. Corderman touched a hand control, and the sheet slid toward him. He operated the foot mechanism again and clipped another strip. The camera kept panning. He glanced up from his work, they saw his profile, then he looked back down at the sheet of aluminum.

"Computer, pause," Gil said. "Replay previous three seconds."

The computer obeyed. Corderman glanced up from his work—

"Computer, pause. Enhance image, magnification four."

The image froze, then enlarged.

Trish looked at him. "What?"

"I think he just saw or heard somebody come into the area. Somebody he knew, because all he spared them was a quick glance, then he went back to what he was doing. Look at his eye. He's glancing to the side, you can tell. Plus, he is wearing earplugs, at least one on this side.''

''So?''

''Watch. Computer, continue to play recording.''

The image came back to life. The cam panned past Corderman. The second he was off camera, Gil said, ''Computer, reset counter to zero.''

The numbers flashing by in white on the bottom of the screen blinked to zero and started over. The camera continued to pan to the left. It reached the end of its arc in another fourteen seconds. Stopped, then reversed, panning to the right. It took fourteen seconds to get back to the shear.

No sign of Corderman.

The camera continued its track. Another fifteen seconds. The fence surrounding the press came into view . . .

''Computer,'' Gil began.

''Don't pause it,'' Trish said. Her voice was calm. ''Let it play.''

''You sure?''

''I'm sure.''

The angle showed Corderman's feet and legs. ''Computer, stop timer.'' The numbers ceased flashing but the camera continued to pan.

There was the body. It was on its back, arched up high in the middle, legs splayed, the feet dangling. The splash plate pressed down hard enough on the upper chest to lever the rest of the corpse up, despite the shattered spine bent into a ragged U-shape. The rest of the body, thankfully, wasn't visible behind the splash plate.

''Oh, God!''

''Computer, blank image,'' Gil said.

''I'm sorry.''

Now she did sob. ''My fault. I shouldn't have asked to see it. Oh, God. David!''

Her voice was pure anguish. Her pain washed over him, thick, bitter, full of grief.

He waited.

A minute or so passed. "Okay. I'm okay now." She blinked tears away, wiped at her face, looked at him. "What is the point here, Gil? Please say this means something important."

"I think it does. Look at the timer. From the last image of David at the shear until we saw him again, forty-four-point-three seconds elapsed, according to the security camera's timer. I saw this machine operate. It took ten seconds for the ram to reach the bottom from halfway down, almost twenty seconds for the ram to travel from its upmost position to the bed. The ram was down all the way when David comes into view again. That means that if David killed himself, he only had twenty-five seconds to do it. He had to be in position, lying face up on the bed and *absolutely still*—because if he had moved once he was there, the press would have stopped and had to be reset—something he couldn't do without getting up, opening the gate manually, and dropping the shields, then starting over—which he obviously didn't have time to do.

"I find it hard to believe that a man could move the ten meters from the shear to the press, set the controls, take off his glasses and helmet and earplugs, then stick his head under the thing, all in twenty-five seconds. Nor do I think somebody could do it to him, even if he were knocked unconscious the second the camera shifted away from him."

"It must be possible. We saw him alive and then we saw him dead. The police would have checked that, wouldn't they?"

"I expect so, if they knew about the press shutting down if something moved under it. I don't think they knew."

"So what does this mean?"

"I think it means somebody tampered with the recording. I think it took longer than the camera shows, and I think somebody adjusted the camera after it was done. And if that is so, it means we are dealing with people who have access to such things.

"Somebody with security access," he said.

She stared at him.

"If that's true, it opens up a nasty venue. We're talking about Corporate Security or the police."

14

As Gil HAD seen in his locker at work, M. Corderman did not leave a lot in Trish's cube to show for his life. His clothes, packed away, were modest and mostly casual—coveralls, shorts, slip shirts, slippers. He had one formal suit, dark, fairly new, but not particularly expensive, of vat-grown silk.

Corderman had a puzzle computer, filled with crosswords and logicals of the Who-owns-the-zebra? variety. Gil thumbed the little unit on, saw that several of the puzzles were done, a couple of others halfway finished.

There was a membership tab to a gymnasium on LL4. A collection of holoproj action-adventure playits. A digital camera, fairly nice but not top of the line, no recording medium in it. Holographs of various vacation sites, in orbit and on Earth: images of the Great Wall of China, the Tibooburra Nuclear Plant, the pyramid of Giza, the giant Redstone Church in Madagascar. There were also holos of wooded campsites, with hoop tents pitched around a firepit; waterfalls, lakes, mountain trails. Pictures of a couple who looked enough like Corderman so that they must be close relatives, probably his parents.

A box that held what looked to be the contents of a drawer contained two penknives, an electric cigar lighter, a deck of holographic X-rated playing cards. A keytab chain with five magnetic plastic rectangles on it, each coded and colored differently.

"Those are for his locker at work, his cube, my cube, and his gym locker," Trish said. "I don't know what the red one goes to."

"You don't have to do this now," Gil said.

"Yes, I do. I need to help."

Here was a tiny plastic bag of crystal marbles. There a birthday greeting card from Trish. In that corner, a small leather purse full of old coins from different countries and stations. An old com unit with several cracks running through the gray plastic case.

"He did that when the thing malfunctioned," Trish said. "Slammed it against a wall."

"He had a bad temper?"

"Not most of the time. Once in a while if he was really tired, he'd steam up. Or if somebody bothered me. Sometimes after I danced, you know, people tried to get too close. If he saw that, it bothered him. He never turned it on me. Never once laid a hand on me in anger."

Gil filed the information away. Maybe he had turned his anger on somebody with a long memory. You had to check.

There were three more boxes and the rest of the inspection didn't take long. Nothing of great value, nothing you wouldn't find while rummaging in anybody else's junk drawers.

Nothing worth getting killed over.

Gil didn't say anything, but Trish picked up on it.

"David wasn't into things," she said. "He didn't have a lot of stuff. He was more interested in people or places, in doing rather than having."

He nodded. "Okay if I take the keys? I want to check them out."

"Sure. Take anything you want." Her voice was hollow.

"I'll need his inquiry code and password."

"355537-T," she said. "Password is 'green-eyes.'"

He had thought about asking Trish to his model show. This wasn't the right time. "Thanks. I'll talk to you later."

He left.

Back at his shop, Gil put his model equipment on line and waited for the casts and molds to heat up. He logged into the station's mainframe and input the keytab numbers, using Corderman's inquiry code and password. The computer agreed with those keys Trish recognized: Corderman's cube, invalidated since he no longer lived there. The one to Trish's old cube, also invalidated. The key to his work locker, still active. One to the gym locker, also still active. Looked as if nobody had gotten around to cleaning that out, either—Corderman must have paid his membership fee well in advance. The fifth key was to a storage unit on the Engineering Level.

Gil commed Trish and asked her about it.

"Oh, sorry. It slipped my mind. David had some tools, battery and induction things, he made wood and plastic things as a hobby. Chairs, tables, like that. He worked in the communal shop but he kept his own tools separate."

"Okay if I poke around in the unit?"

"Whatever it takes."

"Thanks."

He discommed, saw that the molds were ready. He would check out Corderman's gym locker and tool shed later. Right now, he was in the final stages of the *Dona Paz*. A couple more life preservers, some warning signs in Spanish and English, a couple of trash barrels full of stuff ready to be dumped into the water, and he would be done.

Hand-lettering a sign so small it could fit neatly on the side of a bacterium took a lot of concentration, though. Hard on the nerves, eyes, and hands.

• • •

The incoming call was not screened out by the computer, so it had to be somebody he wanted to talk to.

"Cycle tools. Field sensors off."

Gil glanced at the chronometer inset into the work bench. 0130 hours, into first shift. He'd been up a long time. "Yes?"

"G-G-Gil?"

It was Trish, and she sounded upset.

"I'm here. What's up?"

"I-I-I h-had a little trouble when I g-g-got off w-work. A man tried to grab me."

He could hear the sobs under her voice. "You okay?"

"I am now."

"Where are you?"

"At home."

"I'll be right there. Keep the door locked."

When she opened her door, he saw how rattled she was. She had a wild look about her, like some forest animal chased by a predator. He wanted to hug her and tell her not to worry, but he didn't know her well enough to know if she would appreciate it or take offense.

"Come in," she said.

He did, and she closed and locked the door behind him.

"I've made some coffee. Would you like some?"

"Sure."

He stood next to the couch while she fussed in the kitchen. "Cream or sugar?"

"Black is fine."

She came back with a heavy plastic mug. He took it, sipped at the coffee but didn't really taste it. "Thanks. Okay, sit, tell me what happened."

They sat. She sipped at her own coffee, set the mug carefully on the small table next to the couch. Turned the mug slightly with one hand. Said, "I got off work a little early, left at the end of the shift. Had the bouncer Dadaji walk me to the lift. The halls were quiet, I didn't see anybody following me. The elevator was empty. A couple of women got on a sublevel or two up, got off on the Square. Three teeners, two boys and a girl, got on there, got off on LL3's main. I rode the rest of the way alone to my level. I got off and walked to my cube. I thought I heard somebody behind me but I didn't see anybody.

''As I was opening my door, a man came out of nowhere and grabbed me. I managed to get loose and use my puke spray on him. He took off.''

''You get a look at him?''

''Just his back, and I was in such a hurry to get inside I didn't see much of that. I didn't see his face.''

''Anything you remember about him?''

She shook her head. ''Not really. He was retching, kind of bent over. I couldn't even see what color hair he had. I think I might have smacked him in the eye with my elbow when I was trying to get away. I hit something on his face, and pretty hard. I've got a bruise on my elbow.''

''He say anything?''

''I'm not sure. He might have cursed when I sprayed him. I don't remember. It all happened so fast.''

''Did you call the cools?''

''No.''

Gil looked at her.

She said, ''Sometimes a customer lays hands on one of the dancers. The cools take a report but nothing ever happens. They figure it is our fault for stirring up their lusts. Hazards of the job.''

Gil nodded. ''Call Ray El-Sayed. Tell him what happened. He wants to know anything that might have a bearing on this case.''

''Some horno mauling me?''

''It might be relevant.''

''God.''

''Set your alarms. Get some sleep, if you can. If you have to go out, keep your spray in your hand, and if anybody gets too close to you when you're alone, warn them off. If they don't go, blast them.''

"Okay."

Gil stood.

"Where are you going?"

"There are a couple of people I want to see."

She looked at him. "You need to do that now?"

He could feel it. She was about to ask him to stay. And he much wanted to stay, but once again, it would be like hunting a badly wounded animal, one hardly able to defend itself. "Yes. I have to do it now."

She sighed. "Okay."

Gil untabbed the closure on his pouch, so he could reach his air pistol fast if he needed it. He used his com to check schedules, found out that Base Alicante was working this shift. He initiated a call.

He was on the elevator before the doctor answered. Somebody had left the holowall running, visual only, no sound. Commercial news was up. Gil stared at the current list of buyouts, takeovers, and mergers as he waited for the doctor to come online.

Timeshare automobile brokers were doing a landslide business.

Bioengineered pharmaceutical stocks were up, baseball team stocks were down.

Big Blue was gobbling up another of the hot Vietnamese computer companies. Big Blue was already the largest computer company on the planet and getting bigger all the time.

"Hello, Gil."

"Base. I need a favor."

"Ask. I'll see what I can do."

The wall shifted to Earth Headline News.

A riot in Mecca killed more than a thousand pilgrims visiting the holy city.

The latest Candy Fancy entertainment holo's cost had risen to more than $400 million and was still climbing.

The militant organization EcoPeace claimed responsibility for the destruction of another dam and power station on the Amazon, fortunately without any loss of human life this time: Mean Green, they liked to call themselves in the save-the-planet movement.

"I need to know if a man has received medical treatment in the last few minutes for the effects of nausea gas, or for a bruised eye or possibly a broken nose."

There was a pause. The news wall blathered silently on: the British Prime Minister called for new elections. All of the polls said Labor was going to blow the Conservatives off the map. The pound immediately declined in value against the New Dollar, the mark, the lira, and the yen.

"Such information is confidential," Alicante said. "I assume you have a good reason for asking?"

"Somebody just attacked Patricia Blackwell outside her cube. At the very least it was assault, maybe attempted rape. She hit him in the face with her elbow and with a blast of puke spray."

"Was she injured?"

"No."

"This is a matter for the police, surely?"

"And she is calling them even as we speak. I'm not asking for the name of the patient, just if there *was* one."

Another pause.

Aquaculturist and billionaire George Johnston died at the age of one hundred and six, according to the newswall.

Alicante said, "I don't see how knowing that could hurt anything. Nobody has been treated for either facial contusions or nausea gas on the station in the last few minutes."

"Thanks, I owe you one."

"I sure wish I could wave you at Anton."

Gil thought about it for a second. Said, "Would being invited to an exclusive art opening by the artist help?"

"I am certain it could be made to."

"I'm having a show of my sculpture next week at the

Higgins Gallery. I'll have your name put on the list. Base Alicante and guest?''

''Excellent! Anton adores such things and will have to go, just to be seen, even though he will be very jealous and angry that *he* did not get the invitation and that I did. He will therefore spend the entire time trashing your work, even if he loves it, and he will worry much when I tell him that the handsome and educated and very talented artist and I know each other, and oh, didn't I ever mention that before? I must have forgotten to tell you. No, we have no relationship. We're just *¿cómo se dice?* . . . friends. I'm certain Anton will suddenly see me in a much better light. It will be perfect.''

Gil smiled. ''Is he worth all the trouble?''

Alicante sighed. ''I sometimes wonder. But when he stands naked in the shower, laughing and all full of himself, he melts my heart. I know he loves me, in his own way. What can I say? We have our moments.''

''I'll see you there, then.''

The newswall continued to flash events about which Gil cared little. He had three stops he wanted to make, and they were more important than which oil reserves had been depleted or which holovid star had had her body resculpted for her latest role.

15

THERE WERE THREE men on Gil's list. And he
wanted to see them before too much time passed.

He hurried to LL4, sub 3. The cubicles facing the hallway were not very big, not even the largest units on this
level. *Must be tight, trying to raise four children in a
place like this*, Gil thought.

There was no admittance scanner. He knocked on the
door. According to the station mainframe, his quarry was
off-shift. Gil guessed he would be asleep at this hour,
given his current work schedule.

The door slid aside, squeaked on its track, and stuck
a handspan from fully open. Victor Willow stood there.
He wore a long nightshirt and slippers, and his face was
wrinkled and puffy, but that was from sleep. There
weren't any bruises around his eyes or nose. If he'd been
breathing puke spray anytime recently, it ought to be apparent and it wasn't. He smelled like soap—and not
vomit or the sweet and sour odor of emetic fluid.

He wasn't the man who'd attacked Trish.

It took a second for Willow to place him. "M. Sivart?
What are you doing here?"

Gil said. "David Corderman might be going to Hell,
M. Willow, but it won't be because he was a suicide."

"Excuse me?"

"He was murdered. Sorry to have disturbed your
sleep."

Gil turned and hurried away. Willow was supposed to
be a Christian. Surely he would forgive Gil for awak-
ening him in the middle of his night.

According to his vox, Chaz Wells was, and had been
for the last hour, EVA in a shuttle, doing a security inspection of the Microwave Array. The grids that received
and converted power from the Solar Powercast Sat were
at the top of the station, a long way from where Gil
was—and from where Trish had been attacked.

Gil considered that. Wells was the head of Security
and certainly could have rascaled the recorders on Engineering. He had no motive, either for killing Corderman or jumping Trish, at least none that Gil could see,
but he was the only one of the three men who had the
means to fiddle the security cameras, and so he had to
be considered a person of interest—if not an actual suspect.

What bothered Gil the most about Chaz Wells was
how eager he seemed to be to keep Corderman's death
a suicide.

If Wells was indeed outside the station and EVA, that
would be easy enough to check. Electronic records could
be altered, but there would be a pilot and crew on the
shuttle, dock workers, people who would remember if
Wells had actually been there. Gil could check that later,
if need be.

That left one other suspect.

Gil took the lift to the Square. The air gun gallery was
supposed to be open, but when he got there, the place
was shut up tight.

He asked the computer for Gauthier's cube number
and was surprised to find that the man lived on LL1. How
could he afford that? Gil had never seen the gallery full

of patrons. He couldn't be making much money there, and military retirement pay wasn't that good.

Well. He would ask him.

Gauthier's cube was in a row of six, each of which was at least twice as large as Gil's. How interesting.

He waved his hand over the door announcer. Ten seconds passed. He waved again. When another ten seconds went by, he started pounding on the door. In this neighborhood, it wouldn't be long before somebody called the cools or security, maybe even a private patrol paid for by the residents. Rich people had more to lose and they usually didn't get—or stay—rich if they didn't protect what they had.

If Gauthier was in the cube, Gil had a feeling he wouldn't want the cools arriving anytime soon.

The door opened. Gauthier stood there. In his right hand, hanging down alongside his leg, was a military-issue deep-space dart pistol. Gauthier's face was pale, his eyes watery, his nose red.

He had a red swelling around his left eye. He smelled like Chinese take-out.

"What the hell do you want?" He started to raise the pistol.

Gil stepped to his left, snapped his left hand out and grabbed Gauthier's right hand, gun and all, then twisted and pivoted left. He brought the man's hand up and out, away from Gauthier's body, a short, tight arc. Gauthier yelped, tried to turn into it, but the leverage was against him. His fingers splayed, he dropped the gun. It hit noiselessly on the thick carpet of the cube's entranceway. Didn't go off and shoot anybody, fortunately.

Even as he moved, Gil looked around for other possible attackers. He'd learned that lesson, at least.

Using the wristlock, his thumb firmly against the back of Gauthier's hand, he backed the man into his cube. When they were into the large room beyond the short hallway, Gil let him go.

Gauthier glared, rubbed at his wrist. "I'll have your

ass thrown into jail! This is assault! Breaking and entering! Trespassing!''

''You want to call the cools, be my guest. And you should know, I've got a pistol of my own I can get out real quick if you make any sudden moves when you make the com.''

Gauthier started at him. ''Dammit, you have no right to bust in here and—''

''Let's bottle the scat, Gauthier. If the cools show up here, I'm going to tell them you tried to rape Trish Blackwell. She caught you in the eye with her elbow and a blast of puke spray. You and I both know a chemstat will show matching tags on the emetic fluid in your system— I can still smell the spray—and that black eye you're going to have will add a lot of weight to the evidence against you.''

''Doesn't prove anything! I bumped into somebody in the hall! They got spooked, started flailing and spraying. An accident.''

''You think that story will stand up to a truthscan?''

''You can't get a scan on shit like that!''

''Somebody killed Blackwell's SO. I think the cools could convince a judge to let the brainbreakers put their hands on you.''

''You're fuckin' crazy! I didn't kill anybody! Yeah, yeah, okay, I wanted a taste of Red, but that's not murder!''

''How is it a man like you lives in a place like this?''

''None of your fuckin' business!''

Gil pulled his com from his belt. Saw Gauthier tense and gather himself, as if to jump him.

''If you try it, I will rearrange the furniture with your face,'' Gil said. He was surprised at how angry he was. He *wanted* Gauthier to try it. ''Shall I call the police?''

''Hold up, hold up. I—I made some investments while I was in the service.''

Gil looked at the man. Investments.

''What was your job in the military?''

''I was a quartermaster.''

That would explain it. A lot of military supplies wound up on the black market, and who better to get them there than the man in charge of distributing such supplies?

But why, other than a grudge over a fistfight, would Gauthier have any reason to kill Corderman? Did he want to get next to Trish that much? That he would kill her SO to leave himself an open field? That didn't make a lot of sense. Somebody with a mind that devious should be smart enough to come up with a plan better than grabbing Trish from behind in a public hallway. The one did not lead to the other, not even with the most warped logic Gil could fathom.

"Now what?"

"Nothing," Gil said. "We're done."

He turned and headed for the door. Paused long enough to unload Gauthier's pistol. He tossed the weapon onto the couch, the magazine into the kitchen.

As soon as he was outside in the hall and the door closed behind him, he called El-Sayed.

Gauthier being the killer really didn't make much sense—unless there was another reason entirely.

True, crooks were sometimes incredibly stupid. There was an entcom on the net that consisted of nothing but reenactments of particularly dumb crimes, from people who tried to mug somebody by pretending a banana was a pistol, to those who left their ID at the scene of a theft. Gil's favorite was the would-be robber who walked into a crowded hotel ballroom and demanded everybody's credit tabs. It turned out the hotel was the site for an international convention of peace officers. There were four hundred men and women in the room, and half of them pulled guns.

Gil wondered what the sound of that many safety catches clicked off at once sounded like. Or if the robber had had a heart attack when he saw and heard all those weapons come online pointed at him.

El-Sayed came on the com. "Small world, isn't it? I've got your girlfriend on another circuit."

"Not my girlfriend. I thought you'd be interested to

know that Emile Gauthier, the guy who runs the air gun gallery, is the man who attacked Trish Blackwell.''

"How would you know that?''

"I happened onto him. He's got a bruised eye and he stinks of puke spray. I bet the tags match.''

"Dammit, Sivart—''

"Listen up. Gauthier is in his place on LL1 along with a military-issue handgun, a piece I would bet is not legally registered. If you hurry, you can probably catch him before he cleans up and tosses the weapon.''

"What is it, Gil? Is it that you *want* me to tab you for obstructing justice?''

"I'm not obstructing anything, Ray. I just called the police to pass along information about a felony. And he might even be connected to another crime—which isn't a crime, according to certain high officials.''

"Anything to support that?''

"No. You might see if you can get a scan.''

"You know better. You need a boxcar of evidence and a capital crime for a truthscan. Murder one, murder of a police official, murder during a major felony, station sabotage in the first degree.''

"And officially, there was no such crime,'' Gil said.

"Officially, no. But we can pick up Gauthier for the assault on M. Blackwell. Maybe he'll volunteer something.''

"Right, he will.''

"You like him for the crime-no-crime?''

Gil said, "Not really. Could be just another of those nasty coincidences we keep running into.''

"I'll drop by and pick up M. Gauthier. Go home, Gil. I'd feel a lot safer if you were there.''

Gil broke the link, headed for the lifts. He was almost all the way back to his shop—not likely he was going to be able to get to sleep just yet, so he might as well do a little more work—when his com chimed. The ID read showed that it was Trish.

"Hello,'' he said. "Are you okay?'' He tried not to make it sound too much like *Should I come over?*

"Better. I talked to the detective. He said they knew who the attacker was and were on their way to pick him up. I told them I couldn't identify his face."

"They've got some pretty good circumstantial evidence," Gil said. "Your defense spray has tiny bits of colored plastic in it, tags that show up under an electron microscope. The tag combination is altered with every lot. Even if he ditches his clothes and takes half a dozen scalding showers, they'll find a tag match in your attacker's lungs or blood. Plus he's got a big bruise where you whacked him with your elbow."

"How do you know this?"

"I paid him a visit. His name is Emile Gauthier."

"How did you know who it was? Why does his name sound familiar?"

"He apparently bothered you one night in the club a few months back. Your SO took exception. I spoke to the man earlier this week."

There was a short pause. "Oh. I remember. The man who put his hand on my butt. Short-haired, kind of old and oily. David spoke to him and the man tried to punch him. David knocked him down."

Not the same as Gauthier's version of the event, no surprise there.

"Do you think he is connected to . . . what happened to David?"

Gil thought about it one more time. "No. I think he knew your SO wasn't around anymore and he tried to take advantage of it." And his conscience made him add, "And that was my fault. I told him about David when we talked."

"It's not your fault. You didn't make him sneak up and grab me."

"Unless he had a criminal record I couldn't find, it isn't likely they'll put him in jail. He'll probably plead it out and get a fine. But I don't expect he'll be bothering you again. The cools know who he is; besides, his last visit couldn't have been very pleasant for him."

"More trouble than I'm worth?"

"Unless you're wired differently than most people, it is kind of hard to keep erotic thoughts going while you are throwing up."

She laughed.

It was the first time he could remember her doing that, laughing, and he much enjoyed hearing it.

"Get some rest if you can," he said. "I'll call you next shift."

"Thanks."

He headed into the Square. Maybe he could get the model finished. He sure didn't seem to be getting any closer to solving the murder. If anything, the waters seemed muddier than before.

16

GIL FINISHED THE *Dona Paz*.

Normally, completing a project was cause for a certain amount of satisfaction, if not elation. Each part of a model had its joys. Beginning, middle, and end. The final few hours as he pushed ahead to get done, like finishing a race, he usually enjoyed that a lot. Of course, there was always the worry that he'd missed something, that people would look at his efforts and find them unworthy, but he'd learned to live with that worry. Done was done, and it was too late to fret much then. Mostly, he felt a sense of accomplishment when he scanned a finished model. This time, his concern over the investigation he'd taken on overrode his usual feelings. The model was more something to complete, to get out of the way, so he could get on with other business. A terrible way to think about art, or even craft.

Well, he was finished. And while he had other commissions waiting, he could take a week or two before he had to start. He usually added a cushion when he projected a delivery date, based on a formula given to him

by an old architect he'd met at conference. Figure out
how much time you'll need to do a job, the old man had
said, double that—then add thirty percent for the shit.
That ought to give you just about enough room to get it
done without people squawking.

Gil smiled at the memory as he locked up the shop.
He usually didn't pad his estimates quite that much, but
he did give himself plenty of time for most of his dead-
lines. Now and again, he'd get overextended. He always
offered to give the customer's deposit back when that
happened. So far, nobody had taken him up on it.

He looked around, didn't see anybody waving a knife
or a gun at him as he left the shop. It was an hour before
shift change, so the elevators were easy on and off. He
went home, locked his door, set his alarm, and took a
shower. He fell into bed and slept.

He dreamed about the collapse of Big Black again.

When he awoke, eight hours had gone by. He got up,
made his cup of coffee, checked his messages. Did a little
yoga and a short form. He had a class later, but plenty
of time before that to check out the next items on his
Corderman list: the tool storage unit and gym locker. He
didn't expect to find a confession signed by the murderer
at either place, but if you didn't check, you would never
know.

But before he could get dressed to leave, he got a com.
It was William O'Connor, the art collector who had one
of Gil's first models, the jet hovercraft ferry *Mbutu*. The
ferry, carrying more than three thousand passengers
across the channel between Maputo and Androka, had
been sunk by a terrorist's bomb off the coast of Moz-
ambique in 2051. Only a hundred and fifty passengers
and crew had survived.

"My nephew was visiting from Earth with my sister,"
O'Connor said. "He's five. He somehow managed to
knock the model off the display stand. I'm not sure, but
I think he also might have stepped on it."

"Ouch," Gil said.

"It isn't too badly damaged," the man said. "In fact,

you can hardly tell, it's mostly some deck chairs on the stern that got crunched, but, well, if you could see your way to repairing it, I'd be happy to pay whatever the cost. It's such a great piece."

"No problem," Gil said. "Bring it by or have it messengered to the shop's security box. I'll fix it."

"I'll send a credit voucher number with it, fill out whatever you think is fair."

"No need. It sounds like a couple hours work. No problem."

"That's not right."

"My models come with a lifetime guarantee," Gil said. "Station decompression, fire, even five-year-olds, they're all covered."

"Thank you, Gil."

Gil smiled. He remembered a story he'd heard once about Rolls Royce, a high-end luxury English automobile maker in the early to late 1900's. Seemed a customer driving one of the cars in the 1930's ran into a ditch in the middle of nowhere and snapped the rear axle. He hiked to the nearest civilization and wired the factory. A few days later a team of mechanics arrived with a new part. They repaired the vehicle, tipped their hats, and left. Some months later, when the driver had yet to receive a bill for the parts and service, he called the factory and inquired about the matter. He wished, he said, to pay for the broken axle repair. Came the cool British reply: "I'm terribly sorry, sir, but you must be mistaken. Rolls Royce axles do not break." And that ended the matter, as far as the manufacturer was concerned. It was probably an apocryphal story, but Gil liked it anyway. If his models couldn't take being trodden upon by a five-year-old, he must not be building them well enough.

Corderman's tool locker held, as far as Gil could tell, tools.

There were two small electric saws, one battery-powered, the other induction, for shaping wood. There was a hand-sized project computer, the Big Blue Tool

Baby, with specs for various projects; a drill with a case of bits; a sander; a router; a power socket wrench and power screwdriver. He had some unpowered tools: two hammers, a socket handsaw, pliers, wrenches, screwdrivers, wirecutters. In addition, there were measuring devices, levels, screws, bolts, pegs, stickers and assorted furniture hardware, pulls, clasps, hinges.

Gil spent an hour and a half going through the storage unit, but he didn't find anything that seemed to be anything other than it appeared. He had seen the rocking chair Trish had in her cube, the one her SO had built, and pictures of some of Corderman's other projects, and the man had seemed to be a fair craftsman. Certainly enough to justify the tools he'd owned. Very hands-on. Without taking the saws and drills and drivers apart, there was nothing else to be found here. The Big Blue Tool Baby was a stupecomp, with just enough RAM to load and run furniture programs. There were two playits, one for chairs and tables and lamps, another for cabinets, dressers and other boxlike items.

He sighed. Were this investigation a rugby match, Gil would be getting his butt kicked.

As Gil headed for the gym where Corderman had his membership, he went over the list Trish had given him of a typical week for the couple.

They both worked the same shift, usually third, so that portion of time was spent apart. They had to sleep and eat and attend to other bodily functions; that accounted for another large piece of their day. They spent the remaining chunk of their lives in such mundane activities as going for walks and stair-climbs around the station, dinner out with friends, reading, watching entcom on the holoproj, making love. Five or six times a week for the last, Gil noted. On average.

He felt a pang of something when he thought about that.

The couple had taken one offstation vacation trip in the last year, a week in the gambling resort wheelworld *Sinatra*. There they went to shows, lost a little money playing the games, swam in the hyperox bubble pool and spent a fair amount of time and energy in bed.

How did Corderman have the energy to work out, after a shift doing heavy work in Engineering, plus all that carnal congress?

Nothing in any of these activities that suggested a reason for murder.

The gym where Corderman trained was a small one. There were half a dozen computerized resistance machines and a few sets of barbells and dumbbells. You opened the front door with your membership tab, stowed your clothes in a locker inside the dressing room, worked out, showered or sat in the spa when you were done. There were privacy cubicles in the unisex dressing room if you wanted to use them, and the shower stalls and toilets were also enclosed. The hot tub and sauna were communal.

When Gil arrived there was a muscular woman in a perspiration-soaked gray flextard sitting in one of the exercise machines, doing shoulder exercises. Nobody else working out.

In the dressing area, a naked fat man sat enjoying bubble jets in the spa. There was no attendant.

Gil went to Corderman's locker and opened it. First thing he noticed was the smell of stale sweat.

There wasn't much to see: depil cream, shampoo, soap, a toothbrush. A couple of clean, folded towels, two jockstraps hanging on a hook. There was a tube of analgesic gel, a sleeveless sweatshirt, and sweatpants cut off at the knees. A pair of weightlifting gloves, training shoes, and a few pairs of thick socks. On the top shelf was a beat-up flatscreen, and for a second, Gil thought he might have something, but when he powered up the small computer, all that it appeared to contain were files of workout and diet charts, showing what exercises and kilogrammage Corderman performed, what supplementary vitamins and amino acids he ingested. He looked at the flatscreen. The amounts of weight it said Corderman could lift and press were large. He had been a very strong man.

It was possible there was a hidden program buried in the computer somewhere, but he didn't really think he was going to get any help from Big Blue. Too bad.

He went through all the locker's contents again, looking for something he might have missed, but the socks were just socks, towels and jockstraps no more than they appeared to be.

He kept the flatscreen. He knew a man who was a whiz with computers; maybe he could find something Corderman had stashed inside his log of bench presses and squats.

The woman who'd been working her shoulders came into the dressing room. She peeled the flextard off and tossed it onto the floor, bent and removed her shoes and socks and dropped them next to the workout suit. Naked, she opened a locker and removed a towel and a pair of rubber sandals from it, along with a tube of shampoo. Slipped her feet into the sandals, hung the towel over her shoulder, started for the shower stall.

Gil noticed the fat man in the hot tub shift his attention to the woman. She had wide shoulders, narrow hips, and small breasts. She wasn't as heavy as a professional bodybuilder, but she was more muscular than an aerobics fitness competitor. Her abs were deeply outlined, and her thighs and buttocks flexed as she walked. She was flushed, and a sheen of sweat shined on her. Her hair was short, black, and the color matched above and below.

Well, well. Another woman who didn't seem to have any trouble wandering around naked in front of people.

Gil said, "Excuse me, can I ask you a question?"

She looked at Gil somewhat warily but not afraid. She glanced at the fat man in the hot tub, who stared at her openly, grinning. "What?"

"Did you know David Corderman?"

She raised her eyebrows. "Sure, I knew him. We used to train together sometimes. He was in good shape."

"You know anybody who might have a grudge against him?"

"No. When he came here, he came to work out. Didn't

talk to anybody, didn't hit on anybody, minded his own business. Why do you ask?"

"His SO doesn't think his death was an accident."

"The dancer. Yeah, we met a couple of times. She's in pretty good shape for somebody who doesn't lift. Nice-looking woman." She scratched just under her left breast. "Why are you asking?"

"I don't think it was an accident, either."

"No shit? Tell you what, if somebody deepsleeped him, I hope you catch them. David was all right."

"Thanks for your help."

"No problem." She went to the shower, hung the towel over a rack, stepped into the stall, and shut the translucent plastic door. The water began to run, and hot vapor rose. She wet her hair, put a glob of shampoo in it, worked it into a lather.

Gil wandered over to where the fat man sat in the bubbly water. He couldn't see the man's hands under the roiling surface, but the fat man was still staring at the woman in the shower stall, what he could still see of her.

"Excuse me, did you know David Corderman? Used to work out here?"

The fat man frowned. "Nope. I don't pay much attention to the men. The women I know. That's Kat in the shower. Has she got a great ass on her, or what?"

Gil shook his head. A gym locker room must be a great place for a voyeur.

He caught Gil's unvoiced disapproval. "She knows I watch her. She likes it. She'd like a little more, too, if you know what I mean."

Gil shook his head again. He had a feeling that if the hot tub watcher here ever tried to do anything more than peep at the woman he called Kat, he would probably be very sorry.

He turned away, headed for the door.

Means, motive, opportunity.

So far, he didn't have any kind of hard evidence pointing at anybody. If it wasn't a crime of passion, not a jealous suitor or angry coworker, why anybody would want to kill Corderman was still a complete mystery. From what Gil had learned, the man had no real enemies. If it hadn't been personal, then the other reasons got a little nastier. Several possible motives came to mind: Maybe the killer was psychotic, just wanted to kill *any*-body, and Corderman was in the wrong place at the wrong time. Some kind of twisted thrill. Or maybe he caught somebody swiping spare parts, and they wanted to keep him from reporting it. People had been killed for less.

Maybe, maybe, maybe.

Means, motive, opportunity.

Perhaps Gil needed to shift his focus. Who had access to the section in which Corderman had worked? Yes, the police would have checked that, but they wouldn't have spent much time on it because they would have trusted the security cameras and gate records. Certainly he could understand the police's actions—no point in checking on somebody who couldn't have been there, was there? But those records could have been rascaled, and Gil thought for sure they had been. He hadn't wanted to mention that to El-Sayed yet.

So, he should find out the names of all the workers who might have been in that area on that date, records notwithstanding. That might be altered, too, but if he did a broad enough search, he might be able to cross-reference the names. Finding a name on one list that wasn't on another and ought to be could be a major clue. Since the investigation was officially closed, Gil wouldn't be getting into police business by contacting people and asking questions.

It was as good a way to go as any.

17

HIGGINS CALLED TO say he had the show set up, and Gil went by to inspect it.

A pair of taser-armed guards inspected his ID tag very carefully before they allowed him into the gallery's showroom. Good to know his work was being so carefully protected.

Nicholas Higgins was there, waiting. He smiled, extended his hand. A tall, gray-haired and bearded man, gaunt almost to the point of emaciation, Higgins wore a blue silk suit handmade by one of Hong Kong's best tailors. Probably cost half as much as one of Gil's models, but he could afford it. The man had some of the best artists in space as clients; Gil was a small fish in his pond.

''Gil.''

''Nicholas.''

''So, what do you think?'' He waved one thin hand at the displays.

Gil looked around.

Each of the twenty-five microsculptures had been mounted under protective denscris domes bolted to a pedestal, and multiple-view holographic macros floated above each model, showing port, starboard, bow, stern and overhead angles. A viewer could zoom in for a detailed inspection of any of the views by touching a panel under the display case. A caption ran underneath the holoprojections, detailing the history of the ship upon which the model was based, the date the sculpture was completed, and an acknowledgment to the current owner for allowing its inclusion in the show.

The models were arranged in chronological order of their construction, from the earliest to the most recent.

"Looks good," Gil said.

"Does, doesn't it? But it gets better. Check them out."

Gil knew them all well, but he walked around and examined the models with a certain pleased interest. He had never seen so much of his work in one place at one time. Almost made him feel as if he were a real artist.

Most of the models were NFS—not for sale—and the five new ones would not have prices posted on them. If you were interested, you inquired politely and were told the cost. A couple of Higgins's patrons supposedly didn't even care to *know* the price. They were wealthy enough that if they saw a piece they liked, they bought it and didn't bother to ask what it cost. *That* was rich.

Gil came to the display of the ferries *Brahmaputra* and *Prajatantri*, the only double sculpture he had done. On a bright summer day in 2041, on a run between Calcutta and Bangladesh in the Bay of Bengal with visibility forever, the two vessels had plowed head-on into each other. Both sank within minutes. The combined loss totaled 3,800 people.

At the end of the caption was the NFS notation.

Gil turned toward Higgins. "Not for sale? Something wrong with them?"

"I'm afraid the show is going to be just for the critics," Higgins said. "You won't make any money from patrons coming to shop."

Gil felt his bowels twist. What was he talking about?

Higgins looked grave, then smiled. "All five of the new pieces have already been sold."

"Really?" That surprised Gil.

Higgins enjoyed his reaction. "It gets better," he said. "I upped your prices. This pair sold to a collector in Zurich. Fifty thousand."

"Fifty thousand—?!"

"You were way underpriced. I also asked and got twenty-five each for the *Sultana* and the *Principe de Asturias.*"

Gil shook his head. He was stunned.

"It gets better still," Higgins said. "I asked for forty-five for the *Bismarck.* I had to knock five thousand off as a professional discount, since the piece was bought by another artist, but your days of peddling models for eight or ten grand are over, Gil."

Gil still couldn't relate to it. He did the math. Take out Higgins's thirty percent, that would leave . . . ?

₦ 98,000. Good Lord! Even after taxes, he could live on that for more than a year.

"But wait, it gets better *still*. Well, at least you'll think so, though it won't put any more money in our pockets."

Gil stared at him.

"The *Bismarck*'s buyer? Johann Wöhler."

Gil blinked. When he found his voice, he said, "No."

"Oh, yes. I mentioned to a few people I know down below that a certain up-and-coming miniaturist had built a quad-Z model of the *Bismarck*. Wöhler is a German military buff, did you know that? His agent asked for holos, I sent them, he bought it."

Gil walked to the *Bismarck*'s display and stared at it.

Technically speaking, the *Bismarck* was not a disaster ship, at least not in Gil's definition of such things. Civilian ships sunk by military vessels during war made the cut, but naval vessels themselves did not. In the case of *Bismarck*, however, Gil had made an exception, given the pocket battleship's short but spectacular career. The 52,000-ton vessel with its eight 15-inch guns and speed of 30 knots sneaked out past Norway in May of 1941.

The British sent half their home fleet out, found it, engaged it. The *Bismarck* blasted the English battleships *Prince of Wales* and *Hood*, blew the latter out of the water, and ran. Everybody and his kid sister started looking for the ship. Less than two days later, they found it. A torpedo attack crippled the *Bismarck*'s steering enough so that the battleships *Rodney* and *King George V* were able to engage the German ship. The *Bismarck* couldn't run. They spent all day and night hitting it with everything they had. It took that long to finally sink it . . .

Johann Wöhler! The best in the world or any wheel-world, and he had bought one of Gil's models!

"It gets better," Higgins said.

Gil grinned at him. "Come on. It can't get any better, Nicholas."

"No? Want to know what he said? Wöhler?"

Gil felt his stomach twist. It was one thing to know that Wöhler had bought one of his pieces, something else to hear his opinion of it.

Higgins's grin was huge. "He said, 'The kid does nice work. Let me know if he does any more German warships.' "

Gil couldn't stop grinning.

It was with that flush of joy that Gil called Trish.

"Hi. Anything new?"

He had to pull himself in, remember that she was still grieving over the death of her lover. But even so, he wanted to share this with somebody. He said, "No, nothing we haven't already discussed. I'm working on some new ideas. Listen, the reason I called is, I'm having a show of my models at a gallery in a couple of days. I was wondering if maybe you'd like to go to the opening? With me?"

It seemed like a couple of eons went by, but it couldn't have been more than a second or two. "Sure. Should I dress up for it?"

"It's an arty crowd. People will be in everything from coveralls to formal, you can do anything you want."

"You have a dinner jacket?"

"I think I can dig one up."

"Wear that," she said.

After they broke the connection, Gil found himself leaning back in his chair and grinning like his brain had shorted out. He had commissions and he'd honor the prices he'd set for them, but somewhere in there, he was definitely going to make another German warship. Yes, indeed.

He grinned. He couldn't imagine a better day.

18

GIL HAD NEVER owned a tuxedo; he rented one when the need arose—and it seldom did—but given his newfound wealth, he decided it might be a worthwhile purchase.

Especially since Trish wanted him to wear one.

He went to the men's wardrobe store, across the Square from his own shop, stood there while the measuring lasers painted him and the tailor asked him if he dressed left or right, then he transferred five hundred New Dollars from his account into the shop's. The basic black suit and cummerbund would be ready by that evening; was that acceptable?

It was. And he bought a new silk shirt, shoes, a black tie, a couple of pairs of socks, braces, and what the hell, some black silk briefs. Set him back another hundred and fifty. Oh, well. It was only money. And found money, at that. He never imagined that Higgins would ask for—and get—more than three times what he'd been charging for his models.

And that *Wöhler* would buy one and be interested in buying more.

Man.

Back at his shop, he opened his computer access and began the process of cross-referencing the workers, visitors, and security personnel who might have been on sub-1 of the E&M Level on the date Corderman was killed.

"Computer, list all third-shift Engineering and/or Manufacturing employees at work on E&M Level this date."

The computer gave him a list. Total number: 4536.

"List all third-shift vendors and/or delivery workers logged in and out of E&M Level this date."

Another list. Total: 176.

"List all Corporate Security staff."

Total: 50.

Who else? "List any persons checked through security gates not included in the previous three groups, give their identification."

Sixteen more. Two inspectors from Hazards, two technicians from Computer Systems Repair, one technician from Recycling. One policeman. Ten people visiting spouses or SO's for assorted reasons—lunch, delivery of forgotten items, in one case, a locked-out daughter came to get a keytab from her mother.

Gil didn't recognize any of the last few names.

Total number of people officially on the level during the period when Corderman was murdered: 4778.

He hunted up the file on his previous search, the one he'd done for the man who'd attacked him in the hallway. Said, "Cross-reference these lists with the file 'Black-haired assassins.' How many possible matches?"

"Eighty-eight," the computer said.

Ah. That narrowed down the earlier list by almost ninety percent. Eighty-eight men. Maybe he could get it even narrower?

Playing a hunch, he said, "Of the eighty-eight, how many are employed by Corporate Security?"

"Three," the computer said.

Gil pondered that. "Hardcopy ID information and holographs of the three men."

On its stand next to his work table, the color holo-laser printer whispered and dropped three sheets into its bin. Gil moved to the printer, removed the sheets, looked at them.

Carl Ball, 31, a gate guard on S-4, at the main entrance to Precision Castplast laser cutting. The holograph presented a swarthy man with heavy features, a thick brow, wide nose, deep-set eyes.

Michael Flannery, 34, surveillance technician. Probably worked on the security cameras and systems. Flannery had his hair combed straight back and to his collar, and a weak chin.

Armando Jefferson, 28, SI-3. Armando was a Security Investigator, third class. SI-3s did low-level investigations, background checks, malingering by injured workers, theft on the job, like that. Armando's ethnicity leaned toward Mexico or maybe Puerto Rico. His hair was set in a wavy style, neatly trimmed over the ears.

Could one of these three brown-eyed, black-haired men be involved in the murder? And the attack on Gil? It wasn't much of a reach to guess that one was connected to the other.

He needed to view them in person to find out. If he could see their hands, he was pretty sure he'd recognize the chewed fingernails of his assailant.

But Gil continued asking the computer questions. One list for all the official workers and visitors on S-1. Another for S-2, the sublevel directly above. Another for people who had called in sick. It was a long and slow process, more in the question of what to ask than in the actual listing. He would keep thinking of ways to throw the lists at each other. Maybe a name or names would crop up often enough to stand out.

The door chime sounded.

Gil looked up, saw a young man in a messenger's blues standing there. Gil had the computer open the door as he untabbed the pouch with his pistol in it. Just in case.

But the messenger was from Gil's client, the one with the heavy-footed nephew, and Gil took delivery of the shipping box he included with all of his models. After the messenger left and he'd relocked the entrance, Gil opened the box and put the model on his work table, turned the viewer on and examined the damage.

Most of the injury was to the stern section. The deck chairs, the railings, a tiny section of hull caved in. Not too bad. He had the specs in his computer; he could cast new parts and replace the fractured ones easily enough. It would take a couple of hours, but he had plenty of time before his suit was ready.

He heated up the table.

The next couple of days went by without any progress on the investigation. Every time Gil was ready to go poke around in it, something else came up. There was a new form he needed to learn for his martial arts class. Some shop business with the tax assessor that couldn't wait. A neighborhood association meeting to do something about teeners running wild in the halls. Little fish, nibbling away at his time.

The evening of his show arrived. He went to collect Trish.

"Wow, you look great," Trish said. "You should dress up more often."

Gil had never been a proponent of clothes making the man, but he accepted the compliment with a smile. "Thanks." At least the tuxedo fit well, and he couldn't tell the difference between the cloned silk of his shirt and underwear and the genuine worm- or spider-produced stuff. Looked and felt the same to him.

Trish was stunning. She wore a strapless green gown that showcased her eyes and her figure, with the hem of the dress nearly touching the floor. She had unbraided her red hair and combed it out long; it fell almost all the way to the middle of her back.

"You are gorgeous," he said. "Thanks for coming to this thing with me. I hope you aren't bored."

"I can't remember the last time I was bored," she said.

When they opened her door to leave, the electric cart and driver were waiting. She raised an eyebrow at him.

"We wouldn't want to work up a sweat in these nice clothes," he said.

She smiled, and he enjoyed the expression.

The main hallway in front of the gallery was clogged with other carts, some of them quite fancy. Seemed there were other people who didn't want to mess up their nice clothes. Gil's driver let them off a hundred meters away. "I guess we can walk that far," he said.

The doorman must have been given Gil's holograph, because he smiled and nodded and ushered Gil and Trish in without asking to see an invitation.

The gallery was nearly full of people. They ranged from artistic types dressed in colorful spandex shorts and shirts to rich people wearing suits and designer gowns from Rio. The old money tended to dress conservatively, the new money a little more showy.

"Here we go," Gil said.

"Are you nervous?"

"Yeah, a little. I'm in the hot seat, so I can't stand back and be amused, I have to smile and be affable."

"I expect you'll manage."

"I'll give you the cheap tour," he said. "See that skinny man in the charcoal tux, smiling like a baboon? That's Nicholas Higgins, this is his gallery."

"Who is the dark-skinned woman in the red taffeta he's talking to?"

"Holly Mbutu, she owns several of my models. Nice lady."

He pointed out several other customers, plus a couple of movers and shakers in the art community.

"Gil! How is it going?"

Gil looked up, saw Chaz Wells in a purple zoot suit. Even had a chain hanging looped from the pants pockets.

"Chaz. I believe you know M. Blackwell?"

Wells extended one hand. "I don't believe we've actually met. I have seen you dance a couple of times. Sorry about your SO."

Wells didn't sound particularly sorry. He continued. "Word is, Gil, you're playing in the big leagues now. Looks as if I got a real bargain on my model. Good thing I ordered it when I did, I can't afford the new prices you're getting. Congratulations."

"Thanks."

A tall man with dark hair graying at the temples moved next to Wells. He wore a plain black tux, much like the one Gil had on, and his smile was perfect. He was about fifty, though he looked younger.

Wells said, "Gil? This is—"

"Manager Brock," Gil finished, extending his hand.

Mario Brock was the Station Manager for the *Robert E. Lee*, a position more or less the equivalent of a mayor or city manager on Earth, though he had been hired by the Corporation and not elected. Maybe CEO might be a more appropriate term. He came from a wealthy family and supposedly worked only because he enjoyed it.

"Very nice work," Brock said. He waved at the interior of the gallery.

"Thank you."

A waiter came by bearing a tray with glasses of chilled champagne. Gil took two stems, gave one to Trish. He introduced her to Brock.

Trish saw somebody she knew. "Excuse me for a moment, would you?" She went over to say hello.

Brock said, "I was wondering if you might consider taking a commission to do a public piece? Something for the Art Walk? We like to support on-station artists when we can."

"Certainly I'd be happy to talk about it," Gil said. "Though it might take a while to get to it."

"I'll have our art buyer contact you."

A thin woman in a black sheath and enough diamonds to fill a bowl came by and caught Brock by the arm.

"Mario, I have someone you simply *must* meet!" She dragged him away. Wells smiled and offered a silent toast to Brock as he was led off. Brock gave Gil a wry grin. You understand how this is . . .

"Ah, Señor Sivart, how is it with you this evening?"

Gil turned and saw Base Alicante, resplendent in a white cutaway coat with tails. All he lacked was a cane and top hat. Next to him stood a handsome young man of perhaps twenty-eight or -nine. He wore a red puffy-sleeve shirt with a large pointed collar, tight blue pants tucked into red leather boots, and a red beret set at the perfect rakish angle. Very flamboyant. He had short, styled brown hair and a thin moustache. This would be Anton.

Indeed it was. "Gil, my friend, Anton. Anton, this is Gil. Sivart, the artist."

Anton's handsome face was set in an expression just a tad short of a frown. Trying to appear lofty and blasé, Gil decided, but he wasn't quite tall enough to look down his nose.

"Anton. How delightful to meet you. Base has told me so much about you." Gil smiled, took Anton's hand in a firm grip, gave him a slow nod, almost a short bow.

Anton did not seem particularly pleased that Base had told Gil so much about him. He said. "Interesting work, your little models."

Gil wanted to laugh. The young man was so insecure he probably had to stop every time he passed a mirror to check on himself. He covered his fear by being snotty. He had met Anton's like a dozen times. He had been like that himself when he was younger. With any luck, he'd grow out of it.

Gil turned toward Base, subtly shifting his attention away from Anton and said, "Thank you so much for coming, Base. Perhaps you and I can have a drink later, when the crowd has thinned a bit?" He glanced quickly at Anton, as if to indicate that the crowd of which he spoke was composed of one. He returned his gaze to Base and smiled, but watched Anton peripherally.

Jealousy flared in Anton's eyes. He said, "Pardon me, I must go and speak to someone I have just seen!" He marched off, his back so stiff it might as well be made of fused vertebrae. Gil and Base watched him go.

"Oh, that was wicked!" Base said. "I won't have to wash dishes or do laundry for at least a week. Thank you. I'll give him a minute before I go and fetch him from the fresher where he'll be hiding. I may have to leave early. To comfort poor Anton."

Gil shook his head. "I'll probably pay for that. Bad karma."

"Gil, over here!"

Gil glanced over, saw Higgins waving at him. "Got to go," he said, taking a big sip from his champagne.

Base gave him a military bow. "Gracias, Gil."

The rest of the evening at the gallery was a blur of congratulatory faces, smiles, and small talk. He met artists, professional and amateur; critics, professional and amateur; fans, collectors, and people who had come for the free wine and hors d'oeuvres. Trish came back and spent much of the time next to Gil. He caught more than a few people, men and women, looking at Trish with interest. She was a striking woman, to be sure.

Finally, it was over. The last champagne stems were carted away, the crowd dwindled to the diehards who didn't want to go home.

"I'll call for a cart," Gil said.

"Why don't we walk?" Trish said. "Reason the dress is so long was so I could get away with comfortable shoes." She lifted her hem a bit to show him her molded slippers.

Good. He'd like to stretch out a little. He didn't have his gun with him; there wasn't anywhere he could put it and not have it show under the dinner jacket, at least not without some fancy holster, but he had a small cannister of pepper spray in his pocket. It wasn't as effective as a dart pistol, but neither was it as messy as puke spray if he had to use it. And he was definitely paying more attention to his surroundings these days.

The walk to her cube was fairly quiet. It was late, people were either at home asleep or working, not much traffic.

"So, how did you do? Sell anything?"

"Well, sort of." He explained what had happened with the new sculptures.

"Wow. I'm impressed. I had no idea you were a rich and famous artist."

"Neither rich nor famous. But I must confess, it sure beats working for a living."

She laughed. "Making those models isn't work?"

"It started out as a hobby. I did it—I still do it—because I really enjoy it. Making money at it is just gravy. If I wasn't getting paid, I'd still do it for fun. Probably not as much of it, but still . . ."

"I feel that way about dancing. It amazes me that I can earn a living doing something I love, something I'd do anyway."

"We're lucky that way. A lot of people show up at a job, put in their time, collect their pay. Suffer through work they hate."

It didn't take nearly long enough to get to her door. She turned to face him. Said, "I had a great time. Thanks for inviting me."

"I'm honored that you came with me."

He started to turn away, but she caught his shoulders, raised up on her toes and kissed him lightly on the mouth. She lingered for only a second before she pulled back. They both looked at each other and sighed.

"Gil, listen, I'd invite you in, but—"

He put his finger on her lips. "Shhh. I know."

Her door slid open and she stepped inside. Before the door closed, she said, "Would you like to go on a picnic?"

"Yes," he said. A picnic?

"I have a couple days off work, starting day after tomorrow. How about Friday? That be okay?"

"It would be great."

"Wear something lightweight, shorts, T-shirt, like that."

He said, "All right." He wondered about that. Somebody had decided a long time ago that the optimum temperature for people on a space habitat was around three-quarters that of a normal human body. Plus or minus a degree, that was what the average station climate was, with a humidity of around twenty-five percent. Lamps in public areas were tuned to solar frequencies. The parks scattered throughout the REL had sprinklers that could be made to simulate rain, and in the largest couple of green belts, wind, harmless lightning flashes, and thunder could be added, to give the "rain" the feel of a thunderstorm. Scheduled rain showers usually drew a pretty good audience.

Theoretically, Climate Control, under the direction of Life Support Systems, located just under the Microwave Array, could even produce snow, but that had yet to be done.

Nobody tried to attack Gil on his way back to his own cube, which was just as well—his attention wasn't nearly focused enough on that possibility. Not nearly enough.

19

GIL ARRANGED IT so that he was watching the guard station when the first of the black-haired men on his list, Carl Ball, reported for work at the Precision Cast-plast entrance.

Ball's fingernails were neatly clipped.

Not him. Logically speaking, he could have been one of the *other* attackers, but there was no reason to make that assumption. He didn't know if either of the other pipe-wielders had black hair.

The surveillance technician, Michael Flannery, was offshift. Gil knocked on his door, a utility cube on LL3.

The door opened. A chase scene blared from a holo-proj entcom in the background, lots of shooting, yelling and engine noises. "Yes?"

"Excuse me, but are you M. Flannery?"

"That's me. What can I do for you?"

"I'm Gil Sivart." He looked at the man's hands. They wouldn't win any prizes at a cosmetology competition, but neither had they been whittled and splintered by teeth. "Oops. I seem to have gotten the wrong Michael Flannery. Sorry to have disturbed you."

"No prob," the man said.

Gil went to class, worked up a sweat and managed to pull a ligament in his right knee when he twisted too sharply during a spring hip throw. His attacker for the exercise, Abdul, flew satisfyingly through the air to land and slap the mat, but that was small consolation. If you hurt your *self* while defending, nobody had any sympathy for you. Gil took a mild anti-inflammatory and pain killer and slipped a neoprene compression brace over his knee. He ought to go home and prop his leg up and ice it, but he didn't have time.

Instead, after he showered, he went to find Armando Jefferson.

Security Investigator third class Jefferson was in the main Security Office on the top sub-level of the Square, according to the query.

The relationship between Corporate Security and the REL Police Department was sometimes a bit tricky. While the police were supposed to handle all criminal matters and Security confine itself to those civil happenings that pertained more specifically to the Corporation's interests, there was some . . . overlap. An employee of the Corporation involved in an illegal incident might just as easily call Security as the cools, reasoning that Security would pass things along to the police, if it was the appropriate thing to do. And in that process, the employee would demonstrate his or her corporate loyalty.

The cools, after all, didn't pay your salary, now, did they?

Sometimes it worked the way it was supposed to work. Something criminal happened, Security got called, they handed it over to the cools, no problem. Everybody was happy.

Sometimes, the Corporation decided that their interests might be better served taking care of the problem themselves, and things didn't go quite that way. If, say, hypothetically, a Corporate exec got drunk and slapped his wife around, well, that was a family thing, wasn't it? And maybe the police didn't really need to get involved with a little domestic squabble when an apology and a box of candy would fix things right up.

Or say, hypothetically, the son of a Stores Vice President borrowed his father's fuel cell cart and accidentally ran over an old lady crossing a main hall. It would be a terrible thing, such an accident, but which would be better? A promising and very regretful young man languishing in jail with a black mark on his record, or a large influx into the poor woman's credit account? Which would benefit everybody more? A truly repentant boy who got a little reckless being punished, or a chance to visit the grandchildren down below, maybe take them for a nice all-expenses-paid week at Disney World?

Life was full of choices. Some were better than others.

Of course, the cools, being concerned as they were with a strict enforcement of the law—which was not always the same as justice, everybody knew—well, they wouldn't be empowered to . . . negotiate the proper settlement the way a Corporate Security official would be. Sometimes justice was better served if the laws got bent just a little.

The police Gil knew didn't much like the system, but as it did everywhere, money talked. In the end, it was the Corporation that paid the cools' salaries, too.

If you opened a lock and stepped out into the vacuum, you died. Everybody knew it, there was no point in railing against it. You might wish it was otherwise, but, hey, that was the nature of the beast. Simple.

Gil arrived at the Security entrance, told them the purpose of his visit, was given a temporary ID tag and ushered into a large communal office.

Armando Jefferson sat at a desk plugging a report into the computer. There were twelve or fifteen other investigators also working, making calls or keyboarding reports.

When Gil rounded the desk, he felt a sudden rush, a

tightness in his belly and bowels. Jefferson wore gray
shorts and a gray sleeveless shirt, gray socks and slippers,
the casual uniform most of the other people in the room
wore.

When he'd lived in South America, Gil had once gone
to an outdoor market. While buying bananas from a fruit
stand, he'd heard a young mother admonish her child, a
boy of maybe four or five, who had been chewing his
fingernails. "Don't do that, Jaime! You are gonna get
worms!"

"Worms?" Gil had questioned the woman.

"Sí. From the dirt under his fingernails. You get worm
eggs in there and if you eat them, they grow in your
stomach."

At the time, Gil wondered if it was true. If it was,
Armando here was probably going to get worms, too.

Jefferson's fingernails were chewed to nubs.

Armando looked up and saw Gil. His eyes narrowed
slightly but he gave no other indication that he recognized him. "What?"

This was the guy, Gil was sure of it. He hadn't really
expected him to be, or at least he hadn't made any plans
in that direction, so he had to decide how to play this.
Maybe Armando was a believer in coincidence, but Gil
couldn't count on that. He would be suspicious, seeing
Gil here, and since he would be, Gil thought that the
thing to do was push it, to make him nervous. Nervous
people made mistakes.

"How's your head?"

Gil looked but didn't see a bruise or cut. Maybe the
pipe hadn't hit him as hard as he remembered. Or maybe
he had the damage covered with makeup.

"What are you talking about? Who are you?"

"You don't remember? We ran into each other in the
hall near my cube. You were with a couple of your
friends. We exchanged pleasantries, I bounced a pipe off
your skull. Surely you haven't forgotten?"

"I don't know what you're talking about. I don't know
you, never seen you before. You better get out of my

face.'' He raised his hand and pointed his index finger at
Gil. There was a colorful tattoo wrapped all the way
around his arm, from the wrist almost to the shoulder.
The design seemed to be based on some kind of fantasy
animal, like a tiger with wings, a whole pack of them.
The image was mostly orange and black.

Gil had a sudden jolt of memory:

—*a flash of color under the upraised arm? What was
that? Orange? A tear in the coverall that revealed something under it? Or some smear on the fabric? He couldn't
tell*—

''Sure, Armando. See you around.''

Gil left.

He was tempted to stand outside the entrance to Security and wait a few minutes, but it was perhaps a little
much to hope that Armando would rush out of the complex and lead a cleverly hidden watcher to whoever it
was who had hired him to thump that cleverly hidden
watcher.

Especially since whoever had hired him might work
right there in Security with old nail-biter Armando.

Gil headed for the elevators, put in a call to Ray El-
Sayed. The detective was off work and Gil asked that his
call be forwarded, since his private number was unlisted.

''This is Ray.''

''Ray, Gil Sivart. You somewhere we can meet?''

''I'm at home. There's a little pub near here. Pete's
Place. I'll see you there in thirty minutes.''

''Right.''

Gil linked his com unit to the station's computer and
asked for directions to the pub. It was on LL3, Sub-2, a
solid middle-class area, about right for an honest cool
living on one income. He headed that way.

It took only a few minutes to get to the pub. It was a
neighborhood place, room for about fifty people if they
didn't mind closeness. A bar that seated ten, a few small
round tables and chairs. In one corner was a virtual game
rig and music system. Another corner held a smoking

booth, a space big enough for four people, surrounded by air walls to keep the smoke from getting out into the rest of the bar. There were a dozen people scattered around, mostly drinking beer or ale.

Gil ordered iced tea and sat at the bar.

A short woman with curly hair went to the music system, ran her credit tab through the reader, and made her selections. A half-scale holoproj of a man in a cowboy hat and white suit with spangles on it appeared in the air over the music box. He sang mournfully about his woman leaving him. A steel guitar cried three basic chords for him in his misery. The curly-haired woman sighed, then went back to a table where two other women sat. The trio drank their beers and talked, watched the holoproj of the soulful singer.

A pair of young men went to the virtual center, ran a credit tab through its reader, put the helmets on. Gil sipped his tea and watched them. A virtual pool table, he realized, as he watched one man chalk an imaginary cue and line up for the break.

A dark man wearing a turban and robe and a blonde woman in a tube top and short skirt headed for the smoking booth. Gil watched their hair ruffle and clothes balloon from the floor-to-ceiling air stream as they stepped through it. The pair lit cigarettes with an electric lighter. Bluish-gray smoke rose but was quickly dissipated by the uprushing air. Gil imagined he could smell the cigarette smoke.

The country western singer finished his dirge. A young woman took his place, a woman with a lot of unnatural red hair piled up and sprayed into a single unit. She had large breasts mostly revealed by her tight, low-cut white dress. She twanged, flat and nasally, about how her man had done her wrong.

Gil smiled. Some themes never got old.

Ray El-Sayed came into the pub. He saw Gil without looking directly at him. Glanced around, took in the rest of the place. Cataloging, sorting, putting everybody into the layout. He wore a loose shirt hanging over shorts and sandals.

The bartender nodded at him. "Hey, Ray. Usual?"

"Yes, thanks, Tom." He moved to stand next to Gil. The bartender drew a draft beer, something pale amber, and put it in front of Ray. He picked it up, sipped it, nodded at Gil.

"Want to go sit at a table? Over there?"

Gil picked up his tea and followed the cool.

Once they were seated, El-Sayed said, "So, what's up?"

"One of the men who attacked me in the hall is named Armando Jefferson, he's an S-3 investigator."

"How do you know this?"

"I went to see him. I recognized him by his hands. He chews his fingernails."

"So do a lot of people."

"He fits the profile I came up with. Right age, size, hair and eyes. Plus he was on the E&M Level at the time when Corderman was killed."

"Not conclusive."

"It's him. He's got a tattoo on his arm I recognized."

"What tattoo? I never heard this."

"I didn't realize it was a tattoo until today. I might not have enough proof to take to a judge, but it's him."

El-Sayed sipped his beer. "You could have told me this over the com."

"Maybe that wouldn't have been such a good idea."

El-Sayed shook his head. "I don't like what I'm hearing here."

"But you aren't so sure I'm paranoid, are you?"

"I would like to believe that you are, but, no, I wouldn't bet my pension on it. And I'm not going to *risk* my pension on it, either. Not unless you have enough proof to bury a mountain."

"I understand."

He waited a few seconds, as if debating whether or not to say something. "If you're right about the com, chances are the mainframe's files have lurkers, too."

Gil nodded. "They already know about me," Gil said. "It won't hurt for me to keep poking at this. I don't owe the Corporation anything, they don't have any handles on me."

"You are a civilian, you ought not to be taking such risks."

"I think it's too late to start worrying about that. When I get enough, I'll bring it to you."

"If you get enough."

"Oh, I'll get it. I'm not going away. It might take a while, but I've got a thread. If I pull on it without any sudden jerks, this will eventually unravel."

"If somebody doesn't take a sharp knife to the thread. Or to you."

"Well. If they do, at least you'll know where to start looking for them."

Another singer, a man dressed in black, but without a hat, began yodeling about how the perils of love led to the perils of dope and booze, which led to the perils of assault and jail. The singer's voice sounded as if it had been pickled in strong whiskey for thirty years, then taken out and left to bleach in a desert for thirty more. El-Sayed shook his head. "Cowboy music, it's all the same. Love hurts, life stinks, why bother?"

"Could be worse," Gil said. "You a fan of Nigerian Boom-Boom?"

"My daughter plays that crap. Got all the appeal of a bowl full of dead roaches. No rhythm, no point, no skill required to play it. No brain required to listen to it. Boom-boom-boom-boom-thud! A chimpanzee whacking the ground with a stick would sound better. What is the matter with children today? They wouldn't know real music if it bit them on the butt."

Gil smiled. Apparently Ray had had this conversation with somebody before. Probably his wife, concerning their daughter.

"What did you listen to as a kid?"

"Retro-jazz. Now there was music," El-Sayed said. "It had melody, harmony, style."

"What did your parents think about it?"

The cool grinned. "My father thought it was an abomination. He threatened to smash my player unless I used earphones."

"'What goes around comes around,' " Gil said. "You don't hear echoes of yourself from your daughter?"

El-Sayed sipped his beer, shook his head. "Yeah, I guess. Somehow, I thought it would be different with me and my kids. That I wouldn't be an old fart like my father. None of that 'When I was your age' crap my father laid on me. No, I was going to be different. Guess that's not how the game works."

Gil nodded. "Guess not." He raised his tea glass. "A toast," Gil said.

El-Sayed raised his beer stein. "Not to raising children?"

"Something about which I know nothing," Gil said. "No, here's to crime."

"At least I can understand that."

They clinked their glasses together, then drank.

20

GIL FELT AS if there was something he was missing, but of course, if he knew what it was, he wouldn't be missing it. At least he had Armando, although exactly what he was going to do with him was still something of a question. He wouldn't get any official help, and since Armando himself was in Security, he might be able to give Gil some grief if pressed too hard. If Armando was connected to Corderman's killing, he surely had help—for he surely wasn't the brains of any operation.

Gil locked his shop, adjusted the pistol in its pouch on his belt, and walked across the Square to catch the local to the Security sub level. Armando would be getting off-shift in a few minutes.

When Armando appeared in the doorway, Gil was directly in his line of sight. He waved and smiled. *Hey, Armando, you murdering scum! How's it going?*

Armando frowned. Before the man could make a move toward him, Gil turned and walked to the nearest elevator. He wasn't as interested in provoking Armando into taking a swing at him—at least not yet—as he was in spooking him. He wanted his attacker to be uncomfortable. Wanted him to know that he knew who he was and what he had done. Even if you started with a real low heat, you could turn it up and eventually bring things to a boil.

Of course, you could get scalded if you weren't careful, but Gil was looking for trouble now. Expecting it.

He was working on a plate of stir-fry at Matilda's when his com chirped. He had set it to screen most of his calls, so it had to be somebody he wanted or needed to talk to calling. He looked at the ID on the com. Trish.

"Hi."

"Hi."

"You still up for that picnic?"

"Sure. When?"

"How about tomorrow? About 1200?"

Gil looked at the clock hung on the wall by the bar, an antique analog mechanical with sweep hands. It was 1800. Sometimes he lost track of time.

"Sounds great. What do I need to do?"

"Nothing. Where will you be? At your cube?"

"Probably the shop."

"I'll meet you there."

When they discommed, Gil felt a smile he couldn't get rid of—not that he wanted to get rid of it.

"You win the lottery?" Tibbs said as he drifted past on his way to the kitchen.

"In a manner of speaking."

"Lord. I know that idiot grin. Had it myself a few times. It's that beautiful redhead, right?"

Gil just smiled. Tibbs shook his head and went away.

After he finished his meal, Gil went to a public com on the Square's Main Level. He put a coin into the com so he wouldn't have to use his credit tab and thus be traced. Tapped in the number listed for Armando Jefferson.

"Yeah?"

Gil didn't say anything.

"Hello? Who is this?"

Gil still didn't speak.

"Goddammit, you better leave me alone. You'll be sorry if you keep this crap up!"

Gil pushed the disconnect tab.

Sweat, Armando. Sweat.

Back in his shop, Gil considered the case thus far. Yeah, he had a lead with Armando and that was exciting, but that didn't mean he should ignore everything else. That thread might not be enough to unravel the whole thing, even though he was sure it would be a major strand. Best that he keep tugging elsewhere.

Something he was missing, he could feel it. He ran through it in his mind, but it eluded him.

The shop com cheeped.

"Yes?"

"Gil? Chaz Wells."

"Chaz. How are you?"

"Ah, maybe not as good as I should be. You have a few minutes for us to sit down? I'll buy you a drink."

Hmm. "Sure."

"Meet me at the REL Club? Say, half an hour?"

"I'm not a member," Gil said. The REL Club was the most exclusive restaurant and bar on the station.

"They'll let you in. And I wouldn't be surprised if you weren't invited to join real soon. You're a famous artist now."

Wells was there when Gil was ushered into a booth in the REL Club's bar. Gil suspected the place had been modeled after some rich man's club on Earth—the walls were a dark paneling, the booth seats leather, the bar itself polished hardwood. Instead of dispensers, there were liquor bottles lined up on shelves in front of a long mirror. The bartender wore a white shirt with garters, a black vest, and sported a droopy handlebar moustache and slicked-down hair parted in the middle.

"Gil! Glad you could make it. What are you drinking?"

"Tea would be fine."

"Tea? Come on, you can have a real drink."

"Another time I will."

A waiter appeared, took their order. Wells wanted single malt scotch over ice cubes.

"So, what can I do for you, Chaz?"

Wells stared down at the table. The waiter returned with their drinks. The Security chief took a big gulp from the scotch. The waiter went away.

"This is kind of embarrassing," Wells said. His breath was fragrant with the expensive liquor. "But, well, it seems as if there has been a complaint."

"Complaint?" Gil could be as disingenuous as the next man.

"Seems an investigator in our organization has gotten this crazy idea that you are somehow . . . harassing him." He took another sip of the scotch, leaving the ball in Gil's court.

Gil let it lie there. "Really?"

When it became apparent that Gil wasn't going to be forthcoming with any confessions of guilt, Wells said, "Do you know a man named Armando Jefferson?"

"We've met a couple of times."

"It seems that M. Jefferson thinks you have mistaken him for somebody else."

"I haven't. I know exactly who he is."

"Really? And who might that be?"

"One of the three men who came after me with pipes in the hall near my cube."

"I thought those men were masked."

Gil didn't ask how he knew about the attack or that the three perpetrators had been masked. The man was the head of Corporate Security. If he *hadn't* known, that would have been a surprise.

"A man is more than his face."

He sipped more of his scotch. Shook his head. "I find it hard to believe that one of my agents would be involved in such a thing. Do you have proof of Jefferson's guilt?"

"Not yet."

"But you are convinced of this?"

"Yes."

Wells rattled the ice cubes in his mostly empty glass. The waiter appeared as if by teleportation, a second scotch over ice centered on a tray. Wells had obviously been here before.

"This puts me in a somewhat awkward position," Wells said. He took the second drink from the waiter.

"I can appreciate that."

"Naturally, if one of my people is guilty of such a crime, I want to see justice done. On the other hand, until that guilt is legally established, I have a certain responsibility to my employees." He drained half of the second scotch. He was obviously an accomplished drinker, despite his worked-for muscularity.

"Of course," Gil said.

"So, what am I to do?"

"What would you normally do?"

"Well. I'd warn the accuser to maintain a certain distance from the accused. Tell him to be careful he didn't slander somebody unless he could prove his accusation. Advise the parties involved to proceed with caution. And begin an internal investigation."

Gil said, "I don't want to make your life complicated. I'll avoid Armando—until I have proof of his complicity."

"I appreciate your cooperation, Gil."

"No problem. Thanks for the drink, Chaz. I am afraid I have to go, I've got an appointment."

Wells raised his glass as Gil stood. "I appreciate your cooperation, Gil."

Outside the exclusive club, Gil thought about the meeting as he walked. Armando was guilty, no doubt about that. He definitely had something to hide. But even so, he had gone to Wells, a man at the top of the Security chain, to get Gil off his back. An innocent man would have done that, but would a guilty one?

Perhaps more interesting was the fact that Wells had

responded so quickly. A low-level grunt not only got his complaint past all the mid-level managers and to the boss himself, but got a very fast response.

Maybe that didn't mean anything. Maybe Wells would do that for any employee.

Or maybe it meant something Gil had already considered.

Maybe Wells was involved.

How very interesting.

The pot, it appeared, was finally starting to boil.

The appointment of which Gil had spoken was with Base Alicante. He was to meet the doctor in his office and while the meeting *was* upcoming, it really wasn't pressing; he had nearly an hour before he was due. Truth was, Gil didn't much like Chaz Wells, and spending another half an hour watching him drink scotch simply hadn't appealed. Doubtless Inspector Targan would have stayed and wormed some vital clue from Wells, had he suspected any was to be gained. He would have been polite, charming, and ever alert for a slip of the tongue, the slightest error on the part of his suspect. Hearing such, Targan would have intuited worlds from it, built a solid case on a raised eyebrow or an inappropriate sneer. Gil didn't have Targan's insight, and he also didn't think Wells would blurt out anything useful in itself. Not yet, anyway.

"I can't begin to thank you," Base said. "Anton has come to the realization that his bullfighter on Earth is, upon reconsideration, much too brutish, and he was never seriously entertaining the idea of going back to him."

"I'm glad for you," Gil said. He sat in the chair across from Base, who leaned against the edge of his desk.

"Of course, his opinion of your work is . . . well, let us say, less than complimentary. What ever can I possibly see in it? It's so—pardon me—mechanistic!"

Gil laughed.

"His fear was of course, that my admiration was more

for the artist than the art. I confess, I hinted at such.
Forgive me.''

"No problem.''

"But enough of my love life. I found something which
might be of interest to you. I took it upon myself to do
a little checking. It seems Dr. Evans, at the clinic in Fecal
Town, saw a slopworker in regard to an accident recently.
The worker stated that he fell out of a refuse container
while scouring it clean, bounced his torso off a heavy
hydraulic lifting arm on the way down, and banged his
head on the floor. He was treated for a mild concussion
and had orthobond injected into two cracked ribs under
his right arm.''

"Interesting. But why would you think I'd find this
particularly so?''

"This happened the same day as your encounter with
the villains in the hall. A couple of hours after it.''

"Word does get around, doesn't it?''

Base shrugged. "It's big, but we live in a bottle.''

"I appreciate it, Base. And the worker's name?''

"Helas Doyle. I have his stats.''

Gil went over the attack in his memory once again.
The man in the red mask might have sustained such injuries, from the two side kicks to the ribs and the hammer
fist to the head.

"Thank you,'' Gil said. "This is a big help.''

"It is nothing.''

When Gil left Base's office, he pulled his com and
called the station's computer. This information was an
unexpected gift.

Unfortunately, Base's efforts were not going to pay a
full dividend. Gil's query revealed that Helas Doyle, 26,
had quit his job as an R-5 tech and left the station for
Earth the day after his injuries were treated.

Gil played a hunch. He asked the computer for records
of other station employees who had left their jobs and
shipped for Earth on the same day as had Doyle. The
computer gave him two names: The first was one Eliz-
abeth Kelly Mason, 65, who retired after ten years as an

on-station primary ed teacher. The second was one Pablo José Rodríguez, 29, also an R-5 tech.

Both Doyle and Rodríguez had been on temporary contracts. There did not seem to be a record of how long they had held their jobs in Recycling. Both quit on the same day.

My, my.

Gil didn't need to be Inspector Targan to intuit a connection. He was willing to bet ten-to-one that Doyle and Rodríguez were two of the three men who had attacked him. And that somebody had hustled them off the *Robert E. Lee* in a big hurry after they had flubbed the job.

Wasn't *that* intriguing?

He would pass this along to Ray El-Sayed. It wasn't likely anybody could trace the two very far once they hit Earth if they wanted to disappear; fake IDs were cheap enough in any spaceport town. But maybe these two didn't worry about being chased enough to bother. Somebody fairly highly placed on the station must have hired them, if they had cover jobs in Recycling. Ray might be able to inquire discreetly and trace them. Even if he found them, it was unlikely anybody would bother to extradite them offworld for an accusation of assault, and it wouldn't take much of a lawyer to throw state-of-mind at an attempted murder charge, especially since Gil wasn't hurt. But Gil might take a little trip down below himself and have a word or two with M. Doyle or M. Rodríguez if they could be located.

This was getting more and more interesting all the time. And like such things tended to do, once it got rolling, it was like a pebble dropped down a snowy mountainside. It grew bigger very fast.

Gil started for his cube. He would pick up his workout clothes and go to the school for a little practice. There weren't any classes scheduled for several hours; he'd have the place to himself. A good exercise session might help him blow the dust out of his brain. He had more pieces. Maybe it was time to start putting this puzzle together.

21

FRIDAY RIGHT AT noon Gil saw Trish through his new window and got up to let her into the shop. She carried a large, old-fashioned wicker picnic basket with a lid on it. She wore baggy shorts and a short-sleeved blouse and sandals. Gil also wore shorts, a T-shirt, and spray-on slippers. The slippers weren't really sprayed on, but they were thin enough so they looked as if they might be, hence the name. He had his gun pouch on his belt.

"Ready?" she asked.

"Yep. Let me carry that for you."

They left the shop, and he followed her to the main bank of elevators. She wouldn't tell him where they were going, but they got off on the main E&M, took a local to the bottom level, S-1. She led him through a public hallway into a maze of small hallways, ending up at a locked door. She pulled a keytab from her blouse pocket and ran it through the reader, and the door opened. Gil followed Trish into what looked like a little-used storage room, half full of dusty boxes and crates, most of which seemed to be empty.

"Well, I'm impressed," he said. "Very, ah, scenic."
She smiled. "Over here."

There was a hatch in the floor, and when Trish touched
a control next to it, the hatch clamshelled up to reveal
an angled ladder. She climbed down it, and he followed.
It was about a three-meter descent. The area was warm,
humid, and brightly lighted, with the illumination coming
from grow lamps jury-rigged on the ceiling and even a
bit from the floor, which appeared to be a milky, translucent plastic. Thirty meters away was a miniature forest,
bordered by a meadowlike patch of short but untrimmed
grass, sprinkled with wildflowers—daisies, dandelions,
even a couple of thistles.

"Wow," Gil said.

He realized this was dead space, either a basement for
the E&M's lowest sublevel, or an attic for Hydroponics
& Livestock. The floor light must be coming from the
lamps in the ceiling of the top sub for H&L, which would
also explain the heat.

"How did this get here?"

They walked to the edge of the meadow. There was a
path through the grass and flowers, and Gil followed
Trish along it to a spot that was mostly grass, near the
edge of the trees. On close examination, these proved to
be different kinds of small-leafed or evergreen bushes
that had been trimmed out, much like bonsai.

She answered his question. "I don't know. Somebody
must have moved the earth into the space a little at a
time, either swiping it or making it themselves. Probably
used homemade compost, installed the lamps, planted the
grass and bushes and flowers. One of David's coworkers
told him about it. We don't think that too many people
know about it, but it has to have been here for years."

She set the basket down, opened it, removed a blue-
and-white-checkered tablecloth, and spread it out on the
grass.

Gil went over to look at a clump of dark green sedge
grass. Spotted something in it, bent, moved the grass
aside. Chuckled to himself.

"What?"

"There's a little valve and timer here. Got a small leak in the seal, that's why the grass is thicker and greener here. Looks as if somebody tapped a water line and installed a seepage hose. Timer turns it on and off, keeps the plants hydrated. Amazing. This is a lot of work." And not the kind of place you'd expect to exist on a wheelworld.

"David and I came here a few times," she said. She put plates and plastic chopsticks out, paper napkins, then began to remove little microwave containers of food. "I stopped by Matilda's and got take-out," she said. "I'm not much of a cook."

"It's wonderful," he said.

"I brought a bottle of tea and one of water. I would have brought wine, but I know you're not drinking." She put out paper cups. She sounded nervous, even a little embarrassed.

He said, "It's the nicest picnic I've ever been on."

"Really?"

"Sure. Company counts for a lot, and so does location." He waved one hand to take in the tiny but private park. "This is great."

"Let me serve you a plate," she said. Pleased now, if still a little flustered. After she filled his plate with three different kinds of Oriental food, she did one for herself, then a third plate.

"We expecting company?" Gil asked, nodding at the plate.

"It's for the ants," she said.

"Ants? Really?"

"Well, I've never seen any here," she said. "But it was an old custom in my family. Whenever we went on a picnic, we always put out a plate for the ants."

Gil took a bite of sweet-and-sour tofu. Nodded. "This is good." He wanted to ask, but held off. She answered his unasked question: "I grew up just outside of Cape Town, SoAf. My father was a manager in the Zulu Platinum Mines, my mother a teacher before she stayed home to raise children. I was the youngest of five; I have four brothers, the nearest of whom is ten years older than I.''

She smiled a little.

"I was the change-of-life daughter. I liked to go on picnics, and they spoiled me. We did a lot of family stuff, even though some of my brothers were old enough to be my father. The ones still around got dragged along.''

"How did you wind up here?''

"When my father retired, he and my mother and I emigrated. I was ten. He died when I was twenty, complications of a stroke, some kind of embolus the medicines couldn't dissolve. My mother died three days after he did. The doctors couldn't determine a cause of death. She didn't want to live without him, so she just stopped. They were very close.''

"Sorry.''

"It happens. He was sixty-eight, she was a year younger. My brothers came up from Earth when Dad got ill, everybody got to say goodbye. They were all still here when my mother passed away. Jarred, the oldest, is a vice-president for Zulu Mines. George is a dentist in Cape Town; Lester teaches history at the University of Stockholm; Roger is a computer systems engineer in Silicon Valley.''

He took another bite, chewed it. "Stop me if I get too personal, but how did you wind up dancing?''

"It's what a degree in kinesiology and physical education is good for," she said. She laughed. "It's what I always liked to do. I thought I might as well get paid for it, if I could. When I get too old to dance, I can always teach it.''

He sipped from the paper cup of water.

"How about you, master-modelsmith and knight-in-shining-armor investigator? Where do you come from?''

Gil considered his response. Shrugged. Said, "I was born in NoCal. Raised in a six-family commune outside of Redding. My father was a mathematician, my mother a holoproj producer. Both very successful in their fields. I've got two biological sisters, one older, one younger, and sixteen communal sisters and brothers of various ages. The commune holds a gathering once a year to which all the families are invited, and I usually go if I can make it.''

"How did you wind up here?"

"I loved puzzles, constructing them, deconstructing them. So I went into engineering. I went to a CIT, got a degree, went to work. Eventually, I wound up at a construction company in Buenos Aires.'' He paused, then said, ''It was a big project. There were some problems. I got . . . disillusioned with that line of work. I had some money saved, so I migrated here in eighty-five. Turned my hobby at modelmaking into a full-time job.''

"Oh, no you don't," she said.

"Excuse me?''

''You've been poking around in my life pretty good here, M. Sivart. Asking a lot of questions which I have been answering as honestly as I can. You don't get away with 'some problems' with work and 'disillusioned.' ''

He smiled. *Got me.*

He took a sip of the water, said, "Okay."

Then he told her about Big Black.

When he was done, she said, "That's awful."

''Yep. And unfortunately, that kind of thing isn't all that unusual. Almost every time a bridge falls or a building collapses, the cause can be traced to greed. Sometimes it's cutting corners on the proper material, sometimes it's hiring unqualified designers or construction workers, sometimes it's ignoring something you know is going to cause problems eventually—like building over an earthquake fault line or in a floodplain. We have the knowledge, the skill, and the technology to build structures that will last five thousand years, with a minimum of maintenance. And given the lifespan of the building, we can do it incredibly cheap. But there is always the greed to contend with. I didn't like the idea of helping put up a tower that will come down and kill people because the owner wanted to save short-term money by substituting cheap steel where the specs called for spun-carbon. Since I couldn't control that, I quit.''

"If one of your models falls apart, nobody dies?"

"Something like that."

They ate in silence for a minute.

"Well, look here," Gil said.

There were several small, black insects crawling over the plate of food Trish had put out for them. Ants.

"How did they get here, I wonder?" she said. "I mean, on the station."

"Stowed away in somebody's luggage, maybe there were some dormant eggs in an antique rocking chair, or stuck to the bottom of somebody's shoe."

"I thought everything that came onboard was searched and sprayed to keep pests off the station."

"It is," he said. "But it doesn't matter. We've got roaches in Recycling, mice and rats in Fecal Town, even a couple of sparrows flying around. Remember three or four years ago, there was a small flock of parakeets loose in the LL1 nature park?"

"I remember that."

He said, "Life finds a way to spread itself around."

She reached over and took his hand, squeezed it. "Almost ready," she said. "Not today, but soon."

He nodded. He knew exactly what she was talking about. He smiled at her.

It *was* the best picnic he'd ever been on.

22

SATURDAY GIL WAS researching WWI German U-boats, with the idea of doing a model that a certain top artist in his field might find interesting. The door chimed. He looked up from his computer and saw Ray El-Sayed and his son in front of the window.

Gil admitted them. "Hey, Ray."

"Gil."

The boy walked over to a holo display of one of Gil's models, the Presidential yacht *Lincoln*, sunk by a terrorist's rocket off Martha's Vineyard in 2046. Only forty people had died, but one of them had been the President of the United States.

"Wow, way fine! You *made* that?"

"Yep," Gil said. "You like models?"

"Yeah!"

Gil pointed to the viewer. "That's the only one I have in the shop right now, but you can punch up holos of others, if you want. Under 'Models.' "

"Way fine!" The boy tapped the controls and the holoproj shifted.

"Don't break anything," El-Sayed said. "We can't afford it."

With young Abdul busy, the cool moved over to stand next to Gil. He lowered the volume on his voice. "We're on the way to the fish pond, but I thought I should stop by. I have some news."

"I'm listening."

"I went to have a word with your friend Armando Jefferson. Just a friendly chat."

"Yeah?"

"I couldn't find him. He missed work last shift, didn't call in. He's not answering his com and it is off-line and powered down, so I can't trace it. He's not at home—I used a police override to open the door, under PDCI."

PDCI was the Potentially Disabled Citizen Inquiry, a way for cools to check on somebody who might be ill or injured inside a locked cube.

"—Nor is he anywhere he normally hangs out," El-Sayed continued. "There is no record of him going EVA or leaving the station on any vessel, private or commercial. No sign of him on any public area surveillance cam."

"Maybe he's getting drunk somewhere."

"I've put out a person-of-interest tag on him, in regard to the assault on you, but none of the patrol officers have spotted him and they are usually pretty good about running the pubs and locating people."

"Maybe he's in-cubed with a girlfriend."

"Maybe. But I have to say, it's got a bad smell to it."

Gil debated with himself for a moment. Should he tell Ray about his drink with Chaz Wells? He didn't have anything concrete, but given the sudden lack of Armando, maybe it meant something.

What the hell. The cool could draw his own conclusions.

He told him.

"Dad, you gotta come see this, it is way fine!"

Abdul had the holo of the *Bismarck* lit.

"I will, just a second."

El-Sayed looked at Gil. "So you have a little chat with the head of Security about Armando and two days later nobody can find him. I don't like this at all."

"I'm not quite ready to jump to that conclusion yet, Ray."

"But you're thinking about it."

Gil nodded. "Yeah. I have to consider it. Whoever killed Corderman had some kind of Security connection. Armando and his two buddies look good for it. And I don't think Armando is bright enough to put something like that together on his own. Wells is. Then again, I can't come up with a reason why he would want to. Maybe one of the other two missing workers might be more forthcoming."

"Doyle and Rodríguez," El-Sayed said. "I've got a buddy in the Port Police at the Jakarta Plex where they landed who owes me one. He's checking them out, unofficially."

"What do we know about Chaz Wells?"

"Nothing past his bio and public record. Maybe I could check on that, too."

"Couldn't hurt."

The cool nodded.

"Dad, come look!"

"Coming. You know, if you call me from now on, maybe you better use my private com number. And keep your conversation bland."

"I hear you."

El-Sayed moved over to look at the holoproj of the model with his son.

Gil reached into a drawer under the work table and removed a block of Lucite the size of his thumb tip, with a tiny speck barely visible in the center of it. Grinned. Said, "Hey, Abdul, catch!"

He tossed the almost-clear plastic cube at the boy, who caught it neatly in both hands.

"Put that in the reader slot."

The boy did as he was told. The holoproj of the ship blanked, and the new image faded in quickly.

"Wow! It's Ricky Rat-Rat!"

The image was of a cartoony rat, big pointed ears, a long snout and clump of a nose, with a rotund body and a long tail that wound around and over his feet. He wore a red vest, white gloves, and a Japanese sailor's cap and a big, toothy grin. The image wasn't as sharp as it would have been if the model hadn't been embedded in the plastic, but you could make out the details okay.

El-Sayed looked at Gil. "I didn't know you did anything but ships."

"I fool around with figurines now and then. Nothing really good enough to try to market."

"This looks pretty good." He waved at the image.

Abdul had the holoproj rotating, to view the famous Ricky Rat-Rat's back side.

Gil shrugged. "It was just for fun. I couldn't sell it anyhow, RRR is copyrighted and trademarked and patented and all. I tried to make any money off him, they'd sue me into a hole so deep it would take light a month to get to the bottom."

"We need to be running along now," El-Sayed said to his son. "Eject the cube and give it back to M. Sivart."

The boy did as he was told. But as he got to where Gil leaned against the work table, the model on his outstretched hand, Gil said, "You have a microviewer at home?"

"Uh-huh."

"Tell you what, why don't you keep the model? I don't have much use for old Ricky here."

The boy's face lit like a high-wattage bulb. "Really?!"

He turned to look at his father, who raised an eyebrow at Gil.

Gil said, "It's just occupying a spot in the drawer."

"Dad? Can I? Can I keep it?"

"It must be worth a lot, even if you can't sell it," El-Sayed said.

"I think that smile I just got about covered it," Gil said.

That drew a grin from the boy's father. "All right. Tell M. Sivart thank you, Abdul."

"Thank-you-thank-you-thank-you!" the boy said. He danced in a circle, bounced up and down, clutched the little plastic cube to his chest.

Gil's own smile joined the others. If he could get that reaction from everybody who wanted one of his models, he would build them for free.

After they'd gone, Gil considered the new information. So, Armando was nowhere to be found. Probably he wasn't hiding out on the station. He didn't seem to be the kind of man who had enough money stashed so he could stay squirreled very long, so he'd have to come out, sooner rather than later. Yes, it was a big bottle and there were little hideaways, like the secret garden Trish had showed Gil, but somehow, Armando didn't seem like somebody who was going to live off the land, either.

So. If he wasn't hiding out on the station, that's a couple of other options. He had gotten off the REL and somebody had rascaled a monitor so his exit wasn't recorded. He could be on Earth by now, with his two buddies, laughing at the idiot cools on the wheelworld.

Or maybe he hadn't made it off the station. And maybe he wasn't laying low.

Maybe Armando was no longer among the living.

Given that there was a murder, and maybe an attempted murder involved here, at the very least, maybe the best way to resolve the problem that Armando presented was to simply . . . do away with Armando. He had no family, few if any friends, and nobody to particularly miss him, not that Gil could tell.

Maybe what was left of Armando was liquefying in a slurry tank in Recycling, soon to become plant fertilizer or flavoring for rabbit or fish food.

Gil couldn't jump to that conclusion, either, but it was another possibility he had to consider.

He sighed. Unless they found the missing man, it was going to throw another roadblock in his investigatory path. A path that didn't seem particularly level and open as it was.

This was what Sherlock Holmes might call a three-pipe problem. Unfortunately, Gil didn't smoke. So instead, he went to the kwoon to do a little moving meditation.

Halfway through the form called Spider Spins Web, Gil had an epiphany. Of a minor sort, anyhow.

He stopped the form, bowed to the wall, and wiped the sweat from his face with his sleeve. He was alone in the school, and as he went to shower and change, he ran over the list in his head. He was pretty sure of what he remembered, but not certain. He needed to pull it up on the computer and check it. Those files were not logged into the mainframe, but only on his flatscreen, back in the shop.

After he dressed, he hurried toward the lifts.

His com cheeped.

"Yes?"

"M. Sivart? This is Edward Fellows. I'm the Director of the *Robert E. Lee* Art Purchasing Department."

"What can I do for you, M. Fellows?"

"We are building an exhibition of nineteenth-century commerce in conjunction with the twenty-fifth anniversary of the station's completion."

Gil had heard something vague about that.

"Yes?"

"We wanted to include a seaport on Earth, someplace like London at the height of the sailing ship days, circa the mid-1800s. Someone suggested that a miniature would not only save us a lot of space, it would also be much more portable. The exhibit would eventually be loaned out to other wheelworlds as part of our exchange program, and maybe even shown at selected museums on Earth. We were wondering if you would consider a commission to build such a project. We have just under a year before the exhibit would take place."

Gil blinked. A seaport? The larger ports during that

period might have had scores, maybe even hundreds of sailing vessels in the harbor—not to mention the docks and warehouses and other buildings themselves. It would be a major undertaking. Months of work, even if the ship details were kept sketchy. He could dupe many of the basic hulls, some of the superstructure and sheets—

The man went on: "I must tell you up front that our resources are limited. We would, of course, entertain your bid, but the maximum amount budgeted for this aspect of the project very likely could not exceed one-point-nine."

Gil blinked again. One-point-nine?

1.9 *million*?

Good Lord!

And what was the qualifier? "Very likely"? He might even be able to push that up a little. Two million, maybe?

Man. There was his retirement. And a whole lot more.

"M. Sivart?"

"Sorry. I was thinking about the, ah, scope of such a project."

"You would consider it?"

"Ah, yes, I think I would."

"If you could draw up preliminary plans and jot down a few notes, perhaps we could get together and discuss this further?"

"I could do that."

"Good. Give my secretary a call and we'll set up a time. I saw your show at the Higgins, M. Sivart, and I must say I think you would be perfect for this project."

Gil stared at his com after the connection was sundered. The rush of astonishment he felt was almost enough to make him forget what he was doing, where he was going. He had a sudden desire to hurry to his shop to start doing research and making notes about what London in 1850 ought to look like. It would take every spare minute he had to do something this complicated, and a year wasn't any too long. If he held it to say, thirty or forty major ships, replicated the main sections and some of the detail work, he might just be able to pull it off.

Some of his commissions would have to wait. He could offer them their deposits back. He could afford to do that now, even without this.

Of course, his extracurricular activities would suffer. He wouldn't have all this free time to go poking around in amateur investigations. But that would be a fairly small price to pay, wouldn't it? To get such a major project, something that would establish him as a serious artist, shown in museums. Maybe invited to lunch with Wöhler . . . ?

Gil smiled at the fantasy. It was awfully tempting to drop everything and rush into this. Awfully tempting.

But he had a murder to solve first, and a new thought to check out. He'd see where that led, *then* he'd play with this new toy.

23

BACK IN HIS shop, Gil ran through the inventory of Corderman's effects. There was the list of the dead man's electronics: his personal flatscreen, the com units, the puzzle comp, and the little unit with the furniture plans in his tool storage unit. He also had a digital camera and the old flatscreen he used for his gym workouts. While it wasn't listed, there would have also been the desktop unit in his cube.

Gil made a call.

"Housing."

"I'd like to talk to somebody about viewing a cubicle."

"Hold the link, please."

Gil waited.

"This is Felicia Peters. How may I assist you?"

"M. Peters, Gil Sivart."

"The artist?"

That surprised him. It always did whenever anybody not in the art world recognized his name. "Yes, ma'am."

"My husband loves your work!"

"Thank him for me."

"So, what can I do for you, M. Sivart? Are you interested in going uplevels?"

"No, ma'am, not just yet. I'm helping a friend out, she lost her SO recently, and I was wondering if his old cube has been rented yet."

"I can check. The name?"

"David Corderman."

There was a pause. "No, I don't show a new tenant for that unit. It is on the schedule to be cleaned and refurbished, but apparently Housekeeping hasn't gotten around to it yet. Big surprise."

"I wonder if it would be possible for me to take a look at it. My friend thinks she might have left something of hers there."

"I don't see any reason why not. The cube is up for rent, I'd be happy to show it to you."

Gil wondered if she'd be happy to show it to somebody her husband didn't admire, but what the hell, fame had its uses. Might as well take advantage of it.

They arranged to meet later in the day.

He discommed, then considered calling Trish and asking her for another bit of the information he needed. No, he decided, he could call and arrange to meet her, but better not to discuss what he wanted over the com.

If his com was tapped, his wanting to poke around in Corderman's cube wouldn't surprise anybody. They wouldn't know what he was looking for, and likely they would have gone through the place pretty thoroughly anyhow. But getting specific with Trish where somebody might hear it, that was another matter. He supposed he could get one of those encryption programs, give Trish a copy of it, and they could talk without worrying they might be eavesdropped upon. He grinned. He'd just as soon see her face to face.

Before he called her, he had another chore he could accomplish via com. He did so, then he called Trish.

"Hi."

"Hi."

"You got a few minutes? I'd like to see you."

"I'm at the club," she said. "I'm rehearsing a new routine. You have something new?"

For the sake of anybody who might be monitoring them, he said, "No, not really. Just need to dot a few i's and cross a few t's."

"I can take a break anytime."

"I'll see you in half an hour."

He closed up the shop and headed for the lifts.

As Gil entered the club, the bouncer nodded to him.

Onstage, Trish did a gymnastic dive, rolled out of it, leaped up into a Russian high jump, legs extended, toes pointed, came down, then dropped into a full side split. She paused, shook her head as if angry. "Music, stop!" she said.

The driving beat cut off.

Trish frowned.

Instead of the artificial skin, she wore baggy black sweat pants, a black jog-bra and matching ballet slippers. She had a rolled handkerchief tied around her head, a red bandana, and it was barely keeping the perspiration out of her eyes. She glanced up, saw Gil, and the frown disappeared.

"Hey."

"Hey, yourself," he said.

She moved to the edge of the stage, picked up a towel, mopped her face and neck. She pointed at a table nearby. "Want to sit?"

"Sure. Rough day at the office?"

"I'm working on a new combination. It doesn't feel right, my balance is off."

"Looked fine to me."

"Thanks. It's almost there."

They sat. "You want something to eat or drink?"

"No," he said. "I won't keep you. I just need to know if David had any other computer equipment I might have missed."

She thought about it for a second, wiped more sweat

from her neck and shoulders. "Other than what was in the boxes or at his gym or tool storage, I don't think so."

"It's important," Gil said. "Anything else at all?"

She thought about it for a minute. Shook her head. "No. He didn't have any other computer gear."

"Thanks. That's all I needed. I'll let you get back to your practice." He started to stand.

"Whoa, hold up a second. This doesn't sound like any i-dotting or t-crossing to me. What's up?"

He said, "I'm not sure. I've got one other thing I need to check out, and even then, I don't know if it will mean anything. I don't want to give you the wrong idea until I know a little more."

"You couldn't ask me this over the com?"

"I'd rather not say anything of substance about all this unless we're face to face."

She wiped at her face with the towel again. "You think somebody is listening to our communications?"

"I don't know. I have to consider the possibility. If they can rascal a security cam's recording, they can probably scan com conversations. And they are worried."

"Man," she said.

"Yes. Listen, do me a favor. Let me hire a cart to haul you to and from work."

"You think things are that serious?"

"Yes, I do."

"Why? What has changed?"

He told her about Armando.

She was shaken by the idea that there might be another death, even if the man might have been connected to her SO's murder.

"So you'll let me have a cart pick you up?"

"All right."

"The driver's name is Howie," Gil said. "He'll be waiting for you when you're ready to leave. He's tall, wide, and has one blue eye and one green eye." He didn't mention that Howie was an ex-rugby player, tough as a box full of rocks, and that he owed Gil a favor.

"You already set this up? Before you asked me?" He heard her anger begin to flare.

"Yes. I—I don't want anything to happen to you."

She caught the tone in his voice. The real concern. There was a long moment, then she said, "All right. Howie."

"I'll get back to you as soon as I know anything about this."

"Okay. Listen, you watch out for yourself, too."

He reached out, caught her hand, squeezed it lightly. "Thanks. I will."

M. Felicia Peters was a bleached blonde who, in an earlier age, would have been called Rubenesque. She wore green silks draped into a baggy shirt and billowy pants and too much makeup, but she was affable enough.

The tour of Corderman's cube didn't take long, and Gil had what he wanted in the first thirty seconds, as soon as he saw the unit's computer console, but he went along so as not to give that away. In case somebody came by later and began asking M. Peters questions about this little visit.

That thing his friend was missing, well, it wasn't here. Too bad.

But there was something he wanted. He had M. Peters go and search the fresher and while she was out of sight, he used a sharp knife to collect his trophy.

"Not in the fresher," she said.

Gil thanked her for her time, autographed a hardcopy holo of one of his models for her husband, and headed back to his shop to consider what he now knew.

This was a wild hair, no doubt about it, but it was as good as anything else he had.

24

IN TRISH'S CUBE, Gil stood in front of the dining table, upon which were piled the computers that David Corderman had owned. As were most of the computers on the station—and just about everywhere—these were all Big Blue hardware. Each one of them had the stylized logo for the company on it, a little metallic sticker with a shallow-view hologram gleaming up in blue and silver.

Before he started, he pulled a device about the size and shape of an old-fashioned pocket watch from his tunic. He pressed his thumb against the device and looked at it.

"What—?"

He waved her to silence. Ten seconds passed.

"Okay, we're clear."

"Clear of what?"

He held the little device up. "This is an aardvark. It's a scanner, able to detect a wide band of electromagnetic, laser, or microwave emissions. If there had been a bug planted in your cube, the aardvark would probably have sniffed it out and told us where it was."

"You do think somebody is spying on us."

"I can't say, but I don't want to take the chance. It takes only a few seconds to check. My shop and cube are clear, and I didn't think anybody would put your place under direct surveillance, but it didn't hurt to see. It seems as if we are alone. Now we can get down to business."

"I'm not sure I understand what this business is," Trish said.

Gil explained it. "When I was going through David's locker at work, I came across one of these stickers." He held up the little hologram he'd pried off the computer in what had been Corderman's cubicle. "This isn't it, this is the one I got from his old cube. I figured the other one must have peeled off his flatscreen when he tossed it into the locker."

"Sounds reasonable to me."

"Right. Thing is, I also remembered that the two flat-screens—the one he carried and the other one in the gym—they both still had the logos in place. As did the games computer and the camera." He paused. "They used to inset the design into the plastic, back in the old days, but somebody realized they could save a couple of pennies on each unit by pasting the design on instead of stamping it in."

"And your point is . . . ?"

"All of David's computers are Big Blue products, and each of them still has the sticker in place." He waved at the table.

She looked at the flatscreens, the puzzle computer, the camera. "I can see that. So what?"

"So, where did the sticker in the locker come from? None of them is missing from his gear. It's an extra one."

Trish shook her head. She was bright, but she couldn't see the connection. "I don't know. Maybe he picked it up on the bottom of his slipper? Maybe it was there when he moved in?"

Gil nodded. "That could be. But we need to check and

make sure this doesn't have some significance."

He began to pry the sticker from the flatscreen Corderman usually carried.

"What are you looking for?"

"I don't know. Something small."

"Wouldn't it be on the extra sticker, the one in the locker?"

"I don't think so. If I'm right about Security being involved in all this, they would have gone over everything in the locker pretty thoroughly."

"What is it you think is going on?

He peeled the sticker loose, turned it over, looked at it. Didn't see anything but adhesive. "I don't know. But what I'm thinking is, these things are somehow connected to this business."

"That's kind of far-fetched," she said.

"I know."

"What could you hide there—assuming something is hidden? It would have to be real little."

He smiled. "I can pile all the micromodels I've ever constructed in the palm of my hand," Gil said, "with room left over. You can stuff a thirty-volume encyclopedia into a microdot so small you could hide it under a flea's egg."

"Ah. But if it is there, how are you going to see it?"

"A portable viewer," he said. "Tool of the trade." He waved a device the size of a coffee mug. "Not the sharpest resolution, but enough to see something down to the size of a big virus."

The viewer lit the air above it with a holographic image. The colors were a little washed out, but the image was clear enough. Gil set the viewer to scan for particles larger than a micron, but smaller than a hundred microns.

The image looked like the ground viewed from a fast jetliner—a liner that went one way for a while, then swung a sharp U-turn and headed back the other way. When it came to something larger than a micron—one-thousandth of a millimeter—but smaller than a tenth of a millimeter, the viewer stopped and focused on it, until Gil tapped the resume search command.

The back of the sticker from Corderman's cube, however, was devoid of anything save glue, dust, and small particles of the plastic computer box itself—at least down to the limits of the viewer's vision.

The sticker he had just removed from Corderman's normal flatscreen was also lacking any military secrets or plans for a perpetual motion machine.

Well. It was a pretty wild shot.

The logo from the old flatscreen Gil had found in the gym locker went under the viewer. Plastic from the case, adhesive, lint around the edges . . . hello?

The holoproj floating in the air was large enough so that the little oval shape was obvious. The architecture wasn't complicated, mostly straight lines and crosslinked ridges, but definitely a man-made construct. He looked at the scale along the edge of the image. Seven microns long, a little more than two microns wide and two deep.

"What is that?" Trish asked.

"It's a hardware lozenge," he said. "A computer chip."

"That small?"

"That large. You could see this under a child's light microscope. It's about the size of a mycobacterium. They are doing work on Earth with viral-molecular computers that would make this thing look like a brontosaur compared to, oh, say, a dog." He waved at the image.

"What does it mean?"

"What it means is, we've probably just found a motive for David's murder."

"How are we going to find out what the chip does?" Trish asked.

They were in the Square, having expresso at the Accept No Substitute Coffee Shop. The booth was cramped, but it was also close to the expresso machine, and the noise of the steam would make it hard for anybody to overhear them talking. Gil allowed himself a shot of the dark expresso, figured it wouldn't hurt his reaction time any.

"We get somebody to look at it and tell us what it is," he said. He sipped at the expresso. It was slightly bitter, not as good as his own brew, but not bad.

Trish drank from her café latte, a beverage that was more milk and foam than coffee.

He said, "Didn't you say one of your brothers was a computer engineer?"

"Roger. He's the closest in age to me. He works for a place in Silicon Valley. They build and program computers for sporting events, timers, like that."

"Would he be willing to take a look at our discovery, you think?"

"Sure. I'm his favorite kid sister. Also his only kid sister."

"All right. Here's what you do. Record a playit for your brother, ask him to check this out for us. Put the playit and the sticker in a packet and seal it. Have somebody you know mail it to your brother, special delivery, only he can sign for it. And tell him to hurry. We need it yesterday. Use somebody you trust. Ask your brother to send a playit or a hardcopy note with what he finds out back to whomever you had mail it to him. No e-mail, no com calls, nothing directly to you."

"You still think somebody is watching us?"

"I don't know. I hope not. But at least one person is dead for sure, and maybe another one is, and I am pretty sure the lozenge we found is tied into it. I don't want anybody to know we found it. If somebody *is* watching, it would be a bad idea if you or I waltz into the post office and send a high-priority packet to a computer engineer on Earth. That would definitely arouse suspicions."

"I understand."

"Do it now," he said. He glanced at his chronometer. "Howie should be waiting outside for you. It would be a good idea to visit several people, before and after you pass the packet for your brother along. If somebody is watching you, they won't be able to mark it."

"You really are serious about this," she said.

He turned his expresso cup in a slow circle where it sat in a wet ring on the table.

"We've lifted up the edge of a big flat rock," he said. "And some nasty, crawly things are stirring under it. We want to be careful they don't sting or bite us when we get the rock up a little higher. They are almost certainly poison."

She stared at him.

He continued: "Somebody killed David. Somebody jumped me in the hall, and I believe it was probably Armando Jefferson and his friends Doyle and Rodríguez who did both. Supposedly, Doyle and Rodríguez left the station and went to Earth, but we don't know that for sure, and we haven't been able to find them if they did. After I talked to him and he complained to the Chief of Corporate Security, Armando Jefferson disappeared."

Gil stopped playing with the expresso cup.

"We're dealing with murderers here, Trish, at least one of whom is well placed enough to hinder any official police investigation. I don't want you to be the next victim. I'm serious about it."

She swallowed. "I understand."

"Good. Just stay cautious. A couple more pieces, and we'll have enough so the police can't ignore it, regardless of how much pressure is on them to leave it alone. But we need to stay alive to finish it."

"I'll be careful. I promise."

He nodded. "Okay. I'll walk you out."

"What are you going to do now?"

"Go find Ray El-Sayed. I promised I'd keep him up to speed."

"Won't he want to see the chip? Wouldn't it be evidence?"

"There isn't any police investigation for it to be evidence *in*, not now. I think he'll go along with us on this.

Before he sticks his neck out, he wants to make sure it is armor-plated.''

"I—thank you, Gil. For all you've done."

"Don't thank me yet. Let's wait until we wrap it up."

25

R AY AND G IL met at Matilda's. They sat at the
end of the bar and drank tea. The place was crowded but
everybody was interested in their own business, at least
so that Gil didn't see anybody paying attention to them.

El-Sayed was surprised, and very interested by Gil's
new information. "You think this chip is the reason behind Corderman's death?"

Gil said, "Once we find out what the chip does, we'll
have a better idea. Right now, yes, I think this is the
reason."

El-Sayed nodded. "Why do I have the feeling this
might get real sticky?"

"Anything new on the missing men?"

It was El-Sayed's turn to nod. "Doyle and Rodríguez
checked into a port hotel a couple of hours after they
arrived on Earth," the cool told Gil. "My buddy says
the clerk remembers them, enough to match faces to the
holos I sent him."

"So they made it that far," Gil said.

"Yeah, but it's not that simple. They didn't check out,

they aren't in their rooms, and nobody in the hotel has seen them since. There are no records of them using their credit tabs anywhere.''

''Why am I not surprised?'' Gil said. ''Once you have a couple of killings under your belt, a couple more don't make any difference.''

''You think they're dead,'' El-Sayed said.

''Don't you?''

The cool considered his tea. ''Well. Economically speaking, it would be a lot cheaper to hire some port rats with jack handles to whack them over the head than it would be to pay Doyle and Rodríguez to go away and stay away forever. *If* they did something on the ship somebody wants to keep secret that bad. And if that's what happened, we've got ourselves a real can of worms here. Multiple homicides. That chip you found must be worth a boxcar of boola.''

''We'll see.''

''Speaking of money, I hear you're about to join the ultra-wealthy yourself.''

''Oh?''

''Didn't the station just cut a deal with you for some big art display? Or in your case, a *little* display?''

''How did you hear about that?''

He shrugged. ''I have a squeal on your file. Anything concerning you hits the station computer, it gives me a call.''

''Is that legal?''

''Strictly speaking, no. But I wanted to see if anybody was checking you out. You have murderous enemies, remember? Anyway, somebody in Corporate Contract spat one through with your name on it. I read it. So sue me.''

Gil smiled and shook his head.

''You don't seem too thrilled about it.''

''Oh, I was, when I first heard it. But I have some problems with it.''

''What, too much work?''

''Not exactly. Not to change the subject, but what did you find out about Chaz Wells?''

El-Sayed pulled his flatscreen from his belt and lit the little holoproj above it. "Charles, 'Chaz' Wells, DOB 28 Feb. 2060, age thirty, one hundred and eighty-eight centimeters tall, one hundred and five kilos, blond hair, blue eyes. Before he became Chief of Corporate Security on the *Robert E. Lee,* he was an investigator for CS on *New Madrid.* Mario Brock, our own dear beloved Station Manager, was the Assistant Station Manager on *New Madrid* before he came here. When he took over the REL, he imported several of his own people for key positions. Wells was one of them. Usual spoils system stuff."

"Was Wells that good an investigator?"

"It wasn't reflected in his record on *New Madrid.* No bad marks against him, but nothing especially distinguished, either. Did his job, kept to himself, didn't get into any trouble. Apparently a steady light, not particularly high wattage. My guess is that he's personally loyal to Brock, and that counts for more in the corporate sector than brilliance in the work itself."

Gil nodded. He knew that was true.

"I've had to work with the guy a couple of times," Ray continued. "He doesn't come across as stupid, he tries to be pleasant but he's not the guy I'd want holding the other end of the rope if I were dangling over an abyss, if you know what I mean."

Gil knew. Wells didn't feel trustworthy. "What about Brock?"

"Brock? What about him?"

"Can you dig around and find out more about his background?"

El-Sayed leaned back and gave Gil a raised-eyebrows look. "You want me to check on the Station Manager? Brock's family has got more money than God, why would he want to get involved in something like this? Whatever this is."

"I don't know. But I met him at my gallery, and it was Wells who introduced us. Brock said something about me doing some art for the station. Then a few days later, I get an offer for a major piece of modelry that will earn me almost two million dollars. The only catch is, it is a big enough project that I'll have to drop everything else I'm doing to get it finished on time. And that would include running around playing detective.''

"Come on. You thinking it was some kind of bribe? Maybe Brock just liked your stuff and nudged the art buyer.''

"Maybe. But at this point, any coincidence is going to ring hollow at first thump. I know a few artists on the station, and Brock's name has never come up as a patron before. If he's got a bunch of models or paintings or sculptures lining his office or home walls, then maybe I'm way off here. Could you maybe find out?''

"I'll see what I can do,'' El-Sayed said. "But I'll have to be very careful. A misstep here, and I'll be on foot patrol in Fecal Town for the rest of my career—if they don't just fire me and pitch me into the void without a suit.''

"I understand.''

El-Sayed left, and Gil ordered a second glass of iced tea. Considered that big contract he'd been offered. After that initial rush of joy, the timing of the offer stuck in his throat, and no matter how much he tried, he couldn't force it to go down. As much as he wanted to believe that Brock had suddenly recognized him as a major artist, a talent to be reckoned with, somehow that did not seem right. Sure, the showing at the Higgins was a big step, it had started Gil on an upward path, but he'd only just begun the climb. Making twenty-five thousand for one of his models was personally very satisfying, but it didn't put him into the rarefied air on the mountaintops. From where he was to a multimillion-dollar project, that was one hell of a big leap. He'd like to be able to make it, but he didn't really believe his leg muscles were that strong.

Too bad.

He finished his tea.

26

MONDAY AFTERNOON GIL was alone in the kwoon working the heavy bag when Trish called.

"What's up?"

"Not too much. You want to drop by when you get a chance? Nothing major, just a . . . little thing I wanted to discuss with you."

A little thing. "Sure. About thirty minutes?"

"That would be good. I'm at home."

Gil headed for the shower in the fresher. Before he got there, his com cheeped again. El-Sayed.

"Gil. When you have a minute, why don't you stop by my office?"

"Sure. I've got something to take care of first." He looked at the clock on the wall. Almost 1400. "How is 1530?"

"Fine. See you then."

He had the water turned on and hot vapor rising when the com bleated a third time. Chaz Wells.

"Hey, Gil, I hear you're not gonna be able to get to my model anytime soon."

"Excuse me?"

"The art contract for the station celebration next year."

"Where did you hear that?"

"What kind of Security Chief would I be if I didn't know what was happening on my station? Hey, good for you. I just wanted you to know it's okay with me if you take your time on my model—this will just make it that much more valuable, right?"

"Could be," Gil said.

"Don't be modest. Anyhow, I won't keep you, I guess you'll be too busy to do much else for the next few months. Congratulations again."

"Thanks."

Gil discommed. He stepped into the tiny shower.

"Hi."

"Hi. Come in," Trish said.

Gil did so.

Inside her cube, she said, "I got the message back from my brother."

"That was quick."

"I'll play it for you, I've already heard it. Listen to this." She paused a second. "There's some family stuff up front."

Gil shrugged. "I don't mind listening to it if you don't mind me hearing it."

"It's okay."

A man's voice came on. "Hey, little sister, always good to hear from you. Let me catch you up.

"I saw Jarred's boy Sammy last week, he's graduating from UCSF, can you believe? Good-looking kid, going to go into mine management like his father.

"Lester's new playit is out. I expect he'll send you a copy. 'The History of Northland Coast Communities from A.D. 300 to A.D. 1500' isn't what you'd call light reading, but if you can't get to sleep, this is just the thing.

"George is mumbling about selling his practice and moving to Australia again, but don't hold your breath.

He's too much a Capetonian to ever leave.

"That's pretty much the family news I have since our last letter.

"Now, the reason for your message. As to this little toy you sent me—where the hell did you get this thing? I thought maybe it was a gag at first, something to pull my leg, but it's a lot of work just to put one over on me, and I don't remember you being that much of a practical joker.

"What you have here, sis—and I'll skip the tech talk because I know that's the first thing you'd say—what you have here is an induction chip. It's what they call a 'remora,' named after a fish that attaches itself to larger fish and lives off the scraps the bigger fish doesn't eat. What that means is, if you stick this little chip on your computer—and that's what it was designed to do, be stuck on a computer—it will draw a little bit of power and turn itself on. It wouldn't use enough juice so you'd notice it, not unless you had some very finely tuned instrumentation looking for it. The lozenge—it's called that from its shape—the lozenge picks up enough spill to operate from a nearby device running on alternating current. When I say 'nearby,' I mean within a few centimeters. And you need some voltage. If you were running a flatscreen on battery power, the thing would probably not be able to suck enough juice to function—though it would if you plugged the flatscreen in to recharge."

Gil and Trish looked at each other. Her brother's message continued:

"What they used to use these things for was industrial spying. You'd slip into your competitor's place, slap one of these onto his mainframe, and it would copy files, wait for the right moment, then transmit the files, using the competitor's own wireless modem. Remoras are harder to detect than a viral program because they don't behave like viruses. Once the stuff is swiped, they shut down. You aren't likely to notice it by accident, and even if you are looking for it, it's hard to find at this size.

"The things worked pretty well for a while, but most

big companies now have programs to detect them or shut off a transmitter without a proper password in place.

"Thing is, what this particular little bastard does isn't that, and for sure, it's not so benign. Staying away from the tech talk, the bottom line is, this thing isn't designed to swipe anything, it's designed to trash the system it's feeding on. It has a timer—set for ten days from now, by the way. When the timer goes off, the chip will turn part of the system hardware into what amounts to a capacitor. A lot of electricity will pile up, kind of like water behind a dam. Then the chip will smash open the dam, flood the system with high voltage, and *wham!* your circuits get fried. Whole sequence won't take more than a few seconds. External surge protectors won't help because it will all take place inside the box and the voltage is high enough so it will run right over internal breakers. Be like trying to stop a river by throwing a handful of dirt into it.

"This is a nasty piece of work, little sister, and while it won't mess up the programs in an affected system— well, most of them, you will lose unstored data and maybe what you are running when your computer cooks itself—your hardware will quickly turn itself into a big, smoldering piece of junk.

"If you happen to be looking right at it when it happens, figure out what is going on and pull the plug, you might save the computer—but unless you find the remora and pull it, soon as you power up again, you're screwed.

"Put one of these on a microcomp and set it off, and you'll be out a week or two's salary to replace the dead box. Set it on a mainframe or supercomp, and you're talking *viel Geld, mucho dinero, beaucoup buckos.* The owner of a super-Cray with this thing on it would be *very* unhappy with you.

"Um. That's pretty much it. I'm going to put this in a locked cabinet and hang on to it. I'd like to know where you got it and why you're having me send this message to somebody else. Let me know when and if you can. If you need anything else, give me a call. Be careful, sis.

People who do this kind of thing are sickos, and I wouldn't want you to get too close to them.''

Gil and Trish looked at each other again.

"So this is why they killed David?"

He nodded. "Yes, I think so."

"You think somebody was going to use the chip and he found out? Maybe shut down the station's computer? Why would they want to do that? Terrorism?"

Gil shrugged. "Could be. The station has backups, and even if all the computers shut off at once, it wouldn't fall out of space. Life support can be run manually, so we wouldn't freeze or run out of air. If that's what they want, sabotage. Could be maybe the plan is extortion. 'Pay us or we'll kill the system.' Something like that."

"But we have the chip now."

Gil shook his head. "No, we have *a* chip." He looked at her. Said, "Maybe there was more than one."

El-Sayed stood in front of the Police Station as Gil walked up to it. "Why don't we take a walk?" the cool said. "The park on LL1 is nice this time of day."

"Okay."

They caught the lift to LL1, watched the newswall with half a dozen other passengers, got off and headed for the greenbelt. LL1's park was the best kept and most lush on the station, no surprise. Rich people didn't like looking at brown grass or dead trees.

"There's a bench by the koi pond," El-Sayed said.

The two men walked along the artfully laid out path as it wound around the park. At the pond, the colorful fish swam back and forth just under the water's crystal surface, black, orange, party-colored blends. Across from them, an old man watched the koi. He smiled and waved at Gil and Ray, then turned and left.

"Two things," the cool said. "First, Mario Brock is not an art collector. He's got a couple of lithographs in his office, not cheap, but his secretary picked them out— to go with the walls and carpets. His cube—it's a twelve-room two-story that overlooks this park, by the way—is pretty bare. There are some expensive paintings and a couple of sculptures in it, but they were there when he moved in.''

"You're pretty good," Gil allowed.

El-Sayed smiled. "Some of my best informants are domestic workers. Brock doesn't have a personal maid or butler, but he uses a cleaning service. They don't pay their workers too well. And rich people tend to think of the help as furniture.''

Gil nodded. "And the other thing?"

"This." He held out two bits of shiny metal. Gil looked at the objects on El-Sayed's palm. They were small, a few millimeters each, and looked like stainless steel, circular bands pinched in the middle, so they resembled small but fat staples.

El-Sayed handed them to Gil.

"Some kind of clamp?" Gil ventured, examining one of the things.

"Yes. Surgical clips, for a vasectomy. Apparently the two vasa deferentia are cut, and these are to make sure no little wigglers manage to make their way across the gap.''

"How interesting. And these are . . . used clamps."

El-Sayed grinned. "Don't worry, they've been sterilized.''

"How did you come by them?"

The cool's grin vanished. "They showed up in a filter in Recycling. I put a notation that anything unusual was to be reported to me. You wouldn't believe what shows up in the filters. They find coins, teeth, even jewels.''

Gil rolled the clamps in his hand, gave them back to El-Sayed. There was only one reason he could think of for Ray to have showed him these. "Let me guess. Armando Jefferson did not want to be a father?"

El-Sayed smiled. "You know, you are brighter than you look. There aren't any serial numbers on these things, no way to be positive, but I spoke to a urologist on Earth who, in fact, did that particular surgery on our boy Armando. The doctor is a relic, he's six days older than God, and he likes to use clamps instead of lasers or microsutures. According to him, almost nobody else still does it that way. I'd say chances are pretty good that Armando is the former owner of this pair.''

''Isn't that a shame.''

''You aren't going to wail and rend your clothes or anything, are you?''

''Armando almost certainly killed one man and tried to smash my head with a heavy pipe. In my mind, that makes his right to use up the communal oxygen forfeit.''

''There's an uncivilized, bloodthirsty attitude. If I didn't know better, I'd be looking at you as a suspect. That, plus the fact that I would never have known the presumably late M. Jefferson even existed if you hadn't brought him to my attention.''

''Could have been a clever ploy on my part,'' Gil said. ''To lull you into not suspecting me.''

''I don't think you're that clever.''

''You might change your mind. I've got some news. We heard back from Trish's brother on the chip we found.''

''And . . . ?''

Gil told him. When he was finished, El-Sayed blew out a big sigh and watched a large black koi as it leapt up into the air and fell back into the pond with a splash. ''I don't like this,'' he finally said. ''Not one damn bit.''

''Neither do I,'' Gil said. ''I don't want to tell you how to do your job or anything, but maybe—''

''—I ought to consider taking a tour of the Computer Section? Yes, I think I might do that. Might be a good idea to peel a couple of logo stickers and run them under a microviewer, might it not?''

''Yeah. We've got ten days. If you find them, it might save us a lot of trouble.''

''And if somebody calls asking for ransom to keep the station from going brain-dead, it would be nice to have disarmed them in advance.''

''Good thinking.''

Gil and Ray split up; the cool headed back for the

Square while Gil meandered along the path away from
the pond, thinking. Through openings through the small
trees, he glanced up at some of the ritzier cubes whose
windows looked down on the park.

Which one, he wondered, did Mario Brock own?

The call he'd gotten from Wells, that was another interesting turn. It was almost as if Wells had called to
remind him he wouldn't have time to play detective—
not if he wanted the fame and money for the commission
put forth by the art buyer for the station. A proposal put
forth at the behest of someone with a fair amount of
power, Gil was almost certain. Somebody like, oh, say,
Mario Brock.

Which, as El-Sayed had pointed out, didn't make a lot
of sense. What, if anything, would the Station Manager
have to gain from a major computer crash on the *Robert
E. Lee*?

There was a question. And one he'd better start trying
to answer.

27

IT WAS TUESDAY, about midway through second shift, when El-Sayed came by Gil's shop. Gil was examining a hard copy of the contract the station had e-mailed him for the anniversary art project. As he suspected, there was a penalty clause if the project was "substantially" late. Essentially, all bets were off if Gil missed the delivery date—the station, hereafter known as the Purchasers, could void the contract and refuse to pay him. The lawyers could argue over that one, but he suspected that the ticking clock was there to remind him to lay off anything not connected to the project.

All that money. What a shame he couldn't go for it.

"You really think that Brock is trying to buy you off?" He nodded at the printout.

"Afraid so."

"Well, here are two more bits of misery to add to your load. I peeled stickers from all four of the station's mainframes, plus their backups. Nothing there."

"Hmm. Maybe we scared them off."

"That would be nice, but I'm not banking on it. I've

got a couple of techno buddies of mine going over the systems—just in case the bad guys decided to put the killer bugs somewhere other than under the stickers. Nothing has turned up yet.''

"And the other piece of bad news?"

"This." He dropped a holograph on Gil's work table. It was a grainy shot of two black lumps lying side by side. There were powdery gray and black ashes piled up near the lumps, but you couldn't tell much from that. It was the scale along the edge that gave Gil an idea of the size. He knew what the things must be, though he'd have never recognized them if he hadn't already suspected what they were.

El-Sayed said, "The one on the left is Doyle. Jakarta Police don't have a confirmation on the other one but, me, I'd bet large that it's Rodríguez. Somebody tried to burn them and they did a pretty good job, but they forgot to knock all the teeth out, that's how they ID'd Doyle. Both corpses had fractured skulls. The way the port cools see it, somebody whacked them over the head, tossed them into a building, soaked them with something very inflammable, then set the place on fire. Both men died from smoke inhalation, though the cracked heads would probably have killed them in short order without the fire.''

"Can I safely assume you're now convinced that Corderman's death wasn't an accident?"

"You can assume that, yes."

"Are we getting any more official help?"

"Not yet. I need enough material so that when my captain opens his mouth to tear my head off for working a closed investigation, I can choke him with what I've got. And what I *don't* have yet is an overriding motive. We have the remora—at least I hope your client's brother has it, he had damn sure better—and we've got all these bodies, but we need to know who benefits from a shutdown of the station's computers."

"I've been thinking about that," Gil said.

"I hope so. Because Wells and Brock don't seem like

particularly good candidates to reap rewards if the station's brains up and go kablooey. Wells is Security, and his head will be the first to roll. Brock *might* survive it, if he pulls a bunch of favors in, but even so, it would be enough of a blot on his record that he wouldn't ever be getting an invitation to the annual Corporate Vice Presidents' Barbecue in lovely Hana, Hawaii. We might ought to be looking at somebody else for this.''

''Maybe.''

''That doesn't sound as if you're in agreement.''

''No, I agree with your assessment. It wouldn't do their careers any good.''

''But?''

Gil shook his head. ''I don't know. I'm missing something.''

''Let me know if you find it. Meanwhile, I'm going to keep checking the computers. I had a thought about that. Maybe they were going to use the thing on a ship's computer. Something carrying valuable cargo or VIP passengers, maybe. I'm going to check manifests for anything glittery coming or going eight days from now.''

Gil looked at El-Sayed. ''That's a good idea.''

''Don't sound so damned astounded when you say that. I have been doing this a while.''

Gil smiled.

With computers, any information available on Earth's public nets could be had by somebody in space—provided they were willing to live with the connect charges to log into a Terran system. What the station had on Brock and Wells was limited, and El-Sayed had already checked that. What Gil needed was more, and he needed to find it in a place where nobody was likely to notice him—either looking for it or being aware that he had found it.

Gil went home and changed clothes, including his shoes. If somebody had managed to put any kind of electronic burr on him, that should take care of that. He turned his com off so he couldn't be located by the computer, rechecked his air pistol for the fifth time that day, then went to the Public Library.

The place was two sublevels above the Square, and he took a roundabout and leisurely path to make sure nobody was following him. Nobody was, or if they were, they were invisible.

The newswall on the elevator mentioned that another teener had died while roofing one of the station's smaller lifts. Third one this year. It was a variation on an old game, and it was not all that dangerous, usually. But some of the lifts had cramped space, protrusions from the walls that could snag the unwary. There was a risk, and that, of course, was why they did it. Teeners thought they were going to live forever. Yeah, some fool somewhere was gonna do something stupid and die, but it was always going to be some *other* fool.

Gil shook his head. When he was fifteen, he had walked across a narrow board between two eight-story buildings. A misstep would have been worth a fatal fall to the alley floor below. He'd been with four of his friends, and he'd never thought twice about doing it. To balk would have been worse than cowardly, it would have been, in the patois of his youth, stale. There was no worse sin for a fifteen-year-old in Gil's circle than being stale.

He had been lucky. Whatever gods watched over children and idiots had stayed the wind and held the board steady for Gil and his friends that day. And on other days when they'd pushed their limits, the Fates must have already had enough foolish teen bodies to process. Gil and his friends could have been killed during the nighttime visit to the whore district in Angkor; or during the race in stolen electric carts through the streets of San Francisco when they flipped one of the carts and totaled it; or scaling a steep and slippery roof in a pouring rain to spray-paint green the genitals of the statue of the Golden Steer in Denver.

Sometimes it was amazing to him that teeners survived to adulthood.

Inside the library, convinced he hadn't been followed, Gil rented a computer console and holoproj, fed it enough bills for three hours worth of connect time to the Earth On Line's People Web, and cranked up the biographical search engine.

It was amazing how many Charles Wellses and Mario Brocks there were on Earth and in wheelworlds. Thousands of them.

Fortunately, he had enough information to limit the search. Date and place of birth, ID numbers. Once he had the proper selections, he had the search engine grind through and locate every bit of information it could find about the two men.

It didn't take long to download the material about Wells. It took somewhat longer for Brock. He dumped it all onto a compact disc about the size of a half-dollar coin, paid extra for the disc, then popped it out of the unit.

With his trophy, Gil moved toward a quiet table in the back of the library. There were only a few people here aside from himself; most of what went on here could be done in the privacy of your own cube. Some people didn't have much privacy there, though, and there were also a few items you couldn't access online, like rare hardcopy books.

He passed a couple of teener students more interested in each other than in studying—doubtless what they told their parents they were going to be doing at the library. The couple sat next to each other, blocked from view from the waists down by the table at which they sat, and their hands were not in sight. Gil could guess what they were doing by the high color in their faces.

Ah. To be young and in lust. Certainly less dangerous and more fun than riding the top of an elevator.

There were two old men using the newsfax scanners. Gil saw a page of the *New York Times* flash past on one of the scanners.

A woman of forty or so sat in a small soundproof listening booth, singing along to music. Gil couldn't hear her or the music, but the woman seemed to be using her whole body to get into the song.

He sat in a padded chair against a wall and put the disc into his flatscreen. He set the holoproj for 2D mode; the only way anybody would be able to see what Gil saw would be to stand directly behind him, impossible with the wall being where it was.

Okay. Wells was the shorter file. He would read about him, then move on to Brock. It would take longer to read in real-time than it had to download it. He could have gone home, or to the shop, but he liked sitting in a library. It brought back memories of his own student days on Earth.

The female half of the teen couple gave a little moan, and Gil grinned again. He had met a girl or two at various libraries when he'd been young and stupid. Even made love to one once, though that had been in the fresher with the door locked.

He began to read.

By the time he finished reading and annotating his download, it was into third shift.

The teen couple, having slaked their lusts, were gone. The woman who would be a music star was also gone. One of the old men still sat scanning papers. Gil hoped that when he was that age, he would have more to do than to sit in a library reading old news about a place tens of thousands of kilometers away.

There you go again, jumping to conclusions. That old man could be a retired professor, researching a book. Or maybe a broker, checking market trends. Or even an investigator, doing background checks on a subject, just as you did. You know that teen couple might have spared you a similar glance when you passed and felt sorry for you, too. Just another old man, all alone in the library, no place better to go, nothing better to do . . .

Gil smiled at the thought. Yes, well, it was true. Appearances *were* sometimes deceiving. There were entire species of animals—insects, fish, birds, mammals— whose survival was in large part due to looking fiercer or more innocuous than they really were. That harmless-looking little spider might carry a deadly venom in its bite.

Best he keep that in mind.

He decided to drop by Trish's club. Might as well bounce what he'd found off her and see what she thought. He could call Ray El-Sayed later and fill him in.

Trish wasn't due to dance for another half hour, and the bartender made a call, then waved Gil back into the dressing area.

Gil passed a couple of the other dancers he had seen before, a couple more he didn't recognize. He nodded at the ones who noticed him.

Trish was in her dressing room, the door open, and he tapped on the doorjamb.

"Hi."

"Hi."

She was dressed in black spandsilk tights tonight, the suit covering her from ankles to wrists but leaving a scoop neck that revealed her bare collarbones and throat. Her hair was pinned into a tight knot.

"Nice outfit," he said.

"Less messy than the skin stuff," she said, "less hassle to put on and take off. Besides, I don't want my audiences to get bored."

"I can't imagine that," he said.

"Thank you. What's up?"

"Not much. I've done a little research. Also talked to Ray El-Sayed again. If it's any consolation, I think that all three of the men directly responsible for David's murder are themselves dead."

He told her about Ray's visit, the holograph of the bodies.

"I'm glad they are dead," she said. "It isn't enough. I want to see whoever sent them punished."

"I'm working on it." He told her about his research into Chaz Wells's and Mario Brock's backgrounds.

"It doesn't sound that promising," she said. "No skeletons in their closets."

"Not per se. But there are a couple of things I want to run down. It will require that I make a trip down below."

"Really? Why?"

"Even with vids, computer information is kind of sterile. Somebody being interviewed and recorded tends to be a little bit on guard, sometimes overly careful of what they say, knowing it is going to be public information. You get them alone, where nobody can overhear the conversation, sometimes they loosen up. Maybe say things you might not hear otherwise."

"You think Wells or Brock have some dark secrets and somebody on Earth knows what they are?"

"I'm sure they have some dark secret—everybody does. And maybe somebody knows about it, maybe not. But I won't know unless I go and ask."

She glanced at the clock. "I have to warm up," she said. "When would you be leaving?"

"In the morning. I'll catch the NorAm shuttle. Probably be gone a couple of days."

She stood. Put her hand on his arm. "Be careful. I've kind of gotten used to you being around."

He felt a small rush from her touch. And from her words. "I will. I've kind of gotten used to me being around, too."

28

SHUTTLES BETWEEN WHEELWORLDS and Earth were commonly called "dropboxes" on the way down and "boxcars" on the way up. The commuter craft—something of a misnomer, since only a handful of people could afford to make such trips on a daily or weekly basis—were bare-bones ships, little more than stasis seats and narrow aisles. Each had a couple of freshers for people with weak plumbing or space sickness, but since the trip only took a few hours, the Corporation didn't waste money on frills. Unless you were used to it, you didn't want to eat in zero-gee, so meals were not an option. You could have an alcoholic drink, but one was the limit. A nauseated passenger who didn't get the barf bag up in time and spewed little globules of scotch in all directions was much worse than a crying baby.

The basic trip was simple: A dropbox loaded with passengers was towed by a tug a couple of klicks from the station; there, the shuttle fired its rockets and headed for Earth in a big hurry. The angle was calculated to use the gravity well for braking, along with some reverse thrust, and a tight orbit spiraled the dropbox down to a landing at one of the three major ports—the NorAm, in Nova Scotia, the Jakarta, or the biggest port, in Rio Nuevo. There was a smaller European port on an artificial island in the Channel between England and France. If you wanted a comfortable and more leisurely ride, you caught one of the big luxury ships, gravity-rigged vessels that took a few days for the trip in either direction. Of course, it would cost you ten times as much and there wasn't a lot to see. Still, a lot of people did it, much as people still took ocean liners instead of suborbitals on Earth. For them, the ride was as important as the destination.

Gil didn't have time for that. A week from now, any of those remoras that might be out there would come to life and start killing computer systems. A slow boat to Earth was not part of the solution.

He leaned back in his seat. He always sat on the aisle, in the middle of the dropbox whenever that seat was available. It was theoretically the safest spot in the passenger compartment, though that point was pretty fine. If a ship massively decompressed in deep space, the shuttle would be your tomb, no matter where you sat. And if for some reason it missed the atmosphere groove and hit ground or water at speed, any particular passenger remains could be buried in a snuffbox. Assuming you wanted to bother.

Having brushed the cold hand of Death a few times, Gil knew it could happen to him. Unlike the teener he had been, he knew he was mortal. It didn't do any good to dwell on it, since as a passenger it was out of his control; still, he thought about it more than he used to.

But the drop was uneventful.

The tug hauled the shuttle out to the launch point and left it there. The pilot gave the passengers a two-minute warning, then lit the engines. The seat absorbed the g-force enough so that it was bearable, if not comfortable. The spiral down was bumpy, but they landed safely at the port eighty kilometers outside Nova Scotia City. Gil went through customs quickly, having no luggage. He caught a hack into town, checked into a hotel, got a copy of the suborbital and bullet train schedules and started making com calls.

There were six people on his list.

One of the hoped-for interviewees was offplanet. One refused to talk to him. Another couldn't be located. But three of those on Gil's list were available. One was local—well, relatively local, in New York City; one was in London; the third was in Spain. Gil used his flatscreen, logged into a routing computer, to make the most efficient connections. New York in the morning, London in the afternoon, Madrid the following morning. If all went as scheduled, he'd be on a shuttle for home in two days.

Connections booked, he set up his appointments.

Richard "Chick" Makepeace was, in theory, a First American. Formerly he would have been known as a Native American; before that, an Amerind and before that an Indian. Before that, he told Gil, he would have been called a godless savage, a cutthroat heathen bastard, and probably a lot worse. At least those were the names from those outside his culture. His people called themselves the Choctaw, then and now.

In Makepeace, the blood had thinned more than a bit. He was about seventy, had pale and much wrinkled sun-damaged skin, white hair, watery blue eyes, and you had to go back to his great-great-grandfather to get to pure Choctaw. But for purposes of casino shares, he said, he was as native as the people who had fought and lost America to the European invaders. Only now, First American casinos were big business. Some of the larger tribes had bought back big chunks of the land they'd been driven off hundreds of years before, and the irony was, they were using the invaders' money to do it. Makepeace found this terribly amusing. His share of the revenues from his tribe's gaming palace on the Gulf Coast must have been pretty good—Gil met him in a Manhattan town house overlooking Central Park that must have set the man back a few million dollars. There was a full-sized grand piano in one corner, a Renoir on the wall over the fake fireplace, and carpets deep enough to use as a bed. A big German shepherd curled up next to Makepeace's custom-made form-chair certainly seemed to be sleeping comfortably enough. The couch upon which Gil sat matched the form-chair, both of a soft and buttery-yellow leather.

"So, son, what can I do for you? You said it was about Mario Brock?"

"Yes, sir."

"I haven't seen him in almost thirty-five years. That was back in my salad days, when I didn't have a pot to piss in and had to work for a living."

"I understand you were his . . . tutor?"

Makepeace laughed. "Tutor? Hell, a glorified baby-sitter was what I was. Mario and his sister Estella. They grew up in London, so they didn't have much contact with the country. His old man hired me to teach his kids 'organic skills.' To 'put them in touch with nature.' When I met 'em, the boy was thirteen, girl was not quite ten. Neither had ever gotten their hands dirty. First night we spent 'camping' was at a private park in the woods in Germany. No wildlife bigger than a squirrel. Big four-meter-high chain-link electrified fence around it to keep the riffraff out. The damned *tent* was wired for electricity. There were showers and flush toilets twenty meters away from the tent. The kids slept on foam pads on cots. Way those two carried on, you'd think we'd packed off into the Amazon and been living there ten years, eating nothing but grubs we found under damp and slimy rocks. They were terrified a lion or tiger or bear was gonna come out of the manicured woods and kill us all. Both spent half the night crying and begging to go home.

"I had 'em for four summers, two weeks each time. I quit after that, the casino was getting built by then and they needed workers down in Biloxi, gave the tribe first chance at the jobs."

A shadow of something passed over his face. It was quick, but Gil caught it.

He took the chance. "Why did you really quit?" he asked.

There was a long pause while the old man stared at him, waiting to see if Gil would look away. Gil matched the stare.

Finally Makepeace said, "You're pretty good at reading faces, ain't you? You got any Blood in you?"

"Not that I know of."

He nodded at Gil. "I've got enough money now so I don't sweat the small stuff, and old man Brock has been dead and cremated for fifteen years, but I need to ask, what are you planning on doing with this? You writing a playit? This gonna show up on the holoproj entcom?"

"No sir, it's background information. A friend of mine's SO was murdered. I think maybe Brock had a hand in it."

The old man shook his head. "Huh. You pretty sure about this?"

"Yes, sir."

"I had you checked out after you called, you know. Found out you're a pretty decent modelist and that you poke your nose into stuff now and then, but usually for good reasons. I never had cause to mention this to anyone before, until it was too late to do any good, but maybe I can make up for it. Okay, son, I'll tell you about Mario and why I quit.

"Last summer I had the Brock kids, we went on a real camping trip. Boy was seventeen, Estella was almost fourteen. Outback of Australia, a two-day hike from anywhere. Well, it would have been, 'cept that the old man had us choppered in and dropped off. Supposed to stay a week." He paused, and Gil could see the memory reflected in his watery blue eyes.

"Long story, short version. Third night we were there, we had a couple of wild dingoes prowling around the camp and I went to shoo 'em off. Told the kids I'd be gone an hour or so, but I circled back five minutes later. We were all sleeping in separate tents, on foam pads on the ground."

Gil nodded but didn't interrupt.

"Thing was, I'd heard something else during the nights besides dingoes. Soon as I sneaked back into camp, I found Mario and his sister in his tent. He was messing with her. I grabbed his ass out of there, slapped him a couple of times and told him if I ever heard of him doing anything like that again, I'd have a little talk with his father."

"Messing with her? What do you mean?"

The old man impaled Gil with a stare. "Son, you know exactly what I mean. Thing was, she was as interested in it as he was, at least it sounded that way. And I didn't get the impression it was the first time."

"I see."

The old man shook his head. "These were rich kids and maybe they didn't use the same rules the rest of us did, but it was hard to understand. The boy got an allowance, at least as much as his old man was paying me," Makepeace said. "He wasn't a bad-looking or stupid kid, he had money and he could have had girlfriends falling all over him. If he didn't want any entanglements, hell, he could have gone to a brothel or had call girls, he could sure afford it. But, no, here he was messing with his own kid sister. And her being happy about it, too, far as I could tell. She wasn't an ugly girl, neither, she could have had boyfriends of her own." He shook his head.

"I thought it was sick, and I didn't want any part of it."

"So you quit."

"Yes." There was another long pause, and a bad memory in the muscles of the old man's jaws as he ground his teeth. "I didn't say anything to their father. I rationalized it to myself. It wasn't like it was rape, he wasn't forcing her, and there were plenty of kids got started that age or earlier. Not my business what spoiled rich brats did, the old man probably wouldn't appreciate me telling him, sure as hell wouldn't be happy I knew about it. He was a shoot-the-messenger kind of guy. So I didn't say anything. I went on my way, worked construction on the casino, made pretty good money for the time. I didn't really think about it much, you know? It didn't affect my life.

"Two years later, Mario went off to school, Harvard or Yale or somewhere. Couple of months after he left, Estella Brock killed herself. I didn't have any direct contact with the family by then, but I knew the guy they'd hired to coach the kids in sports. Coach knew the maid who found the body. The girl took an overdose of pills and left a note, telling all about her and Mario. Didn't sugarcoat it, either. According to the note, they'd started when she was eleven, been at it since. Broke it off when he went to school and got himself a girlfriend there. Estella killed herself because she didn't want it to be over. She loved him."

Gil found himself releasing his breath. "What happened?"

"Not much. The family doctor came out. The Brocks were wealthy and important. The maid left domestic service and bought herself a nice house in Mexico. The note disappeared. The doctor told the press he had been treating Estella Brock for a mild case of the flu and she had an allergic reaction to the medicine. That was how it wound up, a terrible, freak accident."

Gil nodded. Rich people had other avenues upon which they could sometimes travel. No surprise. He'd heard of worse being covered up.

"The old man nearly blew an artery, according to my third-hand information, and his wife, the kids' mother, was angrier than he was. Before the maid packed up and went off to enjoy her early retirement, she overheard that Mario wasn't going to be enjoying the family fortune, not then and not ever. The old man would keep up appearances, get the boy through school, but he was going to cut him off cold after that. So Mario went on about his life, graduated from school, left the bosom of the Brock companies to make his own way in the world, supposedly with his father's blessing at his ambition. But what he had done to his sister was going to cost him something roughly in the neighborhood of seventeen billion dollars when the old man shuffled off. Probably a helluva lot more than that now. Mario's mama still holds the grudge, she must be pushing eighty by now, and when she dies, it all goes to a nephew and to charity."

The old man looked at Gil. "I should have said something. Maybe that girl would still be alive if I had called her father and laid it out for him before I quit. It's one of the few regrets I have about my life."

Gil didn't speak. There wasn't anything he could offer to heal a wound this old.

"This any help to you, son?"

Gil nodded. "Yes, sir, it is."

"Well. Maybe that's something. You know anything about karma, son?"

"A little."

"It always comes round, you know. Mine, yours, everybody's. I've been halfway expecting somebody like you for years."

"Yes, sir."

"See that you don't do anything that merits a visit like this down the line. I just got it off my chest, but I have to say, it doesn't really help that much."

"Yes, sir."

Gil still had two appointments: The first was with one of Brock's former college instructors and the second with a woman Brock had once been engaged to marry. But he had found, he thought, his motive for Corderman's murder.

If what Makepeace said was true, Mario Brock was not heir to the huge family fortune as everyone thought. He had to live on his Corporate salary and stock options, and while that was not an inconsiderable sum for most people, it was nothing to a man who would have inherited billions.

So, somehow, what it was about was money.

Now all he had to do was figure out how Brock planned to profit, and he would have him.

29

GIL CAUGHT A transatlantic suborbital from New York to London, a flight that lasted about an hour, not counting the takeoff and landing.

In a small flat just outside a town called Gilford, Mario met with one of Brock's ex-college instructors at Harvard. The professor was perfectly willing to talk to Gil—though he must confess he had little to offer.

Yes, Professor Wheeless said, he *had* written a glowing report some thirty-odd years ago, concerning the Brock boy's undergraduate paper about the great Greek tragedies, but the truth of that was perhaps a bit more complicated. That was during a period of new construction on campus, you see, and the Chair of the department, a man to whom Wheeless owed his tenure, had been hoping for an additional wing for the proposed Greek Studies building. Brock had been a decent enough student, but the report had been at the behest of the Chair. Perhaps young Brock's very wealthy father might feel inclined to endow the department with a substantial gift if he thought his son had a demonstrated brilliance in that area?

And where had the Chair gotten such an idea?

Dr. Wheeless could not say for certain. Perhaps young Brock had mentioned it. It was so long ago. Did it matter?

And as for the new wing? Well, apparently the elder Brock had not been so inclined, despite the glowing report on his son's prowess in the classics.

If Mario Brock had indeed been the one responsible for getting an unearned accolade, it showed he was self-serving.

So Gil now had Brock involved in an incestuous relationship with his sister, being cast out of the family fold without the cushion of money, and manipulating his university instructors for his own benefit. As the twig is bent, so grows the tree.

Gil spent the night in a small European-style hotel with a bath down the hall, then got up early and caught the bullet train through C2 for France, and then Spain. It was a pleasant enough ride, given the speed at which the countryside and assorted tunnel walls flashed past.

In Spain, Gil called upon M. Louisa Abbington, who had a small villa twenty kilometers from Madrid.

She was a spectacularly attractive woman of fifty, was M. Abbington, striving hard to look thirty. It was his guess that a combination of plastic surgery, hormones, and exercise had gone a long way to helping her achieve her goal—she had even taken the trouble to have her hands dermabraded and vatted so they wouldn't give her away; but though it had been under another name, Gil knew when M. Abbington had been born. She could pass for late thirties easily enough, maybe a couple of years younger in a subdued light. A gorgeous woman, still sure to draw admiring gazes everywhere she went. She must have been stopping men cold in their tracks since puberty. She was fighting hard to hold on to her beauty, and it was a battle she would lose eventually, but for the moment, she was still ahead of the game. Sad, the premium people put on physical beauty, but a fact, nonetheless. And her beauty had been her ticket through life, unless Gil was very mistaken.

They had tea in the courtyard of her villa, in the shade of a white canopy draped over three-sided cedar lattice walls mostly covered with dark green ivy. An electric fan circulated not unpleasant warm air. The flowers in her garden were in bloom and very colorful.

She could only give him an hour, M. Abbington apologized, since she was expecting a young gentleman caller later.

Gil had not told her who he was, other than his name, nor why he was asking questions. If she cared, she didn't ask.

About Mario Brock, she said:

"He was so very ambitious. It was hardly seemly. By the time we met, Mario was in his thirties, not ancient, but of course, much older than I."

That would have been a good trick, Gil thought, given that Brock was forty-nine now and Abbington a year past that. But he said nothing.

She continued, "But he had a certain something about him I found attractive. We got along famously and eventually became engaged. He was very clever, a potent lover, and he could not get enough of me that way. It was quite glorious."

"What happened, if you don't mind my asking?"

"Well—please phrase this kindly when you write about it for your magazine or entcom or whatever—I had to break it off. It wasn't just the age difference, it was that he was so . . . driven to accomplish great things on his own, he had no time for romance. He even renounced his family fortune, so confident was he of his own eventual success." She smiled, treated Gil to teeth that were too perfect to be real. "Life is much too short not to have romance in it, don't you think, M. Sivart?"

Gil returned her smile. *Romance . . . and a few billion dollars.* He wondered if Brock had actually told her about not getting the family jewels. Or if she found out on her own. He could only imagine what M. Abbington must have thought when she discovered that Brock wasn't going to be swimming in money when his parents passed away. Somehow, he thought her fondness for him might have faded pretty fast at that point. He had the feeling that if M. Abbington was going to be some man's trophy, the price was going to be dear, even now. Certainly fifteen or twenty years ago she would have settled for nothing less than a very rich man.

"I still think of dear Mario fondly, you know. He's an executive somewhere, I heard." She sipped at her tea. "A pity my caller will arrive soon. You look like a very athletic man yourself, M. Sivart. May I call you Gil?"

They both smiled.

When Gil left, he considered this new information. Brock was unlucky in his choice of bedmates, starting with his sister and extending at least as far as M. Abbington. He had lost much more than most men because of it.

One might suspect that Mario Brock harbored a certain bitterness as to his lot in life.

Gil considered trying to dig up more background on Brock but decided that he had enough. He wasn't so interested in what perverse or unlucky things the man might have done as he was in a motive for murder, and he had that.

Money.

Gil caught the boxcar from the Channel Port and was back on the *Robert E. Lee* by the middle of third shift. He was tired and he wanted to fall into bed before he talked to Trish or El-Sayed, get a few hours sleep. But before he could do more than step into his cube, his com started chirping.

"Yes?"

"Gil, it's Howie. I'm sorry, mate."

"Howie? What are you talking about?"

"Somebody just coldcocked me outside the club. When I came to, Trish was gone."

30

"GONE? WHAT DO you mean, gone?"

"I was waiting outside the club for her to get off work.
I saw a guy drifting in my direction, and while I was
watching him, his buddy musta got behind me. I heard
him, but too late. When I came around, there was no sign
of Trish. Nobody saw or heard anything, she was just . . .
not there. I tried her com, no answer."

"Where are you ?"

"Emergency room. They say my skull is cracked but
I been hurt worse playing ball with my grandfather—hey,
leave off, I'm on the com here!"

"Let them take care of your head, Howie. You call
the cools?"

"I wanted to talk to you first. But the medics called
'em. There's a uniform waiting to interview me."

"Don't say anything about Trish. Tell them you don't
know who hit you or why."

"Right. What about—?"

"I'll take care of it. Sorry about your head."

Gil grabbed his air pistol, which he'd been forced to

leave behind on his trip down below, and headed for the lifts. He put in a call to Ray El-Sayed as he moved.

"This better be damned good, calling at this hour."

"Trish has disappeared, Ray. I'm on my way to her cube."

"I'll meet you there in ten minutes," the cool said.

The entrance to Trish's cube was locked, and there was no response to the chime or Gil's knock. He was seriously considering kicking the door in when El-Sayed arrived.

"No answer," Gil said. "I don't think she's in there, but I had to check."

The cool removed a small electronic device from his belt, triggered it. "This is Ramses El-Sayed of the *Robert E. Lee* Police Department at the entrance to the cubicle of Patricia Blackwell on LL2. M. Blackwell is not responding to com or entry chime and a resident of the station and close friend, M. Gil Sivart, has indicated to this officer his concern that M. Blackwell could be ill or injured and thus unable to answer queries. Pursuant to SL-3347, I am utilizing police override to enter the cubicle and attempt to ascertain the health of M. Blackwell."

Ray thumbed a control, and the door clicked and slid open. Gil started forward, but the cool caught his shoulder. He pulled his duty weapon, pointed it at the floor. "Behind me," he said. "This is what they pay me for."

Gil followed Ray into the cube, but there was nobody home.

"All right. Explain."

Gil did. "Brock has her. One of the people I contacted or tried to contact on Earth must have warned him I was poking around in his past."

Ray shook his head. "If nobody saw it happen, we can't even prove Trish has been kidnapped. She's got to be missing for at least one shift before we can officially start looking for her—it's not illegal to turn off your com. And we're talking about accusing the *Station Manager* of a major locktime felony. A man who can have me suspended by snapping his fingers. If I took what we have to a judge for a search or arrest warrant, he would laugh me out of the station.''

"Dammit, Ray, they've got her!''

"I know, I know. We'll get her back.''

If she's not already dead, Gil thought.

As if reading his mind, Ray said, "She's alive. If they had wanted her dead, they'd have done it outside the club, end of problem. They took her because they wanted to know what she knew, or—''

"—for a trade,'' Gil finished. He knew. It made sense, but his fear had blocked his reason. He couldn't allow his feelings for Trish to get in the way here. He had to keep a clear head if he was going to save her. He took a deep breath, let it out slowly.

"What did you find out that Brock would risk this for?''

Gil told him about his trip to Earth.

Ray shook his head. "I had no idea. I thought Brock was worth more than some small countries.''

"So does almost everybody else. It wouldn't be in his interest for people to think otherwise,'' Gil said. "We need to know about Brock's financial dealings. How he planned to make money off a computer crash.''

"I have some markers out,'' Ray said. "Looks like it is time to call them in.''

"I'm going to go see Wells,'' Gil said.

"Not a good idea,'' Ray said. "You walk into the lion's den, he just might decide to eat you.''

"They don't know what I know, or if I've told it to anybody. If they kill me, what I have might go public. I don't think they'll risk that.''

"If they are killing and kidnapping people, they've already gone deep into risky territory, Gil. I don't think you should go down this path.''

"I appreciate your concern, but this isn't a situation we can sit back and wait on. There is a clock running here, the remora are set to trigger in a few days. After that, what we've got won't be worth much. You find out what you can about Brock's money. I'll feel out Wells.''

And in the process, stall the man long enough to figure out a way to get Trish back in one piece, Gil thought. But he didn't say this to Ray because he was certain that what he would have to do would be highly illegal. Maybe even deadly so.

Gil went to Chaz Wells's office. He was admitted right away, and found the security man sitting behind his desk, fingers steepled. ''Gil. What a pleasant surprise.''

Gil had his pistol tucked into his waistband, a thin vest covering it. He could get it out faster than from his pouch. But he didn't want to start shooting yet.

''What do you want, Wells?''

The blond man smiled, and it was a wicked expression. ''Recorders off,'' he said. He leaned back in his chair, tapped the side of his face with one finger. ''What do I want? Why, not much. I thought perhaps you and I might . . . barter a bit? A straight-across trade. You give me the, ah, tiny little thing that is actually already mine, stolen by somebody who had an unfortunate accident. I give you the, ah, *package* you, ah, misplaced, and everybody is happy.''

''That's it?''

''Well, not quite. I think it only fair that you include with the tiny object in question any and all research and records connected to it.''

''I see. And if I choose not to trade?''

''Your misplaced package would likely be permanently lost.'' He leaned forward. Waved at the chair. ''Have a seat.''

''I'll stand.''

It was what Gil expected: The chip and any evidence regarding it for Trish. If he did make the trade, they might wait long enough to see if their scheme went as planned, then both he and Trish would wind up dead. People who had killed four times before weren't people you wanted to trust with anything, especially your life.

"All right," Gil said. "Let's trade."

"You have our property with you?"

"No. It's on Earth. It will take a couple of shifts to get it here."

"A fast courier can get here from Earth in an hour or two."

"The problem is getting the thing to a fast courier."

Wells shrugged. "All right."

"I need to see her alive."

"See who?"

"I'm not recording this," Gil said.

Wells tried to look bland. "I didn't accuse you of any such thing, Gil. We'll show you the package when we make the trade." Wells waited a moment, then said, "It's your line. This is where you threaten me if anything happens to your girlfriend." Again, the nasty smile.

Gil said, "Threaten you? Why would I want to do that? We're businessmen here. We've already agreed to the terms, haven't we? No need for violence."

"I'm glad you see it that way, Gil. Because your hand-to-hand training wouldn't do you much good against me. I'm better than you are. Smarter, stronger, meaner. I have the winning hand here."

Gil kept his temper in check. What he wanted to do was jump across the desk and beat Wells to a bloody mess, force him to tell where Trish was. It would have been satisfying—but stupid. Wells might have a hired thug standing ready to kill Trish if he didn't call with some code phrase at a certain time, and Gil couldn't risk that.

Instead, he forced himself to smile in return.

Gil went to his shop, to make his plans. This time, he didn't lock the door. It was out in the open now, and he didn't think anybody would bother him—not until they had the remora and what Gil knew in their hands.

The first thing he had to do was figure out where she was . . .

Ray arrived as Gil was working on how he was going to rescue Trish.

"What did Wells say?"

"They've got Trish. He wants to trade her for the chip and whatever data I've got."

"Damn."

"What did you get?"

"Nothing, yet. Brock's financial advisor-broker is based in Zurich. His accounts are all pretty secure. There's no legal way to get into them, not without a court order, and we don't have enough to get one."

"I hear a 'but' in your voice."

"I once caught a c-geek snooping in the station's computers. Could have put him away but he was just a kid and I let it slide. He was a genius, could rascal anything with a brain. He owes me. He's going to see what he can come up with."

"They'll stretch you out to dry if they find out you sponsored something like that."

Ray shrugged. "Most of the time the law works pretty well. Sometimes, it gets in the way of justice. We have enough dead people in this mess, I'm not going to let them kill any more if I can stop it."

"Thanks, Ray."

"I got mirrors in my cube," El-Sayed said. "And children. How could I look at them if I let this happen because I was worried about my job?" He paused. "So you bought us a little time. I hope it's enough."

"Me, too."

What he didn't tell Ray was that by the time the deadline arrived, this would all probably be over, one way or another.

He had less than sixteen hours to figure out where Trish was and a way to save her.

31

WHEN RAY LEFT, Gil realized he was exhausted. He didn't think he could sleep, but he went to his cube, took a shower and lay on the bed, hoping to at least rest a little.

While turning over the problem of where Trish might be and how to rescue her, he dropped into slumber.

Once again, the giant structure Big Black collapsed.

Once again, he was powerless to stop it.

There came the screams, the smells, the awful sights—

Gil jerked awake. Three hours had passed. He knew he needed the rest and was glad to have gotten it, but time was running down.

He got up, went to make himself coffee.

While the hot water filtered into the cup, he thought about it again.

He didn't think Trish would be in Wells's or Brock's personal living quarters. While either of those cubicles would probably be proof against any legal search—who would dare kick in the SM's or the SC's door?—he doubted that either man would want to hold a captive in his own nest. There were some fairly advanced forensic techniques, even in deep space, that could sniff out molecules, do genetic matches, and by now, they probably wouldn't want to risk it, not if things got to the point where a search *might* take place.

He sipped his coffee. He couldn't concentrate properly on the taste of it, but drank it anyway, for the caffeine it offered.

No, they'd want to stash her somewhere else. Somewhere nobody would accidentally stumble over her, and where she would be secure.

Where they could get rid of her in a hurry, if need be.

Gil figured this would let out most of the Living Levels. He reasoned that while you could certainly hide a kidnappee in thousands of cubicles where nobody would think to look, *if* something happened, *if* by a miracle you *were* discovered, you would be trapped. Any sublevel on the station could be sealed, in the event of a disaster or other emergency, and if the stairs were locked, the lifts shut off, the emergency seals triggered, there was no way to leave. Exterior walls around the Living Levels were multiple, sandwiched layers of aluminum, carbon fiber and insulex, just like the rest of the station, and proof against a micrometeor strike. You weren't going to dig through exterior walls with a kitchen knife or even a power saw to get away. And even if you could manage it, what you would get for your trouble would be sucked into vacuum. A sure problem without a suit on and a getaway craft waiting. Sure, there were emergency exit locks on each sublevel, but the authorities could seal these as easily as shutting off the elevators.

Wells wasn't a genius; Gil was pretty sure he was responsible for most of the more stupid things about all this that had happened since Corderman's death. But Brock was directly involved now, Gil was sure of it, and he was no slouch in the smarts department.

Gil was betting that Brock would make sure Trish was somewhere they could get rid of her in a big hurry.

If they just shoved her through a lock into vac, station

sensors would be able to locate her, so it wouldn't do them much good. If Trish turned up dead before Gil made the trade, they'd have to figure he'd give what he had to the cools. And maybe come hunting them with vengeance in mind—which was true enough.

She might be hidden inside a ship at the docks. That was a possibility. It was a long way to Earth, and unless you were right on a ship's tail, you might not see it dump a body into a long glide that could end with it becoming a shooting star over the South Pacific.

Would a human body burn up like a meteor when it hit thick atmosphere? There was a grisly thought.

Or they could be holed up somewhere in Recycling. They had rid themselves of Armando that way, and as far as they knew, gotten away with it. If they had Trish where they could pitch her into the coarse grinders and slurry her into the acid baths, there wouldn't be a corpse to worry about.

But even if he could narrow it down to a particular deck, a single sublevel, you were talking about a lot of space to check. He needed a handle on it, something to grip. This was important, but it was a puzzle, and he was good at solving puzzles.

Okay. Occam's razor. If she's on a ship, they need more hired killers, plus a tame pilot or captain and a crew willing to turn a blind eye to a lock being opened in deep space and somebody pitched out through it. Possible, possible, but then they'd have to figure out a way to erase any connection between the ship and themselves, and that's another complication. A lot more people to get rid of.

On the other hand, if Wells had Trish tied up in Recycling, all he had to do was kick her down a chute and override the security mechanism designed to stop a human from dropping into the flailing blades. Nobody else to get rid of when it was done.

He didn't think another death or ten would bother Wells or Brock at this point, but logistically, the latter proposition made more sense. When plans went awry, as this one had, keeping things simple was the first rule.

Iffy, iffy. But go with it.

Assume for a minute that Trish is somewhere on the Recycling level. Within a short distance of a big grinder, one big enough to reduce a body into pieces that would fit into a slurry pipe. How many of those were there?

And—were there any security rooms, surveillance stations, interview booths, whatever, that might be close to a big grinder? A space that Wells could control, could make off limits to any intrusion?

Gil could find out about the locations of grinders and maybe the security spaces. Station plans were a matter of public record.

He went to his computer.

When he was done a half hour later, Gil had five possible locations. All were within a hundred meters of a Class-One or -Two Refuse Reducer. All were large enough, according to station specs, to contain a human being. There was an interview room, two general utility storage closets, a camera platform, and a classified waste disposal locker, where corporate documents to be shredded were bundled.

Ray could probably find out if any of these five spots had been marked off limits by order of the Corporate Security Chief. But if Gil told Ray about this, the cool might insist on going along, on doing things legally. It was one thing to have a c-geek rascal a financial computer for information that might show motive for a murder; it was another thing to do what Gil had in mind.

No, he'd hold off telling Ray for now. He could check these places out himself. If he was wrong, well, no harm done. If he found Trish, he didn't want anything getting in his way, certainly not a man he liked and might have to hurt to get past.

And there were a couple of things he would need before he went to Recycling. A couple of markers of his own to be called in.

•   •   •

It was the middle of first shift before Gil made his way downlevels to the bottom of the station. Aside from his air pistol, he had a few items he wasn't supposed to have, and a determination to use whatever it took to find and free Trish.

He took a local to LL5, another local to the lowest sub in Fecal Town, and then a set of secondary stairs into the top sub of Recycling.

The stairs were empty.

Between LL1 and Stores, there were usually people using the stairs, many of them clad in expensive exercise suits, climbing steps to keep their muscles toned. Corporate executives, stay-at-home spouses, or SO's, retirees who would rather walk than go to a gym.

Most of the people who lived on LL5 who might be going there from Recycling didn't need to climb stairs to stay in shape. They took the lifts.

Once he was there, Gil pulled his flatscreen and checked the maps. The first area he wanted to check was another sublevel down and a quarter of the way around the station. This was the interview room, the largest space, and Gil's first choice.

When he got there, it took only a few seconds to see that this wasn't where Trish was being kept. The room was closed, but there was a one-way mirror inset into the wall, and a quick look through the dark plastic showed the room to be empty. Gil hurried away before somebody saw him peeping into the room.

The first storage closet, another level down, was locked. Gil looked around, didn't see anybody. He pulled his pistol and a small electronic device, similar to the police override Ray had used to gain entrance to Trish's cube. This was a bootleg lockpick, possession of which was worth a class-D felony. Gil had gotten it from a man who owed him a favor from a couple of years ago. Gil tapped the control. The door slid open, and Gil jumped into the closet with his pistol ready to fire—

The closet held metal racks loaded with blank playits,

hardcopy security forms, light pens and pencils, and other office supplies.

Two levels down, the second closet was empty, nothing in it at all.

The camera platform, on the same level, overlooked racks of manual valves connected to slurry and liquid waste pipes. Most of the pipes were about the diameter of a big man's thigh. There was a security cam there, but the platform was mostly used for storage of camera equipment and was locked behind a gate. The walls of the enclosure were a thick wire mesh that allowed a passerby to see pretty much everything inside.

Nobody there.

That left only the document locker, a space a meter wide by two meters deep and two meters high. If Trish was there and if she had company, it would be a tight fit.

Gil made it to the locker. He waited until a couple of workers in dirty coveralls trudged past, then pulled his gun and electronic lockpick. He touched the lock control. There was a click, but the door did not open.

Uh-oh.

Looked as if this was it.

Gil moved quickly down the hall. There was a door on the same side, another storage locker, and it was happy to open at his illegal machine's electronic prompting. Cleaning supplies, mops, buckets, dry sweep granules sat on the metal shelves. Gil stepped into the room. He put the lockpick into a trash basket, stuffed it under some old rags and empty plastic boxlets. If he was right, he wouldn't need it anymore, and he didn't want to get caught with it.

From his pouch, he removed a spare magazine for his pistol. He looked at it. Only the top dart of the six was visible in the magazine's feed slot. It and the dart immediately underneath it were different from the other four darts. The tips of these two looked as if somebody had pressed a small ball onto them, covering the sharp points of the flechettes. The little round globes were a putty-gray color, almost exactly the same size as the blunt rounds Gil fired in practice, so they should slide up the feed ramp into the gun's chamber just fine.

Gil took a deep breath, let it out, took another and allowed half of it to escape. What he was about to do was illegal and dangerous.

He slid the door wide, wedged it open with a mop handle. Nobody was in sight. He leaned out, aimed his pistol for the wall directly across from the document locker, and pulled the trigger.

The wall exploded. The blast was loud in the confined hallway, even though he had been expecting it. The Detonex pellet, probably a twin to the one that ruined his shop window, blew a shallow crater in the wall, created a blast of heat and a little smoke, enough to trigger the fire and shock alarms on the ceiling.

Gil ducked back into the locker. Counted:

One . . . two . . . three . . .

He stepped out into the hall.

A man stood in front of the document locker. His left hand gripped Trish's shoulder, and his right hand held a pistol pressed against her right temple. His back was to Gil.

Gil raised his own gun. "Hey," he said.

The man turned, dragged Trish around with him. Gil didn't recognize the man's face. The man frowned, pulled his gun away from Trish's temple and pointed it at Gil.

Gil put the red dot of his pistol's scope squarely on the man's forehead, right between the eyes. Squeezed the Taurus's trigger gently . . .

And fired the second Detonex dart.

32

TRISH DIDN'T SCREAM, but she was stunned. Gil ran to her, sluiced bits of bone and brain and blood from her face. "Are you okay? Come on," he said. "We have to get away from here."

"Gil? What—?"

He could understand her shock. There was a dead man on the deck by her feet, a corpse with half its head gone. Gil's ears rang from the sound of the Detonex, and he'd been farther away than Trish. But the fire and vibration alarms blared and would draw people, and Gil didn't know how many of those people might belong to Brock or Wells. This wasn't over yet.

He grabbed Trish's hand and pulled her away. The sensors wouldn't show that the station was in danger, but they needed to get off this sub before somebody decided to lock it down just to be on the safe side.

Or to trap them here.

There were stairs just up the corridor. He dragged her toward them.

They reached the landing. There was a security camera

mounted on a shelf two and a half meters up, high enough to keep small hands from fiddling with it, but otherwise not particularly secure itself.

While Security had long lobbied to have all surveillance equipment on-station tied into a central net, it hadn't yet happened. Many of the cameras in obscure locations where nobody expected trouble were simple and ultra-cheap units using chip matrices that recorded, then erased themselves every six shifts, then started recording over again. These units had low-cost wide-angle lenses, bottom-of-the-line electronics, and fixed foci. Image quality was poor at best. Teeners sometimes pulled them down and stomped them, usually when they wanted to smoke or screw and they didn't feel like going somewhere more private. Or, in the way of teeners, just for the hell of it. The throwaway cams weren't worth stealing, and almost nobody ever did. What would you want with a camera that only recorded bad images at one particular distance? When you could get a much better unit from Stores for what you paid for lunch?

Gil removed the cam from its mount. He popped the recording chip out and stuck it in his pocket, then put the camera back in position. If somebody looking for them noticed the cam's chip was gone, they might guess that Gil and Trish had been here, but they couldn't be sure. They didn't put these units on every flight, usually just every five sublevels, so even if they *were* sure Gil and Trish had been here, they couldn't know which way they had gone. That gave them ten sublevels, five in either direction, where they might have left the stairs unnoticed. And it would take a long time to check every other set of stairs and all the elevators on all those levels.

Which way? Up or down? Up would take them toward the relative safety of the LL's, but up was also likely where trouble would come from. Another few subs and they'd be at the bottom of Recycling, in a place of tanks, vats, and huge pumps. Few workers, and right now, that was a plus as far as Gil was concerned.

Decide!

Down.

They had no sooner stepped through the door when the lock clicked and the pressure seals engaged behind them with a high, hydraulic whine.

The sublevel had been sealed.

That had to be under Brock's order, since there wasn't any real disaster. Brock or Wells had probably called their hired gun and when he didn't respond, figured out they were in trouble.

With the door sealed, nobody would be following them from uplevels, so that was good.

Normally in an emergency, the elevators would stop above and below the affected level; if sensors in the shaft detected a drop in air pressure below basic life-support levels, the shaft itself would be automatically sealed by sliding pressure doors. If the problem wasn't completely catastrophic, the shaft would stay open, even though the access doors on the level or sublevel would remain locked.

There wasn't going to be a pressure drop in the elevator shafts, given that the only damage was a small, shallow crater in an inside wall, plus a little smoke. So while nobody could access an elevator from the sublevel Gil and Trish had just left, an elevator could be made to traverse the level, if you had the proper override codes.

Something the head of Corporate Security could easily get his hands on.

But he wouldn't know where they had gone. Not unless Gil did something stupid, like use his com to call for help. Even a public com to Ray El-Sayed might be traced, so that was out, too. No, what he had to do was find them a good hiding spot and sit tight for a while. After things settled down, they could get a message to Ray somehow, maybe call somebody who could hand-deliver it. Wells couldn't monitor every call on the station, couldn't listen to the coms of everybody Gil and Trish knew, could he?

Well, yes, he might. He could instruct the communications computer to listen for Gil's or Trish's or El-

Sayed's name, so that if one of them was mentioned, the computer would red-flag it. Wells might not be able to do that legally, but he could probably do *it.*

Worry about that later. Right now, the thing to do was find a safe place. It was a big station. And unlike Wells had been with Trish, Gil wasn't constrained in his choice of a hiding spot—except that it probably was on one of ten sublevels. Maybe. Wells couldn't even know that for certain. For now, at least, they were okay.

The bottom sublevel of Recycling was a place largely occupied by rows and rows of big plastic sewage conversion tanks. These were cylinders, shaped and ridged on the outside almost like short stacks of coins. The tanks were four meters high and eight meters in diameter. Large pipes fed processed, liquefied waste into the tops of the containers. Once inside, the suspension settled through a series of filters, was further treated by chemical and electrical rectifiers. The resulting liquid was pumped out to pressure distillers, from which it would eventually emerge as pure water. The leftover solids in the tanks were then mixed with dissolvants into a fluid slurry and pumped to giant centrifuges up one level where the various minerals would be separated and reclaimed.

Recovery of water and minerals from such sewage approached 93%. What you flushed down your toilet today might come back from your drinking fountain tomorrow. Tasteless, odorless, and as chemically pure as commercially bottled water.

Gil knew, because he had once taken the tour.

He was as careful as he could be in avoiding other security cameras. There didn't seem to be many of them on this level; no surprise. Most of the work around the tanks was automatic, with robots and sensors filling in for people where possible. Gil knew that from his tour, too, and it was one of the reasons he'd headed here.

Trish picked a thumbnail-sized piece of spongy red-and-white bone from her neck and looked at it.

Gil took the bit of skull gently from her and tossed it away.

She looked at him, still dazed, but more in control. "What did you do to him?"

"I shot him with the same thing they blew out my shop window with."

"Why?"

He wiped a fleck of blood from her cheek. "He was going to kill you."

"He said he wasn't."

Gil said, "He was a kidnapper. He had a gun. You think he wouldn't *lie* to you?"

She shook her head. "Sorry."

"It's okay. I understand."

"What—how did you—?"

"I talked to Wells," Gil said, keeping his voice quiet. "He's responsible for this, he and Brock. What I found out on Earth was, Brock isn't rich, he doesn't get the family fortune. Somehow, this is all about money. Anyway, Wells offered to trade you for the remora chip and what I knew about it. I agreed, to give me enough time to find you."

"I'm glad you did. Why are we here?" She waved her hand at the tank farm.

"Because Wells and Brock are desperate. They know we know something. They hired killers, maybe Wells even had a hand in the actual deaths himself. If we get to the police with what we know, the cools will have enough to open an investigation. They can't take that chance."

"And we can't call for help because they might be listening," she said.

"Yes."

"So now what?"

"We stay here until we can figure out a way to contact Ray El-Sayed without being seen or heard."

"Thank you," she said. "For coming to get me."

"How could I not?"

She managed a small smile. She caught his hands, squeezed them.

"Are you okay?"

"Me? I'm fine. Not a scratch."

"I mean about shooting that man."

He thought about it for a few seconds. He had killed a man, and in a particularly gruesome manner. The slow-motion images of the kidnapper's head shattering would probably stay with him forever. The hand that held Trish had belonged to a person. Somebody who'd had a mother and a father, maybe a family of his own, hopes, desires, some kind of life. Gil had ended all that. However much the man might have deserved it, it was not something he could just shrug off, the killing of another human being. He would probably have nightmares about it. But not as many nightmares as he would surely have had if Trish had been killed. It was a high price, but one he'd pay again.

"I'm okay," he said. "You're safe—we're both safe—and I can live with what it took."

"Come out, come out, wherever you are!" yelled a singsong voice that echoed hollowly through the tank farm.

Gil jerked his hands away from Trish and went for his pistol.

Wells!

"Come on, Gil! Come out and play!"

33

Wᴇʟʟs!? Hᴏᴡ ʜᴀᴅ he found them?

Gil gestured for Trish to stay where she was. He edged around the curve of the tank and looked down the nearest aisle.

No sign of anybody.

"I'm going to go see where he is," Gil said. "If you hear anybody coming this way, don't let them see you. If I'm not back in five minutes, try to get to an elevator and get as far away from here as you can."

"I want to go with you."

"No. If something happens to me, you have to put this together. Get it to Ray El-Sayed."

"Come on, Gil! I've got somebody who wants to see you! Say something for the man!"

"Don't do it, Gil—unh!" The voice was cut off by a grunt and the sound of an impact, but not before Gil recognized the speaker.

Ray El-Sayed.

"Oh, shit," he whispered.

"What?"

"He's got Ray."

"What are we going to do?"

Gil looked at his pistol. "I've got enough air to fire the four darts left in this magazine. If I can get within fifteen or twenty meters of him, I can take him out."

He didn't add that he'd have to hit Wells with two or three of the little missiles to put him down, and even then, the electric charges on the darts might not do it quick enough to keep him from killing Ray if he had a gun or knife on the cool.

He stayed low, moved across the aisle, slid behind another tank.

"Come on, Sivart, come on. You think you can get past all my security gear? We've got cameras hidden where you wouldn't believe. Might as well give it up. I've evacuated this sublevel and locked it tight. Come on. I'll give you a fair chance. You and me, hand to hand. Better man leaves. It's the only way out—I've got the override and you don't."

Gil duck-walked across another aisle, trying to pinpoint Wells's location. It was hard; the sound bounced from all the tanks and hard floors and ceiling. He was close, but Gil couldn't tell where.

"If you don't come out, your friend the overeager cool here is going to have himself a sudden case of terminal lead poisoning!"

Lead poisoning?

Gil went prone, crawled a few centimeters on his belly, peeped around the opposite edge of the tank . . .

There he was. Ray stood in front of Wells, his left hand pressed against the side of his head. Blood seeped from between the cool's fingers and dripped down his arm. Scalp wound; those bled a lot. Wells probably did it with the weapon he had pressed against Ray's spine.

The weapon was the Thompson submachine gun that had been hanging on the wall behind the security man's desk.

Wells must have spotted Gil peripherally. He turned, snatched the weapon away from El-Sayed's back, and pointed it at Gil. Gil jerked his head back as Wells fired.

The explosions were terrifically loud. Bullets spanged off the floor, ricocheted away. One or two of them hit the heavy plastic tank a quarter-meter above where Gil's head had just been. One of the bullets punched a hole in the plastic. A stream of murky liquid squirted out under pressure and began to spatter on the floor. Apparently the reclamation process hadn't removed the stink at this stage—it smelled like a stopped-up toilet.

And also apparently, Terran T&F had not rendered the weapon Wells carried inoperable after all.

Any one of those missiles it fired could kill, and he had at least twenty-five of the thirty the magazine held left. And maybe a spare magazine tucked away.

Gil gathered himself, came up into a squat, then leapt across the space between the leaking tank and the row across from it. He had to lead Wells away from where Trish was.

The sound of the multiple shots came as one long *rippp!* More bullets hit the floor and bounced away, and at least a couple hit the new tank with a drumlike *thump!*

Gil didn't pause, but sprinted past three more rows of tanks, then cut to his right, past three metal pumps mounted with large bolts to an antivibration rack bolted in turn to the floor. He got to the end of the rack, then looked around to see if Wells had moved.

The Security Chief was not in sight. Ray El-Sayed's right wrist was attached to a pipe coming out of a nest of such tubes by a white loop of cufftape.

If Wells had gone down that aisle after him, he would see Trish if she didn't put the tank she was behind between her and Wells.

Time to make some noise.

"Bad shooting, Chaz! My grandma could do better than that!"

Gil darted across the gap where Ray was cuffed to the pipes, but Ray had his back to him and didn't look in that direction.

"You don't think I was trying to *hit* you, do you?"

Wells yelled back. Moving toward Gil. And away from
where Trish was. Good.

"Gil, Gil, Gil, give me credit for more than that! I just
wanted to get your attention, that's all! Listen, it's still
not too late to clear all this up. Weber was no great loss,
we won't hold that against you. You were worried about
your girlfriend, we understand that. You and she and the
fool cool can still walk away from this alive. Give us the
chip. We'll hold you for a few days, until after our party
is over, then we'll let you go. And hey, you won't have
to leave empty-handed. You can be a rich man. So can
your girlfriend and the cool."

Yeah, right.

"Come on, Gil. This is fun and all, playing chase
down in the bowels, but we're talking about serious
wampum here, hundreds of millions, maybe even a billion. We're not greedy, we'll share it with you, there's
enough for everybody."

Gil moved along a horizontal rack of floor-to-ceiling
pipes of various diameters, ranging from wrist-thick to
as big around as his waist. Some of the lines gave off
warmth; one was wrapped in insulation tape and had frost
half a centimeter thick coating it. There were gaps between the tubes, and Gil kept low and peered through
these as he moved. He'd lost track of Wells.

Gil weaved his way in and out of a series of small
evaporation ponds. The shallow pools were covered with
plastic caps, each of which was held up in the center by
a post, so the ponds looked like miniature circus tents.
These were supposed to be airtight, but the smell was
less than fresh.

A power transformer surrounded by a protective orange plastic mesh fence and warning signs loomed ahead.
The unit was man-high, a metal cylinder with insulators
on the top, a conduit and lines coming down from the
ceiling to the insulator and through openings in the top,
with smaller wires leading out near the bottom. Gil
moved toward the transformer. If he worked his way
around that and down the narrow corridor between more

pipe racks just past it, he could get close to Ray. He had a small pocket knife, not much, but the blade was probably sharp and sturdy enough to eventually worry its way through a piece of cufftape. Ray wouldn't have his gun, but two sets of eyes and ears would be better than one.

He reached the transformer.

"Gil, behind you!"

Gil spun, saw Wells ten meters back, just coming from under the pipe rack. Past him another ten meters was Trish. Wells grinned and brought his submachine gun up.

"Trish, get down!"

Gil snapped his pistol into firing position, one-handed. His vision narrowed, and all he could see, all he could comprehend as time oozed into its slow-motion fugue again, was the gun that would chop him down—

He fired, once, twice, three times, and he *saw* his darts hit the magazine and front stock of the tommy gun.

Instinctively, he had focused on the threat and instinctively, he had sought to remove it.

But the low-powered darts were wasted on the gun Wells held. The darts' sharp tips had to pierce a man's flesh to deliver enough of their charge to do any damage—human skin was a great insulator.

Shit—!

Gil jumped, tried to get behind the thick metal transformer—

Wells fired, held the trigger of the weapon down. Five, ten, fifteen, bullets lanced at him, paths rising higher as the recoil drove the tommy gun's barrel upward—

Gil almost made it. One of the bullets hit him on the right forearm just below the elbow. He felt the tug, saw his hand pop open and the gun in it fly away to clatter onto the floor. Had enough time to think to himself that the bullet must have gone right between the bones because he saw a flap of skin tear open on the opposite side of his arm and watched the copper round just . . . fall out and to the deck, where it bounced twice and lay still—

More bullets smashed one of the insulators on top of

the transformer, and sparks flew as wires tore loose.
Smoke and the smell of ozone washed over Gil, but he
was still moving, crabbing sideways, then turning to run
full out—

Wells stopped shooting; he must be out of ammunition. Gil's hearing came back in time for him to hear the
sound of something metal being dropped onto the floor.
Probably the empty magazine—

Gil's arm hadn't started to hurt yet, but he couldn't
close the fingers of his right hand. Or move them at all.
A little bit of blood ran from the entrance wound, a neat
round hole, and a bit more that dripped from the more
ragged exit wound, but not all that much.

He dug into his left pants pocket, found his penknife.
As he crossed the large central corridor where Ray was
cuffed to the pipe, he yelled, "Ray! Catch!" and tossed
the knife.

He saw El-Sayed reach out with his free hand, but
didn't have time to see if he caught the knife, because
he heard footsteps behind him and he jinked left. He
tripped heading into the tank farm, but his training took
over and he turned the fall into a shoulder roll and came
up, still moving.

Sifu would appreciate that one.

Gil ran, and considered his situation. His gun was
gone, his right arm was pretty much useless, and he and
his two friends were trapped on this sublevel with a murderer who had an antique but very lethal weapon. His
options were limited and getting more so all the time.

What would Inspector Targan do in such a situation?

Turn your disadvantages into advantages, the abo's
voice seemed to say in his head.

Yeah, right. I'm shot and bleeding, how do I turn that
*into an advantage? If Wells has enough sense to look
down, he can trail me by following the goddamned blood
I'm dripping all over the—*

Wait a second, hold up . . .

Yes. That might work.

• • •

Wells came around the last row of tanks, walking slowly, his weapon held in front of him ready to shoot. He was grinning as he followed the spatters of blood on the floor, fresh drops every half meter or so, leading right down the center of the aisle toward a dead-end corridor and a row of refuse bins.

Wells reached the last two tanks. Glanced to the left, then the right. The aisle in both directions was clear as far as he could see. He said, "You boxed yourself in, Gil! There's no way out of that cul-de-sac. You can come out on your own, or I can punch holes in those trash cans until I hit you. I've got three more magazines full of bullets. So the only question is, do you want to die on your feet like a man or crouched down inside a dump bin?"

"Neither," Gil said softly to himself.

Then he leapt from the top of the tank where he had been hiding, and came down on Wells.

He aimed a hammer blow at the top of Wells's head as he fell, but the left-hand strike landed on the man's left shoulder instead. Still, Wells hadn't been expecting it. Gil's attack knocked the gun loose.

The weapon clattered into the cul-de-sac. Both men tumbled to the deck—

Wells shook off the fall, came up just as Gil did—

The security man squared himself into a left side stance, hands lifted and held in tight fists. Scooted a little closer.

Gil shifted his own position so that his left side faced Wells, his good hand high and open.

"You've only got one hand," Wells said. "Soon as you block whatever I throw, I got your ass."

Gil didn't speak to that.

"Goodbye, Sivart. I'm gonna enjoy this."

Wells slid in, threw a short left jab at Gil's eyes to draw the block, then a hard, straight right, to smash Gil's face.

Gil snake-blocked—left, using his bent wrist to deflect the jab—right, using the heel of the hand to parry the right punch. Before Wells could recover, Gil did a fast backfist, all snap from the elbow, and caught Wells across the bridge of the nose.

One, two, *three!*

The backfist wasn't the most powerful strike, but it was enough to snap Wells's head back in surprise—

Gil whipped his left foot up in a short counter sidekick and slammed his heel into Wells's solar plexus. He snapped his foot back down, did a back cross-step as Wells tried to breathe and couldn't . . .

Gil twisted in a spinning back elbow strike. The point of his left elbow speared Wells's right eye. He felt the socket go.

Wells dropped as if he had been clotheslined. His head bounced against the floor. He lay still, out.

Gil looked down at the unconscious man. "Maybe you won't enjoy it as much as you think," he said.

"Gil?!" Trish said.

He looked up and saw Ray and Trish coming toward him. Ray had Gil's air pistol. Trish must have run to pick it up after Wells had shot it out of his hand.

Ray looked at the man on the floor. "He dead?"

"No. He is going to need some facial surgery."

"Good. We'll want him to look nice for his truth-scan."

"You think we have enough evidence now?"

"Yeah. I think so. Let's go see my captain. And then our soon-to-be ex-Station Manager."

Trish moved to Gil. "Are you okay?"

"I'll need a little work on my arm," he said, holding it out. "But I'll live."

"I'm glad," she said. She hugged him.

He put his good arm around her, pulled her close. Kissed the top of her head. "Yeah. So am I."

34

BASE CAME BY to assist the surgeon working on Gil's arm. Just as a courtesy, he said.

"Not really my field," he said. "But I patched up a few gunshot wounds when I was doing my ER rotation on Earth. Still a lot of those old weapons out there."

"So I noticed," Gil said.

The surgeon killed the bacteriostatic lamps. "I think that's about got it. Shouldn't be any problems. It'll take a couple of days to heal completely. Use the electropads three times a day, ten minutes at a time."

"Thanks. And thank you for coming by, Base."

"De nada."

Gil flexed his arm and hand. Sore, but at least the fingers were working again. The dermoplex sealing the revised wound was the same material that Trish sometimes wore in her dance routine.

Outside the surgery room in the hall, Trish and Ray waited.

"All fixed," Gil said. He waved at them.

Ray said, "Police policy won't allow you to come

along on a felony arrest, Gil, but if you happened to be passing by the SM's office in, say, ten minutes, well, it is a public place.''

Gil nodded. "You don't think he'll try to run?''

"No. Even if he knew for sure we have Wells, he's used to people hopping when he says 'Jump.' He might not be rich, but he's not poor. He'll throw lawyers at us, he'll call in favors from judges and veeps, blow a lot of smoke, flash a lot of lasers, deny everything right up until we run the scan on him.''

Gil nodded.

"I have to go now, my warrants should be ready. See you around. And hey, thanks.''

"I want my pocketknife back,'' Gil said.

Both men grinned. El-Sayed turned and ambled away. A uniformed cool in a cart waited for him outside the clinic. Gil watched Ray climb into the cart.

When Ray was gone, Trish came over to look at Gil's arm. "I've got some nice red dye that can brighten that dermoplex up,'' she said.

"Might be an interesting effect. You want to take a walk?''

"Yes.''

Brock's arrest was done with a minimum of fuss. Gil and Trish were standing outside the SM's office when Ray arrived, along with his captain and the Police Commissioner. The trio climbed out of a large open cart and went into the office. A second police cart pulled up behind the first, a covered one, and a uniformed officer opened the back door and stood next to it.

Two minutes later, the three policemen emerged, along with Mario Brock. The man chatted with the Police Commissioner. He appeared unconcerned in his expensive silks, looked as if he might be discussing some trivial bit of personal news instead of being arrested. Brock nodded at a couple passing by, smiled. If he was concerned, it didn't show.

Gil and Trish stood silent, watched Brock pass. He was

ten meters away when he glanced over and saw them. His smile faltered for an instant, then resumed. He nodded at them as if they were old friends.

"The bastard!" Trish said. She clenched her fists.

"It's okay," Gil said. "He's smiling now, but that won't last. He's going away forever."

"It's not enough for David's death," she said.

"I know."

They watched him get into the covered cart. The uniformed officer closed the door.

Ray called a few hours later, then he came by Gil's shop where Trish and Gil were waiting.

"It's done," Ray said. "Wells and Brock are in custody pending a court-ordered brainscan. Wells is recovering from the shattered eye bones you gave him. Once he's fit, the scans'll get done. When we get the results of those, they are cooked. All over but the crying."

"I still don't understand," Trish said. "Why did they do all this? Where were they going to profit?"

Gil had finally figured it out, he thought, but he let Ray start to tell it.

"Brock didn't have a lot of money of his own," Ray said. "But he did have access to station funds. With Wells's help, he spent years setting up a theft. A few days ago, they embezzled a little over eight million dollars. We got it because we knew to look."

Trish shook her head. "That's stupid. He had to know somebody would figure that out eventually. Where could he hide? You'd track him down."

"If he had kept the money, yes. But he planned to put the eight million back. Nobody would ever know it had been gone. He just needed to use it for a few days. If some discrepancy showed up in the accounting program later, well, the money wasn't gone, was it? What was the problem? It would be a hard crime to prove."

"I still don't get it. What has that got to do with the computer chip Gil found? Was he going to wreck the accounting system so nobody could tell who stole the money?''

"No. We were thinking too small," Ray said. "We were figuring he was going to kill a couple of systems on the station or maybe a ship. What he had planned was much bigger." Ray looked at Gil. "You want to impress us with your logical skills?"

Gil picked it up. Said, "Brock wouldn't be satisfied with a few million, he came from real wealth; but, because of what he did to his sister, he couldn't have it.

"Thing is, with the way things work these days, you can't really steal hundreds of millions of dollars without somebody noticing. Even if you could, you couldn't spend it or hide it; that much money leaves a trail. So he figured to earn it." To Ray, Gil said, "Your c-geek got into Brock's financial files."

Ray nodded. "Yep."

"Does somebody want to get to a point here?" Trish said.

"The remora chip," Ray said. "It wasn't just the one. There are a lot of them. We put the word out, and authorities have already collected several hundred, there may be thousands still out there. They've found them on major computer systems all over the world, even in a few wheelworlds. Air and maglev train travel, traffic control, hospitals, banks, computer nets, communications, governments, you name it. Brock had a group of Big Blue company technicians on his payroll, they've been slapping these things on systems for months, maybe longer." Ray shook his head.

"They aren't all rigged to go off at exactly the same time," the cool continued. "So far, they are all set for the same day, but at a variety of hours."

Trish looked at Gil.

"Here's the scenario," he said. "In a few days, major computer systems grind to a stop, and all of the affected hardware is from Big Blue. Naturally, people will know it is sabotage, but what they won't know is how many of Big Blue's units might be affected. There will be a lot of worry and a certain amount of panic. They'll rush around shutting down their computers, trying to figure out what the problem is. It will cause a major snafu, but pretty quick, they'll figure it out.

"Immediately, the price of Big Blue stock goes through the floor as nervous speculators rush to unload. Billions of dollars get lost or made, depending on the buyers and sellers."

Ray said, "But when no more attacks take place, the prices will go back up."

Trish nodded. "Ah. I see. So if Brock bought a lot of Big Blue stock when it was priced low, then when it went back up, he'd earn a lot of money. But wouldn't that make him a suspect?"

"Not really. There would be thousands of other people who did the same thing," Gil said. "The stock market is full of vultures who prey on dying companies. Usually they just watch and wait instead of kill things themselves. Brock would be a face in the greedy crowd. But I'm guessing that he was smarter than that." He looked at Ray.

Ray nodded. "Yep. He was set to buy some shares of Big Blue, he had an order scheduled the day after Big Blue's machines went belly up. But the buy was not so big he would stand out. He'd make maybe a few million. Nobody would blink, he was Mario Brock of the billionaire Brocks, they wouldn't think to look at him too closely.

"He had already bought shares of one of Big Blue's competitors, prices of which would tend to rise at least temporarily, so he'd make a few million for a relatively small buy there.

"But where he really stood to gain was his investment in a new company. Want to guess what it specializes in?"

Trish thought about it for a second. "Something to detect and prevent this kind of computer sabotage?"

"We have a winner," Ray said. "Give this woman the prize. Through a system of proxies, and without his name being linked directly to it, Mario Brock owns a big chunk of something called Alert Systems Protection. A struggling Thai company a little less than a year old which just went public on the Asian big board this very month. Stock is valued very low at the moment, a few yen a share. ASP produces a daughter chip that detects and deactivates such things as remoras within microseconds. Does it cheap, too, only a couple hundred, including the installation. Money-back guarantee.

"So while this attack on Big Blue's systems might be a one-time act of terrorism, *maybe* it would happen again. Even with business insurance, the deductible premium and the hassle of having to reinstall your system would be pains in the wallet. An inexpensive little chip to stop such attacks would suddenly become very, very popular."

"And," Gil said, "given the sudden demand for such a product, the stock for the company producing this little jewel would rocket upward."

"We don't know for sure, yet," Ray said. "But probably Brock passed this insider information on to some other wealthy investors willing to round off a few corners to make a killing. I'd guess he got some piece of their action, or a premium for letting them in on the deal."

"Of course, a lot of small investors would lose their shirts," Gil said. "Probably a lot of them would be ruined, given that Big Blue is supposed to be a gilt-edged sure thing."

"What a devious, evil man," Trish said.

"Yes," Ray said. "We'll find out how your SO figured into it when we scan Wells and Brock. My guess is, he found the chip and reported it to Corporate Security. And Wells would have been alert to such reports."

Nobody said anything for a time.

Trish said, "I think maybe I need to go home now."

"I'll walk you," Gil said.

"No. I'd just as soon be alone, okay?"

"Sure."

She left.

Ray shook his head, said, "You gonna just let her go like that?"

"She said she'd let me know when she was ready for anything more. I'll have to abide by that."

"Me, I'd be pounding on her door. You're not as smart as you make out."

"Probably not," Gil said.

"I need to go myself," Ray said. "Tell my wife the good news."

"Good news?"

"Seems there is a lieutenant's job opening up in Detectives in a couple of months. My captain seems to think I could handle the duties."

"Congratulations. You deserve it."

"That's for damn sure. But I wouldn't have gotten the shot at it if you hadn't brought all this to me. I owe you."

"I hope you remember that next time I'm poking my nose around for a client."

"If I don't arrest you for messing in police business, I might cut you a little slack. I might want to be a captain someday."

Both men smiled.

35

Two LONG DAYS passed.

Gil was in his shop again, working on the plans for a nineteenth-century German Navy sailing ship. He was pretty sure that when the investigation surrounding Corderman's death was over, the contract he'd been offered to do artwork for the station was going to be withdrawn. Anything involving Brock and money would be suspect, and the offer had been a bribe.

The com cheeped. He answered without looking to see who the caller was.

"Hi," Trish said.

"Hi."

There was a pause. Not an uncomfortable silence. He waited. He smiled unseen at her.

"I took some time off from work," she said.

"That sounds like a good idea."

Another pause.

"Maybe you'd like to come by my cube when you get some free time?"

"I would like that."

"Gil?"

"Yeah?"

"Bring a toothbrush."

He laughed. "I'm on my way."

His grin lasted all the way to her cube.

And his smile got bigger when she opened the door naked, and invited him inside.

Sharon Shinn

__ARCHANGEL 0-441-00432-6/$6.50

"I was fascinated by Archangel. Its premise is ususual, to say the least, its characters as provocative as the action. I was truly, deeply delighted."—Anne McCaffrey

__THE SHAPE-CHANGER'S WIFE
                 0-441-00261-7/$4.99

Aubrey was a student, gifted in the fine art of wizardry. But the more knowledge he acquired, the more he wanted to learn. But there was one discovery he never expected, one mystery he risked everything to solve.

Her name was Lilith.

Now available *JOVAH'S ANGEL.* An Ace Trade Paperback.
      __*0-441-00404-0/$13.95*